Sutherland

A novel by

M.C. Hall

September Sky Press

An Imprint of 50/50 Press, LLC

Sutherland
© 2018 by Megan Cassidy-Hall

50/50 Press, LLC
140 Quay Rd.
Delanson, NY 12035
http://www.5050press.com

ISBN-13:9781947048188

Library of Congress Control Number
LCCN:
Edited by: Karen S. Cassidy

This book is a work of fiction. The Sutherland Sisters and Anna Louise Roberts were real, historical figures. However, while some incidents in this book did occur, names, characters, places, and incidents are either products of the author's imagination or are used fictitiously. For wholly-faithful, nonfiction accounts of the Sutherland's lives, the author recommends reading materials published by the Niagara County Historical Society.

Printed in the U.S.A. First Edition, September, 2018

Pictured: The Seven Sutherland Sisters with Their Father
Left to Right: Sarah, Naomi, Fletcher, Grace, Victoria,
Dora, Mary, and Isabella

"When we were taught about the Sutherlands in school, we didn't know about anything about this darkness they were involved in. Back then, to us, the Sutherlands were perfect, just perfect. That was all. I wasn't told the rest of it until much later."

~Lois Smith, my grandmother

Part 1

Quite Above Them, Socially

Pictured: Miss Sarah Sutherland

March, 1879

Real ghosts don't lift the rag-covered tables of mystics. They don't fill the hazy crystal balls of charlatan mediums who travel in gypsy carts. They don't rattle chains in the attic or rearrange furniture in the cellar. They don't bend to your will.

The spirits haunt us in much more subtle ways, making their presence known in a sudden frost, lacing across a window pane on a sweltering afternoon in July, or the wafting of lavender and lilacs on an icy January morning. They are the soft moans in the night that mingle with the creaks and groans of house floorboards, the whisper at the base of your neck, beckoning you out into the night without a lantern to guide you.

A moan followed by shrieks and howls of laughter woke me the night I first saw the Sutherland sisters. Back then, there were still seven of them, all living at the Old Miller Place, a failing chicken farm with nothing but a few rusted coops, a weathered barn, and a three-room log cabin.

I woke violently and held in a scream. It took me nearly a minute to realize the moaning had been from my younger sister Faith, who tossed in her trundle bed, unused to the silent cold of our new home. The shrieks and giggles were coming from outside, however, and I padded over to the window to seek out the source of the noise, wincing as my feet hit the frigid floorboards.

It was late March, and our old home in West Virginia had seen the warmth of spring for nearly a month. Now, in Upstate New York, snow still covered the ground in dull graying drifts, and Father heard tell the sun might not appear for several more weeks.

A cloud passed from before the moon. In the light, I could make out seven figures clad in ragged nightdresses, laughing and screeching as they scampered down the icy lane. As I watched, each girl in succession unbound her hair, letting long locks blow about wildly in the winter wind. When the gust of wind subsided, their hair settled onto the snow, and they ran, looking like seven brides dashing to marriage with seven cathedral veils trailing out behind them.

Transfixed, my fingers gripped the window sill. One by one, the girls stole into the church, where my father was to begin as minister the following Sunday. I cracked open the window to better hear their words, but the wind whistled in, stinging my eyes, and Faith moaned again, stirring beneath her heavy blankets. Frowning, I shut the window and pressed my nose to the glass.

The smallest girl paused before entering the building. The stars seemed to flicker as she gazed up at my window. She couldn't have been much younger than me, maybe seven or eight years to my eleven. But as she stood in the cold with moonlight shining on her small, round face, she seemed like a changeling from one of the fairy stories Mother forbade us from reading.

As this thought passed through my mind, another gale of wind whipped through the girl's thick dark hair, encircling her small frame like a dust storm. When it settled, she smoothed back her tresses and grinned up at me wickedly, teeth glinting in the pale light. Giving a quick wave of her fingers, she disappeared into the chapel.

Within a few moments, notes from the church's pipe organ crashed through the wind. Even with the window shut, I could hear voices joining in chorus.

From the other room, my mother's sharp voice cut through my reverie. "What in the name of Heavenly Glory is that?"

I hopped back into bed and saw Faith, eyes wide and knuckles white as they clung to the edge of her blanket.

"That'll be the Reverend Sutherland's brood," my father sighed.

"Reverend indeed," Mother barked out a laugh. The only thing sweet about my mother was her lemon verbena toilet water, and even that held a sour note.

"Ida, hush. The children," Father soothed.

"As if they haven't already woken? All this racket in the middle of the night."

"I was warned of this," Father said. "I'll speak to Sutherland after the Sabbath's ended."

"Goblins and witches every one of them," Mother snarled. Though I never contradicted her out loud, my mother and I disagreed on almost every subject. On this point, though, I was fairly sure she was correct.

"They've had a hard time of it," Father replied. From my bed, I could picture him stroking her hair the way he always did when she worked herself into a state.

I reached down to do the same for Faith, who was now trembling and glancing nervously toward the window. When my hand passed over her forehead, she mewled a little, almost like a baby kitten, and I realized that, though afraid, she was only half-

3

awake and would probably be unable to remember this incident come morning.

Faith climbed up from the trundle bed to join me, the way she used to in the first two years after she moved from her crib to our shared bedroom. She was five-years-old, but stuck her thumb into her mouth, reverting to a habit I hadn't seen her take up since she was two. I wanted to shout at her for behaving like a baby at a moment when I felt small and vulnerable and needed comfort myself. Instead, I held my tongue and instead whispered, "A great big girl like you shouldn't act so." Then, I gave a gentle chuckle of admonishment.

Faith poked my stomach with her chubby fingers, "You were just as frightened as me, Anna Louise." She giggled and snuggled her head next to mine, falling asleep as soon as the organ ceased its tune.

For my own part, I could not rest for several hours, imagining the seven girls returning home like a coven of witches, carried on the wind by their long locks, leaving not even a trace of footprints behind them.

***

The Sutherland magic remained unbroken until Father and I traveled to their small farm the following Monday. Mother did not approve of my going. As we sat to breakfast, she voiced her concerns. "You should hear what the ladies in church were saying about them, William." Mother patted the tight bun at the top of her graying head.

Faith and I exchanged glances. Though not strictly enforced, the rule in our often-somber household was that children were neither seen nor heard, particularly at mealtimes. We found that when we obediently adhered to this rule, we discovered more about our parents' inscrutable adult world than we would have if we insisted on chattering about household chores and schoolhouse playmates. I tapped a finger to my upper lip almost imperceptibly, our silent signal to pay close attention and not breathe a word.

"Women will always gossip," Father said, a hint of a smile playing at the corner of his mouth, "but I do wish they would take a Sabbath of it on Sundays."

Mother raised an eyebrow, "Sometimes we may talk a bit too much, but this is no mere gossip. There was good reason they ousted him as minister. He was a Copperhead, you know, and then there's the matter of his wife's sister..."

"And little pitchers have big ears," Father cut her off, giving us a pointed look that said this conversation was not for us to hear, which was, of course, the very reason we wanted to hear it.

Mother glanced over at us, pursing her lips. "Go outside and run the stink off you," she declared. That was her usual way of saying we had taken up enough time, space, and food, and must take heed to amuse ourselves— either with study or play, she cared not which.

Typically, Faith and I jumped at the chance to play outside. Tonight, Faith looked at me, and I looked at Father, and Father looked outside, and we all laughed. Even Mother joined in. She had forgotten that there was to be no play on the Sabbath, at least until the sunset.

Moreover, in West Virginia, the sun shone daily. Apart from the highest mountain peaks, the snow had melted away, and yellow daffodils were popping up amongst the green. Outside our new house, the wind howled, whipping powdered snow in great swirls of white.

The broadcloth coats Faith and I had worn Sunday would not suffice for us to play in. I noted they were too thin even for that short excursion across the lane to the chapel. Frost had clung to our eyelids and hair while the wind pierced through the coats, chapping our chests red with its bite.

"Go upstairs," Father smiled when our laughter subsided. "There may be a gift to help you warm yourselves, and what with the cold... and everything else disturbing our sleep these last nights, we could all use a few more hours of rest today."

Faith scrambled up the steps as I trudged along behind her, thinking the village gossip an even greater gift than whatever trinket Father had purchased for us. She must have thought so too, for she paused halfway up the stair case to whisper, "Anna, what's a copperhead?"

"A snake I think."

"Why would Mother say that Reverend Sutherland was a snake?"

"I don't know," I considered. "But I can't help wondering what type of man would allow his daughters out of the house after midnight wearing nothing but..." I paused, not wanting to finish the thought. The memory of that night drifted past my eyes like a fading dream I no longer wanted to remember.

"Nothing but a thin nightgown any decent girl would refuse to wear even in front of her own sisters?" Faith giggled.

I couldn't think of the scene any longer. Instead, I elbowed past Faith laughing, "Race you." She grinned a gap-toothed smile in reply, and we bounded up the stairs, falling onto my horsehair mattress in a fit of giggles.

Once we wiped the tears of laughter from our cheeks, Faith pointed to the brown paper bundle on top of our shared hope chest, which sat at the foot of the bed. In an unladylike manner which would have shocked Mother had she been there to witness it, we both flopped forward onto our stomachs, extending our arms to grab up Father's gift. The package was tied with thin red twine, and Faith picked at the tight knot, biting her tongue in concentration.

After a few moments, I tried to pull the package toward me, but one end of the twine was stuck under the lid of the hope chest. Faith looked at me. I shrugged in reply, and together we sat up and moved to the edge of the bed.

Once I slipped the twine off the package, we ripped open the paper. Inside were two slates, slate pencils and two readers, one for Faith, and one for me. My sister looked as if she were going to cry from happiness.

In West Virginia, we had needed to share both a slate and a reader. Father worked among the poor there, and they could not afford to pay him much in the way of salary. In addition to his ministerial duties, he had worked a few acres of farmland. Like most of the children in our town, we often went without, and that which we did have was shared between us. The church served as a schoolhouse. When Faith began school the year before, we sat together in the same pew, passing our slate back and forth and holding open the reader to two different sections.

Before we moved, Mother had said, "Our new town in New York is nearly as small as where we live now, but I hear tell that Lockport, the next city over, is bustling with traffic from the Erie Canal. They called it Clinton's Ditch, but it's brought much business and prosperity to the region. There was even talk of a train station, and it is expected that Lockport might be as large as Buffalo someday."

We weren't to go to the Nickel City, however, for Mother said Buffalo was an "urban forest trembling with angry trade unionists." And she did not want us associating with "those rough city types." Later, I found the city to be abuzz with art and culture. Millionaire's Row on Delaware Avenue was lined with mansions as fine as those on Fifth Avenue in New York City. Furthermore, I spoke with a trade unionist once, and he was quite gentlemanly.

I can only think my mother's opinion was based on rumors of a certain Canal Street, which one of my schoolmates later told me was "The wickedest street in the world" filled with nothing but "saloons, bars and brothels."

Mother had not told us all this the day we moved in of course. She merely remarked, "Cambria is small, but folks from the neighboring towns will come to worship with us, particularly after they hear your father speak. The power of the Spirit shines upon him whenever he takes to the pulpit."

I remembered this exactly because it was the only kind thing she had uttered all that morning, and I smiled again at her words. Father was indeed a good preacher, and we were all proud of the work he was doing. However, I realized that Mother's generosity appeared in part because she knew that a larger congregation in a growing town would also mean more money for the family.

At first, I thought Mother greedy, but I came to appreciate that Father's new position could bring gifts such as the slate, which would make our lives comfortable, if not extravagant.

Faith and I pried open the hope chest and gasped when we saw what was inside—two brand new coats! I drew them out, taking care not to catch the beautiful brass buttons on the lid of the chest.

Faith's coat was a soft gray with red woolen trim around the edges and a detachable military-style cape that was all the fashion amongst little girls just then. She would be the envy of every child in the younger school.

My own gift would cause just as much jealousy—a long cloak of heavy navy wool with brown fur at both the collar and the cuffs. I slipped my arms through the long sleeves, knowing before I stood that it would puddle at the ground, but I could grow into it in a year or two. There was no point in buying two or three such richly-designed garments when one would last through several seasons.

Faith began to sniffle, and I put my arm around her bony shoulders. It was rare that she was given anything new. She had gotten used to wearing my old, threadbare clothing as soon as I outgrew it. Sometimes, I incurred the wrath of our mother by griping or saying precisely what I thought at any given moment. Unlike me, Faith lived up to her virtuous name and rarely spoke a word of complaint. However, my sister was a girl, not a saint, and she had secretly longed for nice things, even if she could never find the courage to say so.

We ran back down the stairs with hugs and kisses, and perhaps a little weeping on Faith's part. It was then that my father stood and declared, "Anna, you'll have the chance to wear your gift tomorrow."

My mouth gaped. We had hardly been in town but a few days. Was I to go to school already? I felt nauseous and dizzy all at once. "School?" was all I could say, trying not to stutter.

"No," Father drew his pipe from its box and filled it with tobacco. "Not for a few more weeks—once we're truly settled and the weather dies down some. I don't want you girls walking into town when a snowstorm could arise at any moment. No. Tomorrow, I must travel down to Reverend Sutherland's to speak with him about his family's nighttime visits."

"And you want me to go?" I gulped, looking over to Mother, who pursed her lips in silent disapproval.

"They have a few girls around your age. I think you could get to know them. I'm under the impression they don't have very many friends in this town. Perhaps you'd be willing to change that?" He looked directly into my eyes.

This was what Father termed a "faith challenge." He did not believe in merely preaching from the pulpit or being a Sunday Christian. Father believed that faith should be lived. He often proclaimed, "The best way to live our faith is to love those around us."

Mother often disagreed with this method, and I once overheard her telling Aunt Ruth, "The best way to live a Christian life is to study the Bible, read the Catechism, sit silently in church, and recite the Lord's Prayer at supper. William is too soft-hearted sometimes."

She had also told Aunt Ruth that I was my, "Father's daughter." She was correct, and under his guidance, I took pains to act kinder and more gracious than I might have otherwise.

Thus, I came to ride alongside Father in the new two-seater buggy the church had purchased for house calls to the sick and homebound. It was a fairly warm day compared to the others we had seen so far. The sky was still gray with clouds, but the buggy was enclosed by clack panels on either side of us, and the fur of my buffalo blanket kept me warm and safe. At least, that is how I felt at first.

As the horse continued the few miles down the road, my hands began fluttering in anticipation. I did not believe in ghost stories, at least not then, but I could not help but wonder if perhaps the girls were witches or imps, as Mother had said. The fact that my father wanted me to accept these mysterious elven creatures as friends was nearly impossible to comprehend.

Still, I didn't feel as if I could ask him to turn back, and so, within a few minutes, we sat before the house, staring at its graying, chinked planks and collapsing roof. Father squeezed my shoulder before stepping down from the carriage and coming around to help me down.

As we walked toward the ramshackle cabin, a thin face appeared in the tall yellowed grasses sticking up in the snow. The girl's eyes met mine for a moment, before she quickly disappeared. Another face peaked out from the house— an auburn-haired girl, silhouetted behind the wax paper serving for windows. Father pressed on, but as his hand reached up to knock on the battered front door, a blast of wind rushed past. One of the gnarled shingles ripped from the roof and struck my face. The slap stung my cheek, and I could not help but feel as if the very house itself was warning us to stay away.

My hand flew to my face, and Father turned to me, mouth open in astonishment. The pain was forgotten in an instant when the door flew open and a ruddy-faced, rather masculine girl of about twenty-four or five glared sternly out at us. "What?" she folded her arms.

Father almost stumbled back. As a respected minister, this was hardly the type of greeting he was used to. "Is your father home?" he stammered.

The young woman barked out a laugh. "Fletcher hasn't been home in three days. If he owes you money, I would try the saloon or the gambling hall, though he may be farther off in Buffalo, Niagara Falls, or even Rochester for that matter. Last time he disappeared, we didn't see him for a month."

She was looking at me instead of Father as she said this, and as her eyes traveled down my new coat, she added, "Not that we missed him."

"Ah, I see," Father said. He turned to me, noting that I had gone unusually quiet and was blushing under the girl's scrutiny. "May I speak to your mother then?"

The young lady softened a little and leaned in the warped doorframe. As she did this, I could see past her to a small kitchen with straw pallets strewn across a dirt floor. In one corner of the room, a coal bucket had tipped over, and another girl of perhaps sixteen, dressed in nothing but an old burlap sack, was on her hands and knees scooping up the small black fragments.

"Mother," the girl paused, "is unwell." She caught me looking at the odd domestic scene behind her and moved her wide frame back into the doorway to block my view.

Then, she turned to address Father directly. "I would let you speak to Aunt Martha, but she's out today, laundering bed linens at the Lockport Hotel. It matters little. I usually speak for the family, in any case."

Father took this in stride, "Well then, my name is Reverend William Roberts. Miss...?"

"Sutherland." She held out a broad calloused hand. "Sarah will be fine. There are a few too many Miss Sutherlands in this house."

He chuckled, "Of course." Father cut off the laugh, and his face grew concerned. "Miss Sarah, I've come to discuss your nighttime visits to our chapel."

A gaggle of giggles burst out behind Sarah. She squared her jaw and shouted back, "Victoria, Isabella, hush. Go find Naomi and Dora. Sit them down to go over lessons." She moved outside and shut the door behind her.

"That chapel was once our own, Reverend Roberts. Singing there is one of the few pleasures we still appreciate. I will not take that delightful diversion away from myself or my sisters, not when they have so few joys in this world." Sarah hugged a torn shawl around her shoulders.

"Nor would I ask you to." My father's eyes glistened, and I could see he was nearly moved to tears in sympathy as he continued, "But I also cannot have you waking up my own girls in the middle of the night. My proposal is that you use the church freely and with my permission during the day. I am usually about town with my work, and other than Sunday services and Wednesday nights when the Daughters of Temperance Society meets, the building is free."

I could tell that Sarah did not quite know what to say. Her shoulders had been tensed up toward her ears, and her fists had been tightened in anticipation of a fight. I wondered how often she was forced into such a stance. If she was surprised then, her shock only grew at my father's next words.

"I hear the town is increasing," he said, turning his head south, where the road opened up as it continued to the port towns along the canal. "There will be many new families as the months turn warmer. Many wealthy families."

"Yes." Sarah lifted her square chin. "And what of it?"

"Wealthy families have wealthy children, and wealthy children require lessons in refinements like art and music in addition to their academic studies. I wonder if perhaps you could take it upon yourself to use the church piano and organ to teach some of the local children in addition to the lessons you give your family."

"For a fee, you mean?" she and squinted her eyes at him.

"Well, you'd have free use of the church, but yes. You would charge *them* a fee, of course," Father said.

Sarah softened. She tucked her raised chin into her chest and looked at the ground a moment. I could see the type of girl she might have been, had her father not been such a fool and her mother such an invalid. Suddenly, her manner shifted, and she glanced sharply up at me, as if hearing my thoughts.

"That will do quite well," she snapped. "I will advertise and begin the week after next."

Sarah paused, pride struggling with practicality on her wide face. Pride won out. "As soon as I have my first student, I will pay for the use of your space."

"A small donation to the church would suffice," Father said. "But I would prefer if you could instead share your talents with us on Sundays... perhaps once a month or so?"

Sarah nodded curtly and moved to retreat inside. I felt Father's foot tap against my boot. I resolved to be brave.

"I saw some of your younger sisters playing out in the yard." I gestured toward the tarnished water pump and the coop just beyond it where three scrawny chickens pecked over scraps of parched corn.

"I have no friends here, you see," I tried to explain. "Except for my own sister Faith, and I thought I might..."

"No," Sarah cut me off. Her tone was harsh, but her face was soft, as it had been before. She reached down to me, her hand pausing to rest on my still-enflamed cheek. "I'm sorry Anna Louise, but as I said, my mother is unwell, and she needs her rest, so you could not come over to visit or play."

"They could come for a visit to our house," I tried again.

Sarah shook her head, sadly. "You have no friends *yet*. However, I've no doubt you will soon, and then, my sisters' presence may not be welcome to you. I'll not break their hearts for a friend easily made but quickly lost," she paused and gazed sorrowfully at Father. "Perhaps someday, when we are older."

"Oh," was all I could reply. Would I be so shallow a child as to make a friend one day only to ignore her the next? I did not know. But her words were a declaration, not an invitation for debate.

"We shall see you Monday after next, Miss Sarah." Father tipped his hat. "I look forward to hearing the strains of your songs."

"Good day then," Sarah crossed her arms again and moved back into the house.

We walked silently back to the buggy and rode forward into town. Father smiled, proud he had procured a suitable arrangement for the struggling family. I frowned in bewilderment. How, I wondered, had Sarah Sutherland known my name when neither Father nor I had ever spoken it?

***

My puzzlement faded as we made our way into town, visiting the lower school where Faith would soon be attending, and the upper school next door where I was to go. I was indeed grateful for Sarah's refusal of my friendship a few weeks later when my sister and I stood in the schoolyard our first day of classes.

The snow was beginning to recede. Freshets of clean, new water rushed down grassy banks into brooks and streams. That morning, as Mother wove the strands of my auburn hair into a single tight braid, she remarked, "Won't be too long before traffic begins along the canal again. I expect plenty of people will arrive, come summer."

"Won't most of them continue on to the West?" I wondered.

"Mayhap." She tugged at the braid in bitter acknowledgement. "But I think that Westward Expansion nonsense is mostly done with. The pioneers realized how foolhardy they were, trying break untamed land out in Indian Territory and most gave up before they started. Others took claims and tried to prove up the land, but couldn't, and they were soon forced to come back to more civilized country."

Mother drew a brown ribbon from her sewing bag to tie onto the end of my braid. "Then there's folks like some of your father's kin, who stayed in the South after the war. Sensible men like your father left the South and fought for the Yankees. The Southerners lost a good number of men in battle. Then, after the Union burned their cities and won the war, the carpetbaggers took nearly every plantation they could get their grubby hands on. Old Southern gentlemen are being driven North, and they're begging the Yankees for work."

I did not know whether this was true, only that I had heard my mother's account of recent history so many times, I could recite it in my sleep.

"There," Mother said, patting my bow, "now you'll be all trimmed in brown for school. Mind you don't get your new clothes dirty and watch over Faith when the supper bell rings. I'm sending some leftover fried chicken and pieces of dried apple pie for you to share, so don't swing your lunch bucket, or it will all be smashed to bits."

I threw my hands around my mother's neck and kissed her pale cheek. "Anna Louise Roberts!" Mother pushed me away. "There's no need to be so demonstrative. For goodness sake, child. Keep your wits about you and be a lady when you go to school. I don't want the other girls to think you're a senseless nitwit."

I withdrew and waited until she finished dressing Faith. Then, with no more kisses or looks backward, I took Faith's hand, and we headed toward town. As we journeyed to school together, the sounds of Sarah Sutherland warming the church organ bellows followed us down the path.

The schoolyard was filled with the noise of play as all the boys, and a few younger, more daring girls, rushed back and forth, leaping over rocks and branches, and hiding behind trees in their games. Faith's sweating palm gripped my hand even more tightly, and I could feel her begin to retreat behind my skirts, the way she used to when standing with Mother amongst the ladies at church. "It will be fine," I whispered. "You've been to school before."

"Yes," her thin voice quavered, "but we were together then."

"And we'll be together now," I said. "I'll be right next door, and as soon as the supper hour comes, we can sit together, and you can tell me all about the friends you've made."

"No one will want to talk to me," she quavered, and I could not help but laugh right out loud. Everyone wanted to talk to Faith. As a little sister, she did pain me sometimes, but the truth was, she was one of the sweetest, kindest girls in the world.

I smoothed the two long braids poking out below her bonnet and moved to whisper some more words of encouragement when a plump girl with bright red curls bouncing all around her face came running over to us. "You must be the new minister's daughters!" The girl grinned. "We go to the Catholic parish down the road, but there are plenty of people in town talking already for me to know who you are."

"I'm Anna." I stuck out a hand. "And this is my little sister Faith."

The girl ignored my hand and pulled me into a big bear hug, nearly knocking me right off my feet. "So nice to meet you," she gushed. "You'll be with me then, and Faith, you'll be in the lower school."

My sister's lip trembled. "Don't worry," she promised, turning to Faith. "I just moved up from that room, and the teacher, Miss Abbott, is ever so nice. She only had to use her ruler twice last year, and that was just because Ed was so naughty. My name is Felicity Rivers, by the way, but you can call me Fliss."

A boy ran up beside her just then. His hair was even brighter than Felicity's. I saw they had identical sprinkles of freckles dancing across their noses. "My name is Edgar. Most people call me Ed, but you can call me Edgar." He bowed in a mocking gesture of gallantry. Then, as his sister let out a peal of laughter and squeezed her eyes shut for a moment, he grabbed my hand, kissed it, and gave me a roguish wink.

My heart beat like a frightened rabbit in my chest, and my cheeks grew hot. I drew my hand to my breast, barely noticing Faith being pulled away by another little girl from the lower school. Faith waved goodbye, smiling for all the world. I looked to Fliss for help, but the cheerful girl had not seen her brother's boldness.

"Oh, Eddie, you're so wicked," a reedy voice called out. "Don't tease her so, and on her first day of school too." A blonde girl in a pale pink coat sauntered over to us. She withdrew a gloved hand from her fur muff and slapped Ed playfully on the shoulder.

His mouth moved into a lopsided grin as though he enjoyed the admonishment, and he winked at me again before dashing away. Only then was the spell of his charm broken, and I was able to sensibly face his sister and her friend.

"This is Nettie Wright," Fliss said as the girl flicked back her golden hair and offered me a limp hand. "Nettie, this is Anna Louise, the new minister's daughter."

"Well, thank the Good Lord." Nettie leaned in toward me. "The last person we had was absolutely dreadful. I never saw such a dour looking man in all my life. The old man's cheeks were sunken in so badly, he looked like a corpse."

"Nettie!" Fliss gasped.

"Well, he did," she shrugged. "And don't even get me started on that Sutherland, the minister before him. My mother could tell you a thing or two about *that* man, I dare say."

"I heard he was removed, but no one would say precisely why." I leaned toward Nettie, hoping at last to hear the full story.

"To begin with, he was a Copperhead," she whispered.

"My mother said that too." I leaned away, disappointed. "But Father wouldn't tell what it meant."

"A Copperhead is a snake in the grass. They're the Northerners who supported the South in the War."

"No," I gasped.

Her blue eyes became dark, like twin lakes after a rain storm. "Where did you say you were from again?"

I straightened my shoulders. "*West* Virginia. Mother grew up there, but Father and his brothers moved when the state split. He was only fourteen then, but he ran off to be a drummer boy for the Union." I felt slightly shamed at bragging this way. My father refused to speak of the years he had served with the army and might not like me to mention it.

"That's fine then." Nettie's eyes cleared, and Fliss let out a breath I didn't even realize she'd been holding in.

Nettie continued, "My father was much too young to fight, but Grandpapa served as a General. He died at Antietam."

"I am sorry," I said, wanting to get back to our previous talk. "We lost a lot of good men there."

"Yes. We did. Which is why it was shameful the way Fletcher Sutherland went about proclaiming that the War Between the States was a mistake. Right from the pulpit, he said we ought to support states' rights. Can you believe it? My mother was the in the congregation that morning. According to Mamma, the man's words gave her such a shock, she nearly fainted."

"So, they kicked him out of the church?" my eyes widened.

"They planned to have a council," Fliss whispered. "But one night, Reverend Sutherland held an anti-war rally in the town square. Afterward, he went into the saloon."

"He always was a drunkard," Nettie interrupted. "Once Sutherland had a few shots of whiskey, he told everyone there that the war was nothing more than 'Northern Aggression' and that 'Negroes ought to be silenced instead of encouraged' because 'slavery was just part of the natural order of things.'"

"Our school was one of the first to be integrated," Fliss explained.

"Yes," Nettie nodded. "A Negro dentist and his family lived in town then. A very respectable family. So, of course, Grandpapa and the rest of the schoolboard voted to let them in." She flipped her hair, laughing. "That Negro family was much more respectable than the Sutherlands. Do you know that even their name means South land? I wish they'd move down South where they belong."

Fliss ignored her and continued, "The men in the saloon didn't take kindly to Sutherland's words. As soon as he left, they set on him and beat him nearly to death."

"No," I gasped a second time.

"Yes," Nettie said, "and they might have lynched him for treachery, too, had Hezekiah Bowman not intervened. He was another Copperhead living in town at the time. He stepped in and took Fletcher back to the parsonage, all bruised and bloodied."

"Had it not been for Mr. Bowman, the minister surely would have perished," Fliss said.

"To beat a man of the cloth! I've never heard of such a thing. Surely, outside of his politics, he was trying to do the Lord's work?" I looked about the schoolyard in bewilderment and saw

Faith chatting happily with her new playmate. Could Father be in such danger just for sharing his beliefs?

"Don't fret," Fliss said. "The war talk wasn't the only reason they beat him."

Here Fliss' voice lowered to a whisper only the three of us could hear. "He had been *alone* with one of the ladies of the church," she confided, "and the girl grew very round about the middle before being shipped off to her aunt over in Ohio."

I felt flames rise in my cheeks. Perhaps Mother was right. This talk seemed too embarrassing and scandalous for my innocent ears.

"Not to mention the business with his wife's sister," Nettie added, raising her voice above the clatter. I could see that, while Fliss cared about propriety, Nettie was all too happy to flaunt the gossip, and I blushed all the more.

"The girls sleep in the kitchen on sacks instead of beds," Nettie said. "Their brother Charlie sleeps out in the barn. But everyone knows Martha doesn't have a room to herself. Fletcher is living with both his wife Mary *and* her sister Martha. It's just like those Mormon men out in Utah with all the wives. I would even dare to say that some of those sisters are actually cousins."

My stomach turned. I worried for the younger children who might overhear our conversation. However, when several stopped their play to listen in, I noticed a few nodding sagely before returning to their games. From their demeanor, I gathered that all this scandal was widely known. No wonder Sarah had said her sisters' friendship would not be welcome to me.

"Will Charlie and the younger girls be coming to school then?" I asked, worried that my impulsive attempt at Christian charity might actually ruin my reputation.

Nettie's light laughter hurdled through the wind. "No. We're quite above them, socially. The Sutherlands don't come to school. They know to stay away from where they're not wanted."

The schoolmarms emerged to ring their bells, calling us in for the day's lessons. "Come with me," Nettie said, grasping my arm. "We can share a desk." She looked back to Fliss who was tugging at her brother's Ed's sleeve, beckoning him inside as he hooted and dodged her grasp.

"I usually share with Fliss," Nettie confided, "but between the two of us, she's getting plumper each day. I fear I'll be pushed off the bench before too long." Laughing, she linked her arm through mine as we went inside.

I returned to the conversation that evening while preparing supper. Mother asked, "Did you meet any nice girls today?"

I wanted to tell her that I had met two very nice girls, and a nice boy as well, but held my tongue as Faith was bubbling over in excitement. In one breath, she exclaimed, "I made a best friend today, and her name is Elizabeth, and she's going to show me everything they've already learned in their speller."

"Ah, now remember, Faith what we read in Mr. Drummond's book." My mother recited, "Happy, happy are they who can truly call *God* their Best Friend! Such will be sure to make choice of good friends and play-fellows, for they will choose none who do not love God, their Best Friend!" She paused, letting Faith consider for a moment.

"I see, Mother." Faith's shoulders slumped. "Elizabeth may be my very good friend, but God is my Best Friend."

"Just so," Mother smiled. I wished for a moment our relationship could be so easy. We always seemed to cluck at each other like two angry old hens, and it seemed I could never do anything to make things be otherwise.

Faith regained her joy and prattled on to detail everything Elizabeth had said and everything she heard about Miss Abbott. By the end of her speech, Mother and I heard tales of everything that everyone in the lower school had ever done in their entire lives.

I tired of Faith's chattering, and when Father came home, the edict of silence at the dinner table allowed me to say nothing. I ruminated about Sarah and the other Sutherlands, wondering what it must be like to never go to school and never have a friend.

At twilight, after my parents and Faith were asleep, I tore a scrap of paper from my schoolbook. It was a dreadful thing to do, and I knew I could be punished for it, but in that moment, I didn't care.

Lighting the lantern, I sharpened my pencil with my small Eagle knife, wrote in small careful letters on the paper, and grabbed up a spare pin. Then, sliding my feet into my new bedroom slippers, I took our two, old broadcloth coats out to the chapel. Folding them neatly on the top of the piano, I pinned the note to Faith's jacket, which rested on top. The note read:

For your younger sisters. In friendship, Anna

I knew Sarah would find the coats early in the morning when practicing, as she always did before giving her lessons. I wanted her to know that she had a friend, even if neither of us were allowed to say so.

***

The days grew warmer still, and I realized New York had not much to speak of in the way of spring. We seemed to move out of winter in seconds, and just as I grew used to my new coat, it was time to cast it aside for the lighter calico dresses of summer. We took our shoes off, too, as soon as we were able, oiling them up and setting them in our bureau. Until the weather turned to frost again, shoes would be reserved for Sundays and house calls. There was no need to wear them to school.

Just as it seemed I was beginning to feel at home in our little school, the year was ending. Lessons would be over until autumn. The bigger boys, like Edgar, and his not-so-charming friends Jonathan and Julius, had already stopped coming to class, for they were needed to help on acres of rich farmland where shoots of corn began to sprout, and apple trees sprang forth with snowy blossoms.

"I shall miss this," I told Fliss and Nettie as we waited for Teacher to ring the bell on our last day. "I suppose I'll not see you for a time."

Fliss nodded, "There's more work to be done in summer than winter. Momma plans to preserve every fruit and vegetable she can get her hands on, and she'll be needing my help. Saturdays are only for mending, though. I can usually find some time to play in the afternoons."

I smiled. "For us too. Mayhap we can go into town together and see the barges pulled along the canal."

Fliss laughed, "The bargemen can be rough, Anna. I don't know if either my mother or yours would allow us to wander down there. But you could come to our house and see the quilt we're making."

I moved to reply, but as usual, Nettie cut in. "I'll be seeing you nearly as often as I do now." She suppressed a satisfied smirk.

Nettie's family lived in a larger brick house on the hill. She invited me over once to see her doll collection, which I had marveled at, though she promised, "I don't play with these anymore, mind you, but they cost a fair bit, and I thought you might like to see them. Do you still play with dolls?"

I lied and said I didn't, though my old ragdoll was still tucked under my pillow, and I still sometimes told her goodnight. What amazed me more than the toys was the collection of servants her family seemed to have. She waved a hand dismissively whenever we passed one. "That's just Bridget, the scullery maid. That's Leah, the laundress."

Guessing I wanted to ask about her family's wealth, Nettie raised her shoulders. "Grandpapa made some investments before he died. He left us quite well off."

I recalled these memories in slight distaste. After a moment, I asked, "Why will you see me often, Nettie?"

"Mamma says that if I'm to marry well, I must be accomplished," she fingered the ruffled lace adorning her skirt.

"She's decided I shall take art lessons in Lockport with Mr. Raphael Beck. He studied in Munich and Paris, you know. And, as there are no Parisian musicians in our parts, I shall begin music lessons here in Cambria with Sarah."

"But you hate Sarah!" I stepped back in surprise.

"Sarah is the best music teacher in town." Nettie rolled her eyes. "If I'm to master the piano, I need to learn from the best."

I looked to Fliss, but she merely stared at the ground and bit her lip, the way she always did when refusing to challenge Nettie.

"You said the Sutherlands were below you," I argued. "You said they lived like heathens, and you'd sooner cross through a swamp than talk with one of them." It was true. This last she had declared not a week before.

"See here, Anna." Nettie poked a finger at my chest. "You don't have servants, so you don't know. It isn't as if I have given Sarah an invitation to *dine* with us. The lessons are a business arrangement. She will be working for me. I'm not lowering myself down to her filthy level, if that's what you're thinking."

It wasn't what I was thinking. I was wondering how I could have sat beside this cruel girl every day for weeks without realizing what she was truly like. I promised myself then that I would sit with Fliss next fall, for Fliss' smile warmed me more than the school's coal oven on any winter day, and all Nettie had to offer were hard candies and porcelain dolls as cold as her heart.

Faith was going home with Elizabeth for dinner that evening, and since I was to walk home alone, I decided to pass by the Sutherland place as I had not seen it since my first visit with Father.

I stopped in front of their rail fence, noticing that it had been repaired in one or two places. Looking beyond the tall grasses and weeds covering their lawn, I saw a glint of silver by the chicken coop and realized that the rusting wire had been replaced. It was clear Sarah's new income was helping her family. I only hoped Sarah and her emaciated siblings were also getting more to eat.

Seeing that glass had also been placed in two of the windows, I looked toward the front door, wondering whether visiting to the house on my own would allow me entry this time. Bracing myself for rejection, I unlatched the gate. As I watched the gate slowly swing open on creaking hinges and took a tentative step forward, a crow suddenly descended upon me.

The creature flew at my face, its feathers so black they blotted out the sun. Screeching, the bird pecked at my arms as I reached up to protect my eyes. I fell to the ground. Crying in pain, I reached an arm back to strike the wild creature as he flapped and pecked at my neck and hands.

I felt my hair being lifted and cried out in pain. Desperate, I rolled back and forth in the dirt, trying to dislodge the shrieking monster, whose talons ripped into the flesh at my back.

"Stop! Stop! Demon bird!" I screamed, trying to slap him away.

With a final caw, the crow bit my neck once more. Rivulets of blood trickled down my neck as the bird careened away. I wiped my tears and looked up into the sky, still shielding my eyes with my hands, fearful of another attack. Instead, I saw the black devil, now as calm as a dove, flying home, my brown hair ribbon clasped in his bloodstained beak.

Shaken, I crawled to the fence. Grasping the wooden rails and raising myself to my feet, I saw a thin face covered by a mass of hair pull back behind the safety of the window.

Clearly, at least one of the Sutherland sisters had been watching. Yet none had come to my aid. I considered knocking on their door and asking for some help directly but knew there would be no answer.

Instead, I sat for a moment, collecting myself. Once my heart had slowed its frightened, skipping beats, I limped down the road, worrying what Mother would think of my torn dress and bloodied hands and face.

For the next four years of school and summers, I never ventured down that path again.

Part II

We're All Mad Here

Pictured: Miss Mary Sutherland

March, 1885

Of all the ghosts I encountered later, I never felt Father's spirit among them. I have, I suppose, that small bit of serenity. He was able to find a peace, which others were not.

I turned seventeen the day Father died. His death was a violent one, particularly for a man who prided himself on bringing amity and kindness to everyone he met. I wish I could say his death was over quickly and he felt no pain, but in truth, he lingered on for days before passing.

One night, his anguished cries grew so loud, I considered breaking both the law and the Commandments by ending his agony myself. I could not bring myself to do it, however.

Thankfully, Christ answered my prayers. Before the doctor came the next morning, God had taken Father home.

Father was not a man to use guns often, particularly given our proximity to both farms and trade routes, which allowed us to purchase meat in town rather than hunt it on our own. However, that March there had been a plague of deer. As more men moved to the area and built homes for their families, the deer had been driven from the forests and were becoming thick throughout town. Father said, "Hunting is needed to thin the herd."

I eagerly replied, "Do go hunting, Father! I haven't had fresh venison in ages."

It was this last for which my mother will never forgive me. Father patted me on the head and answered, "Well then, my Anna, you shall turn seventeen to a feast of venison stew." Those were the last clear words he would ever speak. He got up from the table, grabbed up his gun, and headed outdoors to take a deer before nightfall.

A few minutes later, as Faith and I cleared the dishes from the table, we heard the blast of a gunshot followed by a cry of pain.

I ran out into the cold. The wind blew snow drifts around me. It took a few moments, but at last, I spotted my father's crumpled body. In the waning gray light, I knelt beside him, holding his mangled face in my hands. "Go for the doctor," I called to Mother, as she stood senseless in our doorway. A hand flew over her mouth and I heard her scream before she took up the lantern and raced to the barn.

Father's gun had misfired. The force of the explosion had gone back toward him instead of out toward the deer. There was nothing to be done, the doctor said. Nothing but ease the pain with morphine until he finally passed.

Women from the church came and helped Mother dye all her dresses black. I moved through Father's memorial service as if dead myself. I could not sleep, for I saw nothing but my father's torn flesh each time I closed my eyes.

In my few fitful dreams, I saw Father and I, walking down a cobblestone road together. The Sutherland crow came at us, pecking first at my face, and then at his, our mingled blood staining the path. I did not ask Faith about her dreams, but I felt the trundle bed move and shake under her similarly broken attempts at rest.

After the parishioners and mourners had ceased bringing their dishes of casserole and baskets of bread, I sat with Mother in the parlor. "Something must be done," I said. "With Father gone, we cannot live here much longer. The parsonage belongs to the church, and they will want a new minister. Will you find work in town?"

"This is my work, Anna," she gestured around the chilled room, which felt barren without Father's presence to fill it.

"A new minister will be sent," I tried to explain. "Perhaps we could move back to West Virginia. We can't—"

A faint tapping at the door cut short my words. "Sit," I sighed. "It is probably Mrs. Prendergast with the preserves she promised."

I opened the door to see the ruffled pink skirts of my friend. "Nettie!" I tried to smile. "You and your mother called on us just last week. I would never have expected you back so soon. Whatever are you doing here?"

She smoothed her dress, "Mamma has sent me to discuss something with you."

"Come in." I led her into the parlor.

"Oh," she exclaimed, seeing Mother in the rocking chair. "I didn't realize." Nettie turned to whisper to me, "Anna, this is a rather delicate matter. Do you think there is anywhere we could have some privacy?"

I nodded, "Mother, could you go upstairs to help Faith with her mathematics? I promised her she wouldn't be left behind her class."

If there was one thing I knew about my mother, it was that she did not take lightly to being ordered about. I knew I would pay dearly for my request later, but extra chores and the coldness I was already used to were hardly of any concern anymore.

"I've come," Nettie paused, clearing her throat, "to inquire whether you would like to take a position with us."

The snow on Nettie's tulle bonnet was melting into a puddle on our floor. I stared at the water as it grew from solitary drip to a small circle, to a pool taking on the shape of the black tabby cat which used to sleep at the foot of my bed in West Virginia. I thought of that cat and the possibility of returning home to Mother's people and could not think of a word to say as Nettie continued.

"Our scullery maid was most unsatisfactory. Mamma was forced to let her go this morning. There's not a proper girl to be found, but I told Mamma that you were bright and reliable. I believe you could perhaps even work your way up to the position of housekeeper or governess in a few years. I daresay I'll need one. Mamma agreed to the idea and requested that I come over at once."

"You want me to be your *scullery* maid?" My face grew hot and tears began to fill my eyes. I held them back. In all my sorrow, I had been unable to cry since the night of Father's accident. I did not cry when he screamed in pain. I did not cry during the memorial service. I did not even cry in my nightmares. I certainly would not cry now in front of Nettie, though I felt humiliated.

"Don't be shocked." She untied her now dripping bonnet and tossed it indelicately on the sideboard. "Your father hardly made a dime working as a minister. It was nothing to be ashamed of. He did the Lord's work, and that always requires a sacrifice. Now he's gone, I know you and your mother won't want to live on charity for too long. I thought you'd appreciate the offer."

"You want me to be your scullery maid?" I whispered again. My embarrassment turned to anger, and I nearly slapped the smug smile right off her perfect porcelain face.

There was another knock at the door, stronger than the weak, feminine taps Nettie had used. "That will be your dear Mamma, will it?" I spat each word.

I flung open the door, prepared to scream right in the woman's pale, pampered face. My anger rushed out with the wind when I saw Sarah Sutherland and her youngest sister, Mary. The smaller girl hugged a small Scottish terrier close to her chest, as if it would protect her from my ferocity.

"Did I come at a bad time?" Sarah's alto voice almost laughed. The tiny dog gave a sharp yip in reply.

I gave a thin smile, but didn't dare reach out to pet the dog, worried it would nip my fingers. "No," I said, sweeping my arm for her to come in, "Miss Wright was just leaving." Now she had put me in a place below her, I no longer felt I could call Nettie by her first name.

Sarah arched an eyebrow at Nettie, crossed her arms, and said nothing. She had given Nettie piano and singing lessons for an entire summer a few years before, but the Sutherland Sisters were now a famous music group. Their new-found acclaim and wealth meant Sarah no longer had to work as a simple teacher.

Nettie refused to acknowledge their success, claiming that Sarah had been, "An abysmal teacher. Nothing compared to Mr. Raphael Beck, who truly realizes my artistic talent and understands how to nurture it."

My former friend said nothing of this now, however, but instead stuck her nose in the air. "You can't afford to be a schoolgirl any longer, Anna Louise Roberts," Nettie said. "It's time for you to accept that and grow up. The offer still stands. Think it over and pray on it tonight. We'll look for a new girl the morning after next if you don't come or send word."

Then, looking down at little Mary, Nettie jeered, "My uncle is a doctor, and he says long hair gives women headaches that cause them to go mad. Perhaps if you cut your hair, you wouldn't be as insane as your dead mother."

This time, I did slap her.

The venomous sneer still on her lips, Nettie said nothing, but turned and flounced out, her frilled skirts rustling and hissing around her as she left.

"Well, I can see I was right." Sarah barked her laugh again. "You'll do just fine."

"Fine for what?" I asked. I felt too tired to fight any longer. My very bones ached, and a headache was forming between my eyes. If Sarah was also looking to procure a scullery maid, I might have acquiesced.

"Mary needs teaching," Sarah explained, "as do the twins, Dora and Naomi. They may be a bit older than you, but I expect you could teach them a thing or two, and they need companionship as much as book learning."

I motioned for the ladies to sit on the settee, noting how much things had changed between us. The days of chicken farming were long gone. After Sarah's music tutorials had become popular with young ladies throughout the county, the sisters started a music act, managed by their father, Fletcher.

At first, they performed in churches, singing parlor songs and hymns. By the summer Nettie began her lessons, the Sutherlands began to appear in larger venues around the state. By autumn, they had achieved such notoriety, they were invited to sing in New York City at the Great Broadway Museum.

During that winter, they give vocal and instrumental entertainments to packed audiences in music halls throughout Connecticut, New Jersey, and even New Orleans. From the stage, they had moved on to gain a contract with a small circus, the W.W. Cole's Colossal Show. They sisters quickly became one of the featured attractions, and since then, their fame had grown with every season.

As a result of their success, the Sutherlands returned to Cambria quite wealthy, earning enough money that both their brother and their Aunt Martha were able to move out of the shared house and purchase separate residences of their own, though I had heard the brother died suddenly soon after.

Nevertheless, as the sisters became celebrities, the papers began to follow their every movement, especially when they hired a group of men to tear down the old Miller shack and erect a new house in its place.

Beyond the material, I saw that having money allowed Sarah's natural good humor to surface. The scrappy strength she'd shown in her younger years had blossomed into true leadership as she took charge of her family and their careers. Her newfound charisma also brought a sort of handsome beauty to her plain, almost mannish face.

I wanted to smile at this new Sarah, but the humiliation of my altercation with Nettie and the sudden offer to work with Sarah left me feeling overwhelmed. I sat, pinching the bridge of my nose where a headache was beginning to form. "I thought you were singing in New York."

"We were," Sarah said, "but work on the house is still being completed, so we'll be home a few months, at least until May or June."

"And if I take the position, what shall I do when June comes?" I asked.

Sarah licked her bottom lip and looked to Mary. The fragile girl stared back at her sister with wide eyes. At last, she ceased petting her little terrier and gave me a timid glance. Then, she bobbed her head once. I realized it was Mary, and not Sarah, who was making the decision in this matter.

"When June arrives, you shall travel with us," Sarah declared. "We've had such great success, we have been offered a new contract. A few weeks ago, we officially left Mr. Coles' circus and signed on with Barnum and Bailey's Greatest Show on Earth.

Soon, we'll set off for New York City. With Barnum, we're set to travel across New York, Pennsylvania, New Hampshire, Massachusetts, Maine, and even up into Canada. The people there have been hankering for entertainment for some time, I hear. They'll pay a pretty penny to see the show."

"And you would have me along?" With Nettie's offer, I had felt ashamed. Somehow, with Sarah's, I felt honored.

"Go back to the carriage, Mary," Sarah said, slapping her sister on the back cheerfully. The girl bobbed her head to me this time and quickly disappeared with her pup.

Sarah turned to me, the smile vanishing from her lips, "What your friend said..."

"She's not my friend," I nearly snarled.

Sarah nodded. "What that spoiled little girl said," she paused, noted my smile, and turned grave once more. "She wasn't completely in the wrong. Mary is not well. In truth, I would keep her at home, but Fletcher insists we must all to perform. 'The Seven Sutherland Sisters sounds better than six,' he says. It would seem he has plans to advertise us as the next Seven Wonders of the World or some such." She waved a hand, dismissing the ridiculous notion.

"But Mary is special. Fragile. I don't know if she can stand the pressures of the stage. It's hard sometimes even on the rest of us. And," she stood, readying to leave, "they do need lessons. At least until we go back on tour. Keeping the girls out of school was perhaps not the best idea, but it was necessary at the time."

"If this musical venture falls apart, I want them to have some education to fall back on. Grace has some sense, but she is too motherly and soft to insist the girls do regular schoolwork. Mary, Dora, and Naomi are as witless as three nanny goats. Isabella and Victoria are not much better—concerned with nothing but fashions and men. It's too late for them, but the younger girls can still be helped. We can provide the books if you can provide the guidance."

I held open the door. "I promise to pray in earnest as I consider your kind offer," I said. "I shall let you know in the morning."

On the brass doorknob, Sarah's strong hand covered mine, "You did us a kindness once when none would even glance at us in the street. I have not forgotten that, Anna. Neither has Mary. She still has the coat."

With that, Sarah was gone. I would pray, as I had promised, but my mind was already decided. I would either support Mother and Faith by my earnings, or I would work in Cambria when they returned to Grandmother's home in West Virginia. Both the parsonage and my grandparents' house were places I no longer belonged. I would pack my few possessions and leave for the Sutherland's before the week was out.

***

A house cannot be haunted unless those who dwell there believe in the spirits and give them power. Considering all that happened later, I often picture my short journey to the Sutherland house that morning as a grim one, filled with the thunderstorms and the overcast skies that so often filled my days in the times to come. Those gloomy days were far ahead, however, and the trip was a short and sunny one.

It was strange to be leaving home for the first time without leaving town. I had not thought this day would come for another year or two, when I graduated and ventured out into the world, perhaps to teach at a lower school, or perhaps to go on for college as my father had done. It would be unusual for a lady to attend college, particularly when we had little money, but Father had spoken to me of scholarships and places such as Mount Holeyoke and Vassar, which educated women exclusively.

Secretly, I held no such ambition, but longed to marry as soon as I was able, maybe to someone as sprightly and sweet as Fliss's brother Ed Rivers, or perhaps Ed himself, if he would have me. More than once, I had pictured Fliss and Faith bearing witness as Ed and I stood in the chapel before my father. I would wear my best dress and a new bonnet, and I would carry nothing but a small bouquet of daisies. In my mind, our wedding would be a sun-drenched day of love and laughter.

Instead, I was to go into service for the one family I never imagined would have the money to pay for luxuries like companions or tutors. It nearly broke my heart, for I knew the Rivers family would never permit a man like Ed to court, let alone marry, a mere servant girl.

The sun beat down on Faith and me as we sat side by side in our shared bedroom, silently bundling up our meager belongings. Sarah had given me a small trunk to be used in our future travels. Into it, I folded my navy woolen coat. Several years old now, the fur was matted, and it was worn at the elbows, but I had grown enough that it was finally the right length. I doubted I would grow any taller, and the coat would have to suffice. I would likely not be able to afford another for some time.

Next into the trunk went my Sunday dress and my underthings. On the top of those, I placed my mourning weeds—the black dresses I would wear for the next two years in memory of Father. Finally, I added the old faded dresses and aprons reserved for work days, believing I would be soon wear those far more often than any of the others.

On the very top, I rested the children's Bible one of Father's parishioners had given me the year I turned ten. Faith had an identical copy, and they were our most treasured possessions. We often comforted ourselves by reading over the stories and carefully touching the colored illustrated plates.

As I discarded the things I would no longer need, I saw that Faith picked each item up and lovingly placed it into the hope chest. She folded my other dresses and petticoats first and then my old, forgotten rag doll and the other books Father and Mother had given me over the years. "You can get them when you come to visit." Her voice cracked at the last word.

"I'll not need them anymore, Faith," I replied, refusing to meet her gaze. "I must work now, and I have no need for frilled frocks, dolls, or playthings. But I promise to send wages to you and Mother, so you can have all the nice things in the world."

She clutched my arm, her green eyes fierce. "Is that why you're doing this? Please, don't, Anna. Don't leave. Come to the mountains with us. I shall work too. There are plenty of positions out there for girls with small hands and nimble fingers."

I wheeled on her and slapped her across the face. She was already stunned, but I dug my fingers into her thin shoulders and shook her, "You will not work in the mines, Faith. Promise me! Promise me!"

She nodded and fell against me, hot tears dampening my breast. I had never struck my sister before, but I had heard too many stories of children sent into the coal mines like canaries, never to return. Even when they did, many died of the black lung before they saw twenty. I could not let my sweet sister suffer such a fate, and I could not allow her to work in a sweatshop either, sewing away in the sweltering heat until her fingers bled. All I could do was work to support Faith and pray she married well.

My sister raised her pale face, and I wiped away her tears. "I will travel everywhere they do, Faith," I said, putting on a false smile. "Won't that be exciting? Niagara Falls is only a few miles away, but I've never laid eyes on it. And think of the mountains and rivers you'll hear of in my letters, and all the cities I'll visit. I'll write you so much, you shall feel as if you've gone there yourself."

"Will you write me every day?" she sniffled.

"I'll write every chance I have," I promised. "Come now." I took her trembling hand. "Mrs. Kraus brought three cakes the day of Father's funeral. I think we can sneak a piece or two before supper."

A few moments later, my sister and I sat together in the pantry like two church mice, knees drawn to our chests as we giggled noiselessly and nibbled away at the thickly frosted German chocolate cake. Can others recall so precisely their last moment of childhood? I cannot say.

The train carrying my mother and sister left early the following morning. Once they had dressed in their traveling clothes, and we were ready to depart for the station, Mother pulled me aside. "I ordered these by post for your birthday," she said, handing me a small package. "They came the day after... well, I was never able to find the right time to give them to you."

I untied the string and opened the box. Inside was a vanity set— a hairbrush with an engraved ivory handle, a matching comb and hand mirror, and a small glass bottle for perfume. "It's lemon verbena," she explained, "the kind I always wear. I thought you might like it. My mother gave me a similar set when I turned seventeen."

Words of gratitude caught in my throat. Though neither of us had spoken of the tragedy, I felt she would always blame me for killing Father. This gift seemed a token of peace between us, her way of saying she forgave me, or at the very least, that she would miss me a little. All I could say was, "Thank you, Mother. These are beautiful. I shall use them every day."

At the train station, no more words were spoken between us. She gave me a stiff embrace before boarding, leaving Faith and me alone on the platform. Our goodbyes had also been said, but I helped Faith pull the heavy hope chest into the luggage car. Then I kissed her over and over on both cheeks and promised to write soon.

My heart was cleaved in two, though I shed no tears. As soon as the train pulled from the station and disappeared around the first bend, my bones chilled, and my body went numb, just as it had the day of Father's funeral. Picking up my bag, I walked the long miles to the Sutherland house like an ambulatory corpse, taking no notice when I stepped in a horse pile or bumped past a stranger on the street.

My mind returned to me with a sudden dread as soon as I saw the Sutherland's new house. It was done in the Queen Anne style, but more magnificently than any other home in the county. The large L-shaped frame had been erected, though only the front of the house had been finished. In that completed section of the house, three floors emerged from the still long, untamed grasses, and a turret topped with a witch's cap cast a shadow across the lawn.

Each of the windows was set with an ornate gable, a far cry from the wax paper lining that had served as windows in their former home. Brown gingerbread lattice offset a fresh coat of sickly yellow paint covering the walls, and pillars towering over the staircase provided a grand, but forbidding entryway.

I must admit, initially I noticed almost none of this. What my eyes fell upon first, as they were certainly meant to, was the rotting fence surrounding the manor. The Sutherlands had kept the old fence, even in its decay. On the latch of the gate was a tattered brown ribbon.

I slipped off my gloves and touched the ribbon in wonder. *Could this be my own ribbon from all those years ago?* The silk slid between my fingers, and I noticed a black spot in the center. The silk was frayed and torn at the edges, but otherwise it was without blemish. Not a speck of dirt nor fragment of leaf clung to it. If the ribbon was indeed mine, the dark stain was almost certainly my blood.

I snatched up the strip of silk, then nearly dropped it almost at once, fearing the crow would return to reclaim its hard-won prize. With one arm covering my eyes, I lifted the other, holding it aloft in my fist as an offering to the winged beast. But the wind, which had been blowing east all morning, was gone. The air was tranquil, and the ribbon did not so much as flutter between my fingertips.

I brought my fist back down, feeling like a foolish child on this day when I was taking on the responsibilities of an adult. Instead of lingering in my folly, I hastily tied the ribbon around the handle of my carpet bag and opened the gate.

As my foot crossed the threshold, I heard cawing in the distance, though thankfully no bird flew near. Above me, the iron weathercock atop the witch's cap began to spin round and round with a wild metallic squeal.

There was still no wind.

Goosebumps raised on my arms, and I nearly turned tail and ran away. However, I knew there was no one to turn to and nowhere to run. I could not meet Mother and Faith at the next train station, returning in disgrace, nor could I go to begging charity from our friends in town, who could scarcely afford to give it.

Neither could I stomach the thought of running to the poorhouse, where girls my age only went alone when their bellies grew round, and they were kicked out on the street.

My stomach turned. If I lost this position, Grandfather might no longer be able to afford Mother and Faith. Either or both might be forced into the mines to buy their bread. It was either face whatever was in the Sutherland Mansion or fall at Nettie's feet, crying forgiveness, which I would not do.

47

Nevertheless, I still might have fled had Sarah not come bursting out of the front door, barreling down the stairs like a runaway ox. I would learn later that Sarah always moved with ferocious intensity, and would come to love her for it, even if her sister Victoria did refer to her as "a man in skirts" behind her back.

Sarah was not the most beautiful or the gentlest of women, but what she lacked in graces she made up for in talent, ambition, and keen business sense. Victoria, in contrast, though lovely in face, was shallow in spirit and concerned herself almost wholly with pleated dresses, new shoes, and other trifles.

"Anna, thank goodness you've arrived." Sarah grabbed my elbow and hoisted my bag onto her broad shoulders. It was an odd thing for an employer to carry the bags of a servant, but Sarah had come from less than nothing and didn't stand on ceremony.

Moreover, she was impatient, particularly when she believed her younger siblings were "acting plain foolish," as she said now. "But that's Mary. One minute she's singing like a lark, and the next she was huddling up in the corner, rocking back and forth, screaming like a banshee."

I wanted to ask how she expected me to instruct Mary in mathematics or history if she was feeble minded. But Sarah continued inside, striding up the turret's winding staircase, taking for granted that I was following her. "Take this." She turned and thrust a book into my hands. "Sometimes reading calms her. The rest of us will be down in the parlor, continuing our rehearsal."

"Whatever is the matter with her?" I panted as we at last stood before the heavy door guarding the topmost room of the house.

Sarah said nothing but drew out an iron skeleton key and shoved it into the lock. "Is she... mad?" I asked, looking around the whitewashed room.

"We're all mad here," a deep voice resounded behind me, and I gave an involuntary shudder.

"Naomi," Sarah admonished, "hush. You'll frighten the poor girl to death." Naomi giggled as Sarah gestured to the novel in my hands, "She's quoting from those Alice books. Naomi loves her little jests."

Naomi was darker than Sarah, pretty but for her hawkish nose, though when she smiled, that small defect in her face disappeared, and she seemed to me the loveliest Sutherland I had met so far.

She ran a hand through her thick brown hair. The front had been cut away in what Mother called, "the lunatic fringe," but rather than allowing a few wisps of bangs to grace her forehead like Sarah, Naomi had curled the pieces with a hot iron, so they frizzed all about the crown of her head. I found this almost as bizarre as the weathercock moving of its own accord. That omen could have been explained away more easily than whatever fad was sitting atop Naomi's forehead.

"I haven't read that book." I tore my eyes from Naomi's frazzled brunette locks and looked about the room once more. I didn't want to admit that I had not read most stories as books outside the Bible and children's morality tales were not particularly encouraged in my home.

"You will soon enough," Naomi said, leaving off her joke to put a warm hand on my shoulder. Her voice was as rich as chocolate, and even in speech, I could hear the bass voice the newspaper had called "sweet and flexible." In Rochester, Naomi had been hailed as, "the greatest musical prodigy in the world." Hearing her speak, it was no wonder her performances were praised above the others.

"Enough chatter," Sarah cut in. "Mary's most likely hiding behind the curtains. The new bedframes should be here by week's end. For now, Anna Louise, there are pillows and quilts in cupboard. You may take a few and sit on the floor. Just read to Mary a bit. She'll calm soon enough."

"Am I to sleep here?" I wondered. The room was cold and as white as a bone.

"Good heavens child, no!" Sarah exclaimed. Without explaining where I would sleep, she turned to descend the stairs, calling as she walked, "If you slept there, wherever would we keep Mary?" With that, they were gone, and I was left alone with the mad woman in the attic.

***

As Sarah had predicted, a pair of newly-shined boots poked out from beneath heavy white curtains. I drew the drapes, causing Mary to shriek and run from her hiding place to the center of the room. She had a nose that mirrored Naomi's, but with Mary's delicate structure, the feature added to her fragile appearance, as if she was a lonely sparrow searching for comfort from her mother. Her hair was darker than Naomi's, too, and had clearly never been cut.

I knew the sisters were celebrated for their long hair, but for the sake of propriety, and convenience, they usually wore it up in great, thick knotted braids. I gathered that they took it down during performances, but seeing Mary with her hair down in midday was shocking. Her slight frame hid behind a charcoal cloud of her ebony locks. When Mary saw me staring, she bore her teeth in a cat-like grin, pushed her hair from her face, and wiggled her fingers in a wave.

So, this had been the little imp I'd seen my first night in Cambria. I almost laughed. For all my trepidation, Mary was still very much a child, younger than me by a few years, and probably just as frightened.

As the light dimmed, I lit the lantern which sat on the sole table adorning the room and said a silent prayer that I would come to care for Mary, trying to think of her as a surrogate for Faith, though much less substantial in spirit. Opening my eyes, I looked at the skeletal creature. It seemed at any moment, Mary would float away on the wind.

They often said the mad were dangerous, but after seeing Father's work with the afflicted, I had come to realize that the danger only lay in their unpredictability and the strange habits their minds forced upon them. I reasoned that Mary was required to work each day, singing, and playing music. She had only her sisters by way of company. When she grew weary, Mary retreated into herself. Her fits were merely a way of breaking apart from the others. Once I convinced myself the girl did not pose any threat of danger, I made a nest of pillows and blankets on the floor and began to read.

As soon as I read the opening poem, Mary quieted; by the time Alice was tumbling down the rabbit hole, she was sitting beside me. I did think the book an odd choice to read to someone as tormented as Mary, but she seemed calmer, and so I continued.

While I read, I felt her cold hands reach up to the braid I had woven around my head. She unpinned it and separated the twists I had taken such pains to make that morning, running her

51

fingers through my locks until my hair fell about my shoulders and down my back.

As she calmed, I settled into my role as nurse and governess, thinking perhaps I might not be in such a disagreeable position. I smiled, continuing the tale as Alice cried and flooded her small chamber. "Poor Alice! It was as much as she could do, lying down on one side, to look through the garden with one eye; but to get through was more hopeless than ever," I read.

When Alice's tears fell, Mary flew to her feet and twirled about the room. I remembered doing this same when I was five or six, and the act again made the waifish girl seem much younger.

I laughed at first, but Mary's spins grew ever wilder, as if she was driven by some unseen force. Her hair flew out like a second skirt, but then began to knot and tangle as she spun faster and faster around the room. I fumbled for the words of the Lord's Prayer, hoping that it might pacify her, or at least serve as some sort of talisman for me. As my lips formed the words, "Our Father," Mary began to laugh.

Her shrill cackle skittered across the back of my neck like a spider. It was a noise completely alien to me, and yet, I could not help but think I had heard it before. I closed my eyes, covering my ears. Behind my eyelids, I saw the weathercock, spinning and shrieking its metallic song, just as Mary was doing now.

My sympathies for her vanished and I stood up screaming, "Stop it, Mary! For the love of God, stop!"

She cut short her lunacy and floated toward me, booted feet moving almost imperceptibly beneath her damask skirt. My breath was ragged from my excitement.

I thought the incident over when, without warning, Mary tilted her face up to mine and raked her fingernails down her cheeks. Thin rivulets of crimson dripped down the cords of her neck.

It was my turn to scream. My mind went blank, and I wondered for a moment if I would go insane just from being in this creature's presence. This thought chilled me more than anything Mary had done. In a moment of clarity, I seized her two small hands with one of my own. With my other hand, I slapped the girl across her torn cheek.

It was the third time I had struck someone, and I hoped it would be the last. Mary's blood dripped from my fingers, but she stopped screaming.

Her face inches from mine, she whispered, "My father wants to speak with you."

"Your father?" I looked into her dark eyes.

"He's waiting in the ice house," she pointed down the staircase.

"The ice house?" My voice shook as I looked down the steps leading into the abyss of darkness below. The Sutherlands were wealthy, but I hadn't realized they'd built an icehouse in addition to the grand manor.

"Through the parlor." Mary wrenched her hands out of my grasp and returned to her original position, hiding behind the curtain.

The sun had set outside, though it was not yet time for dinner. Tentatively, I stepped down the stairs. The gaslights along the walls flickered as I moved past.

The thought of seeking help from Fletcher comforted me. He was, after all, a minister. Perhaps the rumors of his wicked behavior were nothing but silly village gossip. If Fletcher was anything like my father, he would help to soothe Mary. If he was like other preachers I had seen, he would give her a stern reprimand. In either case, her wounds would need to be treated.

I did not know whether the Sutherlands had strict protocols against interruption during their rehearsals. Adding to this was my worry about the security of my position in their household. As a hired girl, they could let me go at any moment. Unsure how to proceed, I tip-toed through the house, searching for either Fletcher or Sarah.

At last, I heard voices emanating from the parlor in low moans and whispers. Glints of firelight sparkled under the door, and I imagined a friendly warm scene inside. I eased the door open and poked my face through the crack. Smoke from the burning firewood floated toward me, but it smelled oddly of stale beer and sweat.

Suddenly, I saw a startling flash of white, as if a specter flew through the parlor. The fire, which had been roaring in the fireplace, went out. The room was taken over by shadows cast by the flickering oil lamp behind me.

Perhaps a window had been opened, and wind had rushed in. Perhaps a beer cart had overturned outside. Perhaps there was no specter, and I was still shaken from my encounter with Mary. My senses may have been playing tricks on me; it is true. All those things could be explained away.

What could not be explained was what Mary had called "the ice house."

It was not, as I had believed, a small building outside the house. I realized what Mary meant when I saw the chilling horror sitting within the parlor itself.

In the swaying, bending light of the lantern, six sisters held hands, chanting in an unbroken circle. They stood around a large flat table. Sitting upon the table like a slab of ice was a six-foot long glass dome.

And beneath the dome lay the cold, rotting corpse of Fletcher Sutherland with pennies placed over his eyes.

My stomach turned. Blood rushed through my ears like the waters of Niagara Falls, and the world went black.

***

"You knocked over the lamp and nearly started a fire." Victoria snapped open a vial of smelling salts beneath my nose.

"Don't scold the girl so, Victoria. I'm sure she's had quite a fright – the fire going out so suddenly that way," a motherly voice soothed. I blinked my eyes, noting the fire had been relit.

"I told you Spiritualist rituals were not to be tried today, Isabella." Sarah pushed through her crowded sisters. "What are you doing down here, Anna? Supper won't be ready for an hour yet."

"Mary," I breathed, "said your father wanted to speak to me. She told me he was in the ice house."

The girls exchanged mysterious looks. "And so, he is." Sarah gave an odd smirk and pointed to the strange, glass coffin. "Though I hardly think you'll be speaking to him anytime soon. Father died suddenly of paralysis two nights ago."

Sarah stood up, and her practical manner eased me at once. What ridiculous fancies I had indulged myself with. I should have proved myself to be more practical, particularly now that I was in the Sutherland's employ. Instead, I had acted a fool.

There were no ghosts or goblins dwelling in the halls. Mary was merely a troubled child in mourning for her father, not a ghost in a girl's body. The "ice house" was nothing but a casket (albeit an odd one) for the poor man's wake. And the unholy circle I perceived was simply an experiment with the new Spiritualist Movement.

Nettie and Fliss had joked of playing with Spiritualism on occasion. Nettie had even held a party with a medium. I had no interest in going and would not have been allowed to in any case. Both Father and Mother disapproved of these so-called experiments, and often cited Leviticus, which forbade turning to mediums, necromancers, and any others who sought wisdom from "familiar spirits" rather than the Lord Himself.

Yet, séance parties were quite the fashion, particularly among young ladies, who squealed over tales of the Fox Sisters and the Hicksite Quakers, who were said to have communicated with spirits through mysterious rapping noises.

"I am sorry for your loss," I said. "May the peace of God be with his spirit, and may—"

"This is Grace, Victoria, and Isabella. Over there is Dora, though everyone calls her Kitty," Sarah interrupted. "Naomi, you met earlier this afternoon, and I suppose Mary has frightened you into leaving. She did the same with the last three girls we tried to employ." Sarah rose and walked over to the coffin, running her hand along the smooth glass.

I waited in dread for an introduction to Fletcher, but thankfully, none came. Instead, Grace sat beside me, held my bloody hand, and inquired, "Did Mary injure you?"

I shook my head and remembered why I had sought their assistance to begin with, "No. She hurt herself. I only..." I trailed off, not wanting to admit I'd slapped her.

"You only got some blood on you while trying to aid her?" Grace supplied. Her long auburn hair sparkled like embers in the firelight, and I felt as if I had finally found a friend in this dreadful place.

Looking down at my lap, I nodded, shamed I was lying to her. "I shall tend to her." Grace rose, handing me a handkerchief to wipe my hands. "Perhaps I'll bring Topsy, if Mary is not too violent. Usually, she is careful with him. Sometimes, the pup brings her consolation when we cannot."

I wanted to ask about their father, who was lying on a bed of red silk with strings of long gray hair fanned out to frame his sallow face. My eyes drifted from his sunken cheeks to the stiff arms folded at his breast. His white, papery skin had withered and receded; his fingernails grew unnaturally and dug into his woolen waistcoat. I had some doubt he had been dead only a day or two.

Sarah saw me staring and moved in front of the casket to block my view. "The mausoleum is not yet built," was all she offered in point of explanation. She arched an eyebrow as if challenging me to investigate the matter further.

"Of course," I sighed. Again, what appeared unnatural was easily explained. They would inter Fletcher in the family mausoleum as soon as it was ready. I stood, not wanting to ask anything further. No matter what horrors I might imagine in this place, it was nothing in comparison to what Faith would face if forced to go into the mines. Though I did wonder if I could change my position to that of scullery maid. I wouldn't mind doing that sort of work for Sarah, and though hard physically, it would be easier on my mind than spending every night with Mary.

"Stay in Mary's room the night," Isabella put a hand to my shoulder and ushered me out of the parlor. "She won't leave her upper chamber, and your room is not yet ready."

"We may not need it," Victoria whispered darkly.

As Isabella led me to Mary's bedroom, I pondered Victoria's words. At the time, I thought she meant I was likely to leave soon. Later, I wondered if she somehow knew I would soon be securing a whole other place in the Sutherland's lives, for before the year was out, I would occupy a different space in the house.

***

The next weeks were busy, but uneventful, once I was able to look past the family's odd behavior. Occasionally, a courier from the butcher or a shop boy sent from a store in town would complain of the smell coming from the parlor. Their protests grew so loud that eventually, an official from town was sent to inspect the situation.

I was the one to answer the door when he called, but Sarah pushed in front of me. "We have no want or need of you here." Sarah slammed the door in the man's face. She turned on me, snarling, "No one came to help when he was alive. No bread was brought, nor clothes or shoes, either. They had no care for us then, and I have no care for them now."

"Laws mean very little when you have money," Victoria's airy voice floated up from behind us. "Hire someone to fetch packages, and we'll have no more interference such as this."

The complaints ceased from that day forward, and I found that, after a few weeks, I no longer even noticed the smell.

Another oddity were Martha's visits. Though the Sutherland's Aunt Martha had moved to her own house, she came to the parlor daily, singing songs to Fletcher, reading to his body, and talking to it as if his spirit still dwell within its rotting form.

Martha was a tall woman, who looked much so like Isabella, I could not help but wonder whether Isabella was one of the sister-cousins Nettie had gossiped about. I pondered this, but Sarah had been a model employer, and after a few weeks, I found the younger girls eager and bright students under my tutelage. Wishing to do them no harm, I said nothing of my suspicions, not even to the other servants.

As Martha's visits occurred so often, I began to think very little of them. This was the effect the Sutherlands often had on my psyche. Given enough time and repetition, even their most bizarre behaviors seemed commonplace.

As a result, I stopped questioning Martha's devotion to the corpse, until one morning, when I discovered her attentions went beyond the singing of a few hymns.

I often toured the house and grounds while Mary, Naomi, and Dora completed their schoolwork, finding that my presence inhibited them at times, and caused Mary, in particular, to become so nervous she could not complete simple sums or memorize more than one word of her history lesson. Thus, I would stroll for a quarter of an hour and return to answer questions, examine work, and correct mistakes.

That morning, while passing by the parlor, I heard a loud scraping noise and peeked in, only to discover Martha, straining as she lifted the glass lid off Fletcher's body.

I hid in the doorway, covering my nose and mouth with a handkerchief to block out the retched smell. I held in a gasp when I spotted what looked like a long, silver knife glinted in her hand.

Then, as Martha slowly lowered her hand, I nearly screamed, believing she was going to cut the poor man's throat, though he had now been dead for six weeks. *Surely no one but a madwoman would attempt such a thing,* I thought.

Thankfully, Martha did not cut Fletcher's throat. Instead, she dipped the blade down and cut a few strands of his hair before scraping the silver knife across his cheek. I stared as she proceeded to immerse the razor into a small bowl, which I had not previously noticed. After wetting the knife, Martha wiped the edge of the blade with a corner of her apron, and once again dipped her hand down into the casket. I realized she was shaving his face. The act was eerie, yet incredibly intimate. I turned from the room, blushing as if I had accidentally seen them having conjugal relations.

Rushing back down the hallway, I ran into Sarah, who was too solid to be hurled or even shaken by my small body. "Good heavens, Anna. Whatever is the matter? You look as though you've seen a ghost. And I know it can't be anything to do with Mary, for I only just heard her in the study, repeating your geography lesson."

My voice shook, and I spoke more to my buttoned shoes than Sarah's square, questioning face. "Your Aunt is visiting again."

"Yes, and what of it? She visits nearly every day."

"She...." I could not bring myself to say.

"She... she...?" Sarah tapped her foot.

"She took the lid off the ice box." I finally formed the words. "She's cutting his hair and beard as if they're still growing, but surely—"

I had no more need of words. Sarah's lips went thin, and she stormed into the parlor. Not wanting to interfere, I returned to the study and began to quiz Mary from the "Political Asia" chapter of *Harper's Geography Schoolbook*, which I myself had completed only two years before.

At supper late that afternoon, Sarah at last declared, "Fletcher needs to be put to rest, mausoleum or no." The sisters looked at one another, but no one said a word in protest, and the next morning, the family traveled to the cemetery alone to provide their father with a private memorial service.

Left alone for the day, I lay in bed for nearly an hour, wanting to cry for their loss and my own father's passing. I could not help but feel more sympathy for them than for myself. When Father died, the entire community had mourned with us. Though I wanted everyone gone at the time, I realized in that moment that I probably would not have felt as much peace about his passing if everyone had stayed away and no one but Mother and Faith had been there to mourn with me. We would not have been properly equipped to see each other through the pain alone.

In contrast, no one but the sisters and Martha attended Fletcher's memorial service. Grace told me privately that this was no surprise, as no one had come to the funeral for their brother Charles the year before, either. Although Fletcher had found a bit of fame as the sisters' manager and was idolized by many of their admirers throughout the country, the family patriarch was still considered a pariah in our community.

Both the *Lockport Union* and the *Niagara Falls Gazette* published obituaries on Fletcher, calling him "one of Niagara County's most famous citizens." The pieces focused particularly on his work with President Buchanan, his musical talents, which were inherited by his children, and the business acumen that helped propel his progeny to fame. And of course, they mentioned his hair, claiming it "came down to his shoulders," though I had seen the man in his glass "ice house" and could testify his hair reached his waist.

With all the publicity, Fletcher's former debauched drinking and philandering did not sit well with anyone in town, particularly the ladies. Moreover, those who had lost fathers, brothers, and cousins in the Civil War did not forgive the man his politics, and they cared not a whit for his life or death and wrote letters to the paper's editors saying as much.

Once Fletcher was interred, Martha declared she would leave and travel to Canada for a time to visit some of the family's more distant relatives. I overheard her telling Sarah, "The gossip I've endured under the last thirty years was enough to drive me mad. You girls are old enough to take care of yourselves. I have never been accepted in this town, and now your father has departed, I see no reason to remain."

***

I worried the sisters would feel the same as Martha, and I hoped the Sutherlands would not give up their home in Cambria just when I was beginning to become accustomed to it. However, it appeared the townspeople had relinquished such prejudices against Fletcher's children, whose newfound wealth may have purchased pardon for the sins of their father.

A week after Fletcher's death was formally announced, a letter came in the post inviting "The World-Famous Seven Sutherland Sisters" to perform at the Hodge Opera House at the end of the month.

Sarah opened the letter at dinner that evening. Before she had finished, Victoria wailed, "I don't want to go." She draped her arm across her eyes and leaned back in her chair as if preparing to faint.

"Don't be ridiculous," Sarah slapped the letter onto the table, jolting everyone's soup bowls, and causing one of the kitchen maids to yelp in surprise.

All seven sisters looked at the young maid in disgust. Under their sudden scrutiny, she gave another yelp and scuttled back into the kitchen. I had no doubt she'd spend the entirety of the meal in tears. I wondered again why I was the only servant permitted at the table, but never having been a tutor or governess before, I thought perhaps it was customary.

I had little time to think more of this discrepancy because Victoria began shouting, "They don't care about us. They've never cared. They only want to gawk and stare!" She picked up her soup bowl and threw to the ground, causing the other two maids to jump in surprise and similarly return to the kitchen.

"Stop carrying on. You'll frighten Mary!" Sarah yelled.

"I don't care!" Victoria grabbed up the entire soup tureen, held it high above her head, and flung it against the wall. Soup splattered across the newly-hung wallpaper, and the dining room seemed to shake with her fury.

Mary curled her legs up into her chair. She was covering her ears with her hands and beginning to rock back and forth. I moved to her, placing a hand on her back in comfort, but she swatted me away and began rocking all the more violently. Grace moved to Mary's other side, and Naomi struggled as if trying to think of something to do to help. Isabella smiled amusedly, as if enjoying the tableau and silently reached for another dinner roll.

"Listen to reason, Vicky, and stop being so dramatic," Dora spoke up. "Anna Louise has been helping me with sums."

"Who cares about your stupid sums?" Victoria screeched. Isabella laughed and handed her a porcelain teacup, which Victoria similarly threw against the already much-abused wall.

"Anna has been helping me with sums," Dora continued, "and the other day, she and I realized that when Mr. Hodge rebuilt the opera house after the fire last year, he added five hundred new seats, including twenty in private boxes."

"I don't give a damn!" Victoria swore, hurling a dinner plate to the floor. Isabella laughed again and threw her own plate onto the pile of shattered tableware.

"Bella," Sarah admonished.

"I wanted to join in on the fun," Isabella tittered. She held a saucer on the tips of her fingers and let it slip onto the ground. As yet another costly piece of china broke, Mary moaned loudly.

"Well you should care," Dora ignored the chaos around her, proceeding as if presiding over a relaxed business meeting. "The opera only held fifteen hundred seats before, and the old tickets were fifty cents."

Victoria held a gravy boat above her head, but she paused and looked at her younger sister in interest. "The new opera house holds two thousand seats. The private box seats cost four hundred a year. The rest of the seats are to be sold for a dollar a ticket."

Victoria lowered the gravy boat. "How much is given to the act?"

"Half," Dora said, "Two thousand minus twenty is nineteen hundred and eighty seats, which equals nearly a thousand dollars plus an additional two dollars from every seat in the private boxes."

Victoria was silent at this, but Isabella added her two cents in, "We've made twice that in the city." She shrugged.

"For a whole weekend, not merely one performance," Dora argued. I was proud to see she'd taken my lessons on debate as seriously as the lessons in mathematics.

"And," Dora grinned, "we've never taken so much money from the people in town before."

"Now that is true," Victoria conceded. "They praise us in the papers and denigrate us in the streets. I shouldn't be opposed to fleecing the flock a little."

"It could help pay for those seal coats you've been lusting after," Dora needled.

"Those coats cost a thousand a piece, but they have already been bought and paid for, Kitty, as you well know." Victoria said, using Dora's pet name. "But I would love to buy the matching hats and muffs. They were ever so cunning."

Victoria's lips parted in a strange smile that showed only her eye teeth. "And besides, we're going to need a new set of dishes. I can't bear to look at this horrid floral pattern any longer." She dropped one last salad plate onto the ground before flouncing out of the room.

"Well Kitty," Sarah began, hands on hips, "it seems the matter is decided. You've proven you've a sharp mind and have done quite well managing Vicky's moods. Now, go with Grace and Naomi and take Mary to her room. She deserves to rest after all this fuss. Anna Louise and I will rouse some servants to clean this dreadful mess."

***

As a minister's daughter, I had not been allowed to attend any of the events that graced the Hodge Opera House. My mother did not approve of music halls and would often say, "The Good Book tells us to, 'Speak to one another with psalms, hymns and spiritual songs.' I don't hear anything in that verse about drinking, carousing, or sitting for four hours doing nothing but watching pagans jump about a stage."

It was the operas in particular she didn't approve of, though she felt that any form of entertainment took our minds away from housework and other godly endeavors. It hardly mattered in any case since, when Father was alive, we lived comfortably enough, but had little money for frivolities.

My mother was wrong about the Opera House, just as she had been wrong about many pleasures in life. The theater could not be compared to the bawdy burlesque shows held in seedy cabarets, or even the coarse vaudeville acts, which had been recently advertised in Buffalo's saloons. Mr. Hodge's Opera House was an enormous structure, taking up an entire city block. Unlike other venues on the outskirts of town, it catered to wealthier families and brought crowds from as far as Pennsylvania and Ohio. Besides featuring operas, the stage held dramatic plays, concerts, and ballets. It became the cultural center of the city.

When we traveled into Lockport the morning of the show, I quickly realized that the Sutherland sisters were much less interested in the building's impressive edifice than I was. While I could not help but marvel at the great stone structure, the others, Victoria and Isabella in particular, were completely absorbed in the shops that graced the street level of the overwhelming building.

"Keep up, Anna," Victoria called, glaring at me. Her buttoned boots clacked as she marched down the road to the first of over a dozen brightly colored awnings.

"Don't touch the bricks," Mary whispered, pushing past me.

I started, hand still outstretched to finger the masonry work. I was tempted to disregard her bizarre order. But Mary turned back around, eyes wide and shaking her head so violently, I lowered my hand, fearing I would precipitate one or Mary's fits if I failed to obey her.

I jogged to catch up to the other girls, trying not to gape as Isabella, Grace, Dora, and Naomi pulled frock after frock from the dressmaker's shelves, and Victoria promptly announced they'd be taking all of them.

The milliner shop was next. This time, even Mary joined in on the fun and squealed in girlish delight over a blue velvet bonnet trimmed with peacock feathers. Sarah looked over to me and rolled her eyes. "They're so foolish when it comes to clothes," she whispered to me. "Then again, you remember when they wore nothing but burlap sacks, so you'll understand why I find it hard to deny them anything they wish now we have the money."

I smiled and nodded. Sarah looked almost wistful for a moment, but then squared her jaw as she so often did and admonished her sisters in a booming voice, "Remember, ladies. It's the hair, not the hat, that makes the woman attractive."

67

"Oh, pooh." Victoria waved a delicately-gloved hand at her sister. "Don't go spouting Father's odd notions at us."

"Yes, sissie," Isabella wheedled. "You know, as well as we do, you'd like this on top of your curls." She tossed Sarah a tan hat done in the new flowerpot style.

"That bonnet was blocked over an upturned, galvanized bucket," the shop girl said, grabbing the hat from Sarah's hand to smooth out the wrinkle caused by Isabella's impulsiveness. "The brim is wired and covered with green velvet bias, and the band is piped in striped silk."

The Sutherlands stopped their usual chatter to stare at the clerk, whose lip had begun twitching. "I'm sure you were correct, Miss Sutherland," the shop girl said. "Your hair is attractive enough. You needn't—"

"I'll take it," Sarah grabbed the hat back out of the girl's hand. "And please take care of Anna as well as the rest of us. She needs a proper bonnet, and the one in the corner with grosgrain ribbon and crepe should do nicely."

The girl approached me with a sneer on her lips. She unceremoniously shoved the bonnet into my hands as the others milled about the shop. I gave her a small smile and put the hat on as she flounced away, tending next to Victoria.

"I don't always like shopping," Naomi said, sidling up to me and using her nimble fingers to tie the long, black ribbon. "But I *do* like that these snippy little shop girls are obliged to personally deliver our packages."

"I don't," Dora said, moving in behind us. "It's a waste of money, and it would be easy enough to send young Stephen to fetch them. That is what he was hired for, after all."

"We shall be taking these with us today, at any rate. So, I suppose it doesn't matter," Naomi retorted before turning back to me. She tied the ribbon smartly and patted the bow. "Look in the mirror, Anna. We'll have to get you a new dress as well. You're our friend and companion, not some common servant. You should dress accordingly."

Dora hugged my shoulders while Naomi's warm words washed over me. Naomi hustled out of the shop and went back to the dressmaker's. She pulled my hand, and before I knew it, I was being squeezed into gray taffeta silk dress with a high collar, a long row of neat buttons, and a movable bustle.

"Keep it on," Naomi nodded to me as she signed yet another bill. "I've purchased a seat for you in the balcony tonight. You'll need something nice to wear, even if you are in mourning."

"Absolutely," Victoria poked her head in the door. "There's no reason to forgo fashion for tears. You can be just as sad in silk as you can in cotton, and black is too old for a girl your age. Gray is much more fitting."

"I want to wear crepe for my father, too," Naomi whispered, "but we have to perform, and for a few of the songs, my part is a more comedic one. Sarah and Victoria didn't think black or gray would be appropriate."

I nodded, but had little time to think or thank her, for they had more purchasing to do. I stepped out of the store, for I did not want the embarrassment of watching on as they paid for the extravagances, nor did I wish to further impose on their generosity.

The day was a clear one, and as I strolled down the row of shops, I could not help but notice that the gossip of the day seemed to center around my employers. The street was a regular

69

henhouse of women clicking their tongues in disapproval of everything the Sutherlands did.

Two women hesitated at the entrance to the shop I had just exited. One turned to the other and declared, "Well, those Sutherlands have certainly taken over the place."

"There's barely room to stand, let alone purchase anything," her companion agreed. "Should we leave? I wouldn't want to be associated with such trash." They continued on.

Another group of busty women hustled past me as one of them said, "Vulgar new money. Do you know, just a few years ago, that flashy Isabella came to my back door, begging for scraps!"

My face turned red in fury because I knew this was a lie. The Sutherlands would never beg, no matter what their situation.

As my agitation grew, I heard a voice behind me whisper, "Just like their father if you ask me. My mother had a story or two about him, I can tell you. Including a time when he tried to get her alone in the sanctuary and chased her all around the pews, trying to pinch her bottom."

Her friend gasped. "Edwina, no. Your mother is so respectable."

"Yes, she is," the woman named Edwina continued, "but Fletcher Sutherland was quite shameless."

"Of course," her friend admitted "I have heard their show is good, despite their reputations."

Edwina started, "We've heard much the same. Though I must admit to you, Clara, I was shocked when Homer insisted we purchase tickets for tonight."

"Oh, are you going? You must tell me all about it. I wanted to attend, just for curiosity's sake, but Geoffrey wouldn't hear of it. He said they play with spirits and that going to their show would be like throwing money at the devil." Clara said this with the glee of a young child sharing a secret for the first time.

I considered turning to reply to this particular remark but remembered my place and continued to silently walk in front of them.

"I don't know that Spiritualism is so terrible," Edwina remarked. "After all, Homer and I traveled over to the Cassadaga Lake Free Association last week—that camp for Spiritualists just south of Buffalo?" Her voice raised as if asking a question and I could see she was eager for her friend to approve.

"Well, we sat in on a session or two," Edwina continued. "It was... a bit strange." She laughed awkwardly.

"Do tell," Clara said with a hint of slyness. And again, I thought she sounded more like a child than a mature woman.

I realized the thought harkened back to my former Sunday School classes. At the end of lessons before prayers, Teacher encouraged us to confess our sins and ask pardon. I found that some children took an almost evil pleasure in hearing the confessions, as if storing up the information for later misuse rather than forgiving and forgetting as we were meant to do.

Edwina seemed not to notice her friend's tone but prattled on with excuses and nervous laughter. "A medium there grabbed my hand and told me we would be having a little boy soon. We've been wanting one so badly... But of course, it's all a bit of fun—an amusement only. We shan't be returning, obviously."

"And what about tonight?" Clara asked.

"The only reason I capitulated to attending tonight's concert is that Homer used to live not far from their farm... if you could call it a farm," Edwina said. "I think his wanting to go had more to do with curiosity than anything else... as you said, Clara."

I snuck a quick glance behind me and caught Clara's pursed lips as they relaxed into an easy, sly smile. "Of course," Clara said. "And there is certainly a difference between watching those Sutherlands in performance and associating with them in public."

"Indeed." Edwina tapped her foot, staring into the shop window again. "They go about town, throwing money left and right, buying up half the shops!"

"Mamie Peterson told me not all their money comes from concerts," Clara said. "She lives across the street from that monstrosity they call a house and says a number of gentlemen patronize them regularly."

"I figured as such," Edwina scoffed. "Common sluts."

My blood had been boiling throughout their conversation, but I felt unable to speak. These women were my elders, and, as I had been reminded more than once, my station had changed. As my father's daughter, I may have been able to dissuade two older women from spreading lies. A year before, as a minister's child, my mere presence had been enough to silence a gossip more than once.

In this instance, I did not know what to do or say. As a servant, I ought not to speak, but as Naomi had said, I was no mere parlor maid, and in my fine new dress, no one would mistake me for such.

In any case, as soon as the foul words came hissing out of Edwina's mouth, I flew into a rage. Stomping my booted foot, I rounded on them. "It isn't true, and you shouldn't say such things. You know nothing about it!" Angry tears burned at the corners of my eyelids, and I opened my mouth to say more, but just then, Victoria came out of the shop with a dramatic flourish.

"It's all right." Victoria laughed, pushing her way in between the two women. "We aren't so common anymore, are we Anna?"

"Well, I never," Edwina said.

"Of course," Victoria rounded on the gossip, "the other accusation might not be entirely inaccurate. Tell me, Edwina, does Homer still loll his tongue like a floundering marlin when he kisses? He certainly did when we were courting."

This image was so ridiculous, my anger fled, and I could not hold back a fit of giggles.

"It's why I turned down his proposal," Victoria said to me with a knowing grin.

"Homer would never—"

"You know very well he did, Edwina Barton," Victoria said. "You had your eye on that man for years and snatched him up as soon as I was through with him. Just like a dog waiting for scraps."

"You... you... wretched little witch!" Edwina shrieked.

The other sisters rushed out of the shop to see what all the fuss was about. Victoria laughed again, her mezzo soprano voice tickling the air like a feathery cloud. "Give your Homer thanks for the flowers he sent me this morning. They will brighten up our dressing room quite nicely tonight."

Edwina rushed at Victoria, arms outstretched toward her throat, but Sarah broke through, grabbing first Victoria's arm then mine. "Let us go, ladies. We have much to do before the show tonight."

"Edwina. Clara." Sarah nodded at each woman in turn.

She hustled us away, but not before Isabella leaned in to whisper to the two busybodies, "If I ever see you speaking to Anna or any of our other servants ever again, I will call on every single spirit I know to torment you the rest of your days."

Sarah ignored her sister's remarks, but I noticed she lifted her square chin in approval as she walked us away. I thought the ordeal was over, but Victoria had one last jibe. "Enjoy the show tonight, ladies" she called, giving the women a little finger wave.

For a second time, I burst into laughter, and the others followed. I felt much more like a friend than a servant as we walked down the street arm in arm, laughing and smiling all the way.

When the shopping excursion was over a few hours later, all seven Sutherlands plus myself and two other servants, who had joined us after finishing their housework, carried armfuls of brown paper packages back to the Opera House.

Everyone was laden with purchases, except Mary, who held only one small package in one hand and her dog Topsy's leash in the other. I did not believe anyone would allow the animal into the building, but though those who let us in gave Topsy an odd look, no one said a word as he trotted behind his mistress.

My hand grazed against the brick edifice as we went in. I could not help but reach out just a few fingers to touch it. "I told you before, don't touch the bricks!" Mary warned again, giving me a sharp look.

"Why?" I paused and shifted a parcel under my arm.

"It's hot," her whisper grew louder and a bit more frantic.

I sighed. She had been having a good day. I hoped she would not fall apart hours before the show. "Mary, the wall may be a bit warm," I conceded, "but only from the heat of the sun. There's no harm in touching it."

The crazed look began to grow in her eyes, so I relented. "If you insist, I'll keep my hands away."

Mary nodded in approval, seeming in that moment much more like Sarah or Victoria than herself. "They *are* hot," she insisted with a superior air. "I burned my wrist only this morning when I brushed up against the building."

"You couldn't have," I said.

"You think you're so clever." Mary laughed. "But you don't know everything, do you, Anna?"

I was about to inquire further about her injury when we were whisked upstairs by an increasingly impatient Sarah. "Anna, we need to rehearse before the show. Ask one of the theater boys to take that dog back to our place. It's a trip back, I know, but we can't have Topsy underfoot. The crowd might get rowdy."

I did as she asked and returned to Mary's side.

"Mary, you said you were burned. Do you need me to fetch ointment or salve from the General Store?" I whispered. Mary shook her head, so I let the matter drop.

Glancing around me, I became overwhelmed by the inside of the Hodge Opera House. I marveled as we ascended the grand staircase. Gold seemed to glitter down from every surface, and the rich red carpet was softer than anything I'd set my feet on, other than the creek bed in West Virginia outside our first home. The sisters seemed to see none of this, however, as they chattered to themselves about the show, which songs they would sing, and who would be featured in the quartet and quintet numbers.

As ushers, stagehands, and uniformed servants bustled in and out of the backstage rooms, Victoria sighed dramatically, "I cannot abide all this chaos." She turned to me, "Anna, did you know that when we were with Cole's circus, we had a maid apiece just to tend our hair?"

I shook my head, but in truth I did know, for Naomi had written an essay for me, which had described nearly every aspect of W.W. Cole's Circus. After our English lesson, Naomi confessed that upon joining the Cole's Circus, her singing was praised in particular.

This might have been bad enough, for the group of sisters bickered as much as they hugged, but a second newspaperman had also praised Naomi's looks and called her hair, "The thickest and most luxurious locks of the bunch" at "six feet that could envelop her entire body."

Victoria's hair was substantially longer, though not as thick, and she took umbrage with the editorial, claiming the journalists in question were "a bunch of untalented hacks," and she would "just as soon marry and leave the family forever than go on being ignored."

Naomi and I had a good laugh over this, as Victoria always seemed to put on theatrics, but Dora said it nearly tore the family apart at the time, and they feared Victoria would run off with one of her gentlemen and they'd never hear from her again.

On Sarah's approval, Grace, the most diplomatic of the family, tried to appease the group by going to Cole and asking that their staff of three maids be increased to seven. The plan worked, and for the rest of the season, each sister had a lady's maid, who attended to her every whim. The seven maids were part of their contract with Barnum as well.

I myself could not imagine being petted and fussed over like Mary's beloved dog Topsy. But when Victoria mentioned the seven maids, the sisters flew into a tizzy of excitement, and even sensible Sarah remarked, "I can never do my stage face as well as that Maggie Barton."

"That's because Maggie mixed Sarah's powders with a bit of greasepaint," Naomi whispered to me as I helped tighten Mary's corset.

"Sarah only lets us use white powder or chalk, or burnt cork with a bit of pigment, even though most actresses use greasepaint nowadays. Victoria and Isabella insist on keeping up with the latest fashions, so they sneak a bit of rouge and lipstick in every now and then, but Sarah won't hear of it for the rest of us and says—"

"I *say* that putting lard on your face is ridiculous," Sarah broke in. "Pig fat is pig fat, and I won't have my sisters smearing their faces with pig fat. Besides, it looks too garish, especially in places with those new electric lights."

Naomi chuckled. "You didn't mind so much when Maggie put it on you now, though did you?"

Beneath my hands, I felt Mary tense and she began mumbling to herself. Not wanting Sarah and Naomi to have a wicked row before the show, Grace stepped between them. "But certainly, the circus is different from the theater, Naomi. A painted face would fit in there, whereas here, in our hometown, paint would be unseemly."

"There you have it." Sarah squared her shoulders. Turning away from Naomi, Sarah touched my arm. "Anna, Mary's corset is tight enough. We don't want her fainting when she is trying to sing. Take time to wash your face and fix your own hair. Then, take your seat and enjoy the show."

She walked away, and I wanted to leave as well, but Mary grabbed my arm. "Don't," she whispered. "Don't leave me here. It's hot and cold all at once and my wrist needs tending."

"Mary, I thought you said your wrist was fine." My words faded as she shoved her tormented arm beneath my nose. A red welt slashed across her delicate white flesh, and small blisters scattered both above and beneath.

"How did this happen?" I gasped. "Did you hit your wrist on a curling rod?" I looked across the room where Naomi, Grace, and Isabella curled their bangs with the heated rods. Sarah warned me more than once not to let Mary near the "blasted things." I agreed, for the younger girl was like a child who could not yet be trusted to touch the stove.

"No. It was the bricks," Mary's eyes darted around the walls of the room.

"I touched them, Mary. They held no heat, but for the warmth of the sun. Please tell me what really happened. I can send a boy to fetch some linseed oil and lime-water from the chemist's shop."

Mary pushed me away, angry either that I had not believed her or that I had discovered her deception. Eyes rolling as she frantically looked for a place to escape, she spotted the washroom at the corner of the performers' space. Before I could stop her, Mary sprinted to the small room and slammed the door.

"Not again," Isabella cried, running after her.

"It's fine." Sarah returned to my side. "She gets like this sometimes. Performing can be a bit much for her, but if she did not have the stage and the adoration of the crowd, I fear she'd crumple in on herself like mother. Go and take your seat, Anna, as I said. You can use a night off from my sister's affliction."

"As could you," I could not help but reply. Sarah's lips curled in a small ironic smile at this, but she nevertheless pointed out the main door, indicating once again that I was being dismissed.

I planned on walking past the new bowling alley, which was housed in the same building as the opera house. But I found that once I had visited the ladies' washroom to bathe my face and hands and neaten my hair as Sarah had instructed, I, myself, had little time to again enjoy the grandness of the theater. I was swept along as frenzied patrons were let in like so much herded cattle.

Smoothing my dress, I was glad I would not be embarrassed by my ensemble, though I felt ashamed I had given up my black mourning dress so easily.

A few weeks prior, Victoria had been paging through her *Godey's Magazine*. "Mauve is going to be all the rage soon, but I don't see anything about it in the illustrations here, at least not yet," she informed me. "I shall have to order three mauve gowns from the dressmakers in town—all in different shades, of course."

She sighed dramatically, "Mauve is Lily Langtree's signature color. Since she is the preeminent actress of our time, Miss Langtree has influence in nearly every artistic circle, or at least the ones that count. Wearing mauve will be the trend to follow. And thank goodness too. It looks so much better against my skin than that dreadful gold that was in last season."

The only thing I could think at the time was a deep thankfulness that, as a servant, I would not have to bow to the capricious nature of fashion. Sometimes, I wished to be like a gentleman. A man could purchase one suit and worry about nothing else for the next decade.

Looking around the crowded atrium, I could see that Victoria had been correct about the mauve. Though some still favored the gold she so disdained, and others were clad in folds of crimson and emerald, the more fashionable, delicate, young ladies wore soft shades of mauve, lilac, and lavender. When a group of them stood together, their rustling skirts became a hazy sunset after a long rain.

I would have been envious, but I knew the rich refinements would be discarded in a year or so in favor of chartreuse, dandelion-yellow, sapphire blue or whatever new faddish color Miss Langtree decided to wear.

However, I was envious when I spied their gloves. I clasped my own hands behind my back as I made my way up to my seat, hoping my unclad elbows would not seem a disgrace among so much refinement. Nearly every woman there wore long opera gloves of white or cream silk, and not only was I missing these accoutrements, but my own short gloves were soiled with perspiration, and the right one was missing a button I had meant to mend, but never seemed to remember when I found the time.

For a brief moment, I nearly wished I was watching the performance from the wings of the stage, or merely listening to it in the backrooms with the other servants.

Shaking off my vanity, I hastily made my way down the row to my seat, where I fell upon the velvet cushion with an exhausted sigh.

"Come now, it can't be all that terrible," a deep voice laughed. I looked up to see a man seated beside me. In my estimation, he was older than me, but only by a few years. I took back my earlier thought that all men's suits were alike because his plain bibbed shirt front with its wing-tipped collar looked somehow smarter than other men I had passed in the hallway.

"Pardon me." The man took off his beaver-lined top hat and pulled off his grey kid gloves, placing them inside. "I realize we have not been properly introduced, but as we have..." he glanced at his pocket watch "a full forty minutes before the performance, I believe we should become better acquainted. My name is James Tarkington. And you are?"

He let the words hang in the air, and I nearly forgot my own name for a moment, so taken was I with his kind green eyes and jovial manner. "Anna," I squeaked. "Anna Louise Roberts."

"Well, there you are, Miss Roberts. Now the introductions are past us, why do you alone out of all this crowd, look for the world like you'd rather be cleaning a kitchen floor than seeing a show? Are you not an admirer of the Sutherlands?"

"Oh, I like them very much," I assured him. "I am employed by them, you see. All the morning, I was busy helping prepare for tonight."

"Yes," he laughed. "I can see how that would be thoroughly exhausting. All seven of them clamoring for you to fix their hair?"

I had not spoken to anyone outside the Sutherland family in weeks. I wished to confess everything to someone. About the ghosts, Mary's fits, her burns today... about so many things I had not written to Faith in the letters I censored before sending. Instead of pouring out the words to Mr. Tarkington, I merely murmured, "Something of that sort."

Then, wanting to lighten our burgeoning conversation, I said, "I've never had the pleasure of coming to a show here before."

"Truly?" he brightened. "Well, then you are sitting beside the right person tonight, for I myself have become a student of the theater, and I can tell you anything you'd like to know."

"Anything?" I raised an eyebrow.

"Indubitably." He smirked back.

"How did they rebuild so quickly after the fire?" I tried.

"I don't live in town myself," he replied, "but according to the newspapers, the people of Lockport raised over seven thousand dollars to help pay for the construction."

"And are those electric lights?" I pointed to the stage.

"No, thank goodness." He shook his head. "I detest those new-fangled things. They aren't as hot as the gas, of course, and people say they're a great deal safer, but they remove the mystery from the stage."

"Mystery?"

"The stage should be dark, with lights illuminating only the faces of the actors and actresses. When a director uses gas lights, candles, and chandeliers, light and shadow dance across sets and costumes like ballerinas. The thick softness of a gas light with its motes and specks adds to the ambience of a play."

I felt myself, gaping in admiration as he continued, "In contrast, when I went to the Paris Opera, the electric lamps shone so brightly, the sets looked like a fraud. I could see every fraying hemline on the costumes and every wrinkle on the actresses."

I giggled at his description. "Forgive me again, Miss Roberts," he said. "I have been too candid."

"Not at all." I put a soiled glove over my mouth to stifle my laughter but remembered myself and hid my hands in my lap again. "I appreciate your candor. I have been living among secrets and confidences for far too long." I flushed, hoping I had not said too much.

I feared he would pry and ask about the Sutherlands and their secretive, solitary world. Instead, Mr. Tarkington laughed again. "Ah, yes. Such is the world of women. Confidences and secrets in plentiful abundance. I've no doubt you also have to contend with employers and friends who speak in riddles and never say precisely what they mean."

"Yes," I sighed again.

"That can be exhausting. I know. I have four sisters myself, and I never can keep up with their enigmatic gossip. Women are a mystery, Miss Roberts, even to other fashionable ladies such as yourself."

I felt my cheeks become warm again. I wished for nothing more but to continue our banter, but the lights dimmed, and the crowd quieted as the announcer took the stage. Both I and the rest of the crowd were expecting Mr. Hodge, as he presented and announced all the acts, shows, and performances at the opera house. But gasps sounded throughout the theater when the announcer looked up into the audience, took off his top hat, shook out his shaggy white hair, and bowed.

It was Mr. P.T. Barnum himself.

"Ladies and gentlemen," his voice cut through the crowd. "I have the pleasure of introducing to you seven ladies beyond compare. These beauties have agreed to join me in a few months for what will now truly be the greatest show on earth. Their talents are beyond compare, and I was overjoyed to find they'd be traveling with our circus. We come back to Buffalo next September, and believe me, it will be a performance you won't want to miss!

"And now, in this very building, in the town where their careers started, I am pleased to present seven Lady Godivas, with longer hair and better wardrobes. Seven long-haired songstresses. Seven refined and educated ladies. Seven hirsute women. Seven models of beauty and womanly grace. Seven wonders of the world. Seven accomplished musicians with seven feet of hair each...The Seven Sutherland Sisters!"

Applause burst through the room as the refined audience forgot their manners in their excitement and gave up exclamations and shouts of approval. One man even whistled! I turned to see that it was Mr. James Tarkington himself and could not help but smile, though I should have shaken my head in disapproval.

We grew silent once again as Barnum jogged off the stage. When the curtains slowly opened, nothing could be heard except a large sigh of approval and contentment from the front row. I peered down and spotted one of Sarah's former piano students, leaning forward in anticipatory ecstasy.

I gave a more discreet sigh of my own. The sisters, who looked mysterious and haunted at home and lurid out among the farm folk of Cambria, were radiant on stage. Even Mary seemed clear and unblemished while singing. Once upon a time, I had spent a rainy afternoon staring at the delicately colored illustrated plates in my children's Bible. The Sutherlands looked for all the world like the host of heavenly angels announcing the birth of our Savior.

They began with "What a Friend We Have in Jesus," with Sarah at the piano, and I knew the family matriarch had chosen this particular hymn because it was "conservative, safe, and not too dour," to use her words. What followed was a series of standard hymns, sometimes sung in one accord and sometimes broken into parts, with Naomi's bass blending with Victoria's mezzo soprano or Mary, Dora, and Grace breaking into subtle harmony. The message was clear—regardless of rumors, this was the performance of an upright Christian family, dedicated to praising and worshiping the Lord.

I also knew their plan was that, after calming their audience's anxieties, they would transition into a series of popular parlor songs, followed by a number of comic tunes, which bordered on the bawdy. The apex of this was again to be followed by tamer parlor songs and then back into hymns because, as Sarah said, "Audiences want a show with more than one note in it. If we sat around singing church songs all night, people would claim they could get more out of the chapel choir, and for less money."

Thoughts of the program's organization soon left me, and I even forgot about the handsome Mr. Tarkington seated beside me. Like everyone else in the spacious auditorium, I was enraptured by the performance. Tears came to my eyes when Victoria, Isabella, and Sarah dedicated the song "Abide with Me" to their late father. I found myself putting my hand over my heart at Mary's child-like solo "I am Jesus Little Lamb." I laughed until my sides hurt at Isabella's comic rendition of "John Riley's Always Dry" with Naomi playing the part of John Riley, bending her elbows as if drinking and stumbling around the stage.

The Sutherlands ended the program with "God be With You till We Meet Again." At the final chorus, "Till we meet at

Jesus' feet, God be with you till we meet again," they moved to the edge of the stage. Rather than bowing or curtseying as I had heard most performers did after a show, the Sutherlands sang their last note, and in one accord, stretched their arms up and let loose their hair.

Waves of gloriously thick tresses came spilling over the edge of the stage, and I imagined not even the waters of Niagara Falls could be so glorious. They seemed to glow under the lights, and I harkened back to my first sighting of them and my hidden belief they were elves or spirits.

"A woman's crowning glory is her hair," I heard Mr. Tarkington say over the roars of applause.

His words brought me back, and I heard more clearly the stomping of feet, whistles, and shouts to nearly every girl on stage. Victoria and Naomi's names were yelled with regular frequency, but men were calling for Isabella and Dora nearly as often, and I heard a smattering of calls for Mary, Grace, and even Sarah, though I must admit these last came mostly from women, who undoubtedly took lessons from her as children.

They had performed their homecoming show with a grace and aplomb worthy of actresses from the Paris Opera to the Metropolitan. And they had done it under more scrutiny and skepticism than any of those, higher profile women could claim. Filled with pride, the Sutherlands waved, curtsied, and took one last final bow before walking off stage, their long locks trailing like wedding veils behind them.

I considered returning to the back dressing rooms, but the crowd was so thick, they jostled me about, and I realized meeting the Sutherlands at the rear door where they would be exiting would be much easier.

"If you're thinking of going to the back, I better accompany you," Mr. Tarkington put out an elbow and inclined his head, inviting me to rest my hand in its crook.

"And why would that be?" I was trying to flirt but failing miserably as he answered me in a more serious tone.

"The admirers," he explained. "They're always rushing the back door, trying to obtain autographs, asking the performers questions, that sort of thing. It's quite..."

"Vulgar?" I supplied, smiling, and taking his arm. "I suppose a man such as yourself would never stoop to such things?"

He laughed, "It probably is vulgar at that. But no, it's quite a thrilling tradition of the theater, Miss Roberts. You see an idol upon the stage, and then the idol descends and walks among the rabble like a mere mortal. To speak to such a creature. Such would be the dreams of Pygmalion or—"

"Or Psyche," I interrupted to show my own knowledge of the Greeks. "But Pygmalion shaped his love from ivory."

"And we shape ours with gas lights and set decoration. Sarah Bernhardt may be fashioned into Queen Maria de Neubourg or Cleopatra or a mere chamber maid, and we fall in love with every form she takes."

As we made our way to the street below, Mr. Tarkington gave little sighs, as if still enraptured by the Sutherland sisters, and I wondered whether any mortal woman would be able to fulfill the deepest desires of his heart.

In front of the theater's back door was a line of male patrons, and I could see plainly that, about this, Mr. Tarkington had been correct. It felt to me an odd iteration of that morning.

Whereas I had been bombarded by the tongues of the ladies in town during the day, I was now subjected to the almost uncensored talk of the gentlemen at night.

As the only lady present, I was glad of Mr. Tarkington's company, though he seemed nearly as eager, but perhaps not so dishonorable as some of the other men.

"That hair," one man elbowed another.

"Truly," his companion said. "My Elizabeth only lets hers down at night in the privacy of our bed chamber."

"Well, actresses have different standards," the first man said.

"They certainly do," said the other. "And thank the good Lord for that!"

They laughed coarsely, and I moved away, only to hear a man in a charcoal gray suit mutter, "But how shall I ask Miss Victoria?"

"I don't think she takes much convincing," his heavier friend remarked. "She's said to have courted four beaus in the last month alone. Turned every single one of them down too, when it came to the question of marriage."

"Marriage?" The thinner man went pale.

"Don't worry, my boy. Victoria isn't the marrying kind, if you take my meaning."

"Isabella isn't either," another man in brown turned toward them to enter the conversation. "My friend Orren—"

He was cut off then as the door opened. Sarah came out first, clutching a Bible to her chest like a shield to protect her from the unwanted attention.

"There's the family commander-in-chief," a thick mustachioed man barked, causing a titter of laughter from those around him.

"Now there's one I wouldn't want to mess with," the man in brown said.

"I've heard she's a harsh one," another replied. "Practices and performances and Jesus and temperance all day long. You know she probably stands for women's suffrage, too."

"The day women can vote is the day I move back to—"

These words were cut off as Victoria followed Sarah. Men hollered and screamed, and the swarm of mindless bodies pushed forward inch by inch as each sister exited the building. Isabella, Dora, and Naomi came next, followed at last by Grace and Mary, who hung behind, nearly burying herself in Grace's still-untied hair. I dropped Mr. Tarkington's arm and joined the mob, trying in vain to push my way through.

Unfortunately, someone else got to them first. A thin man with hair as red as a January fire ran through the overcrowded street. His threadbare suit ripped as he thrust past more subdued spectators. He leapt at the Sutherlands, crying out, "Mary! Mary! I love you, my darling!" I could see a glint of silver in his hand, but realized only too late that he was brandishing a pair of scissors while leaping toward the girl I had sworn to protect.

My high-pitched, "No!" cut through the crowd, but rather than help Mary, a group of men's heads swiveled back to look at me, wondering why a lady would attend such an immodest event.

As I watched in horror, the red-headed man grabbed Mary's arm and pushed her up against the wall of the opera house. She screamed in fright and tried to wrench herself away.

89

Grace tried to get to her, but was driven back by one of her own admirers, who held out a paper for her to sign.

I screamed again as Mary's assailant tried to cut a lock of her hair. Just as his scissors were about to close, Mr. Tarkington moved forward, grabbed the man's arms and bent them back.

I used all my might to push the fray in front of me and yell, "Let me through, damn you." It was the first time I had ever uttered a curse in my life, and the men must have been shocked at hearing it, for they parted like the Red Sea.

The mob quieted, but the red-headed man was kicking at Mr. Tarkington and screaming, "Delia, the unkindest girl on earth, when I besought the fair, that favor of intrinsic worth, a ringlet of her hair!" He repeated this odd poem over and over as Mr. Tarkington dragged him away from the scene and gave him quite a stiff punch to the gut for his trouble, which I would have been shocked to see, had I not been attending to Mary.

"That blasted Cowper," Sarah swore under her breath.

"Is that the Irishman's name?" I helped Mary to her feet.

"No." Sarah yanked Mary a bit too firmly and the younger girl winced and began whimpering again. "Cowper is the author of that damnable poem. I've heard it so many times I could spit. Thank the good Lord Mr. Barnum had to leave after the announcements. He might very well have cancelled our contract after a spectacle like this."

Mary screamed, and both Sarah and I turned to see that more men, and one or two ladies, were hurrying toward us. "Our carriage won't arrive for another thirty minutes. Get her out of here." Sarah pushed us back toward the door. I took her to mean that Mary and I could hide and wait in the theater until the melee was over.

"Don't," said Mr. Tarkington, who had returned after disposing of the dishonorable Irishman. "You can take my coach. I shall escort you to the carriage in case anyone else attempts to assail you."

"Then you'll find another method of transport home?" Sarah viewed him skeptically.

"I wouldn't dream of doing anything different, Miss Sutherland. On my honor."

"Go." She said, decidedly, and turned back to her other sisters as they continued walking, waving, and coquetting among the crowd.

I grasped Mary's arm. She winced and moaned, but I ignored her protestations. My heart panged with sympathy, but this was no time to play the delicate flower. Mary could faint and weep later; for now, we needed to get her home as soon as possible. We rushed around the corner, away from the flowers, chocolates, gifts, and clamoring demands for more time, more singing, more stories, more, more, more. I could understand why Mary found it so exhausting.

"This is your carriage?" I could not help but gape at the luxurious coach at which Mr. Tarkington had stopped.

"Yes." He touched the high wheels lovingly. "It's a European design—a Chariot d'Orsay. Vanderbilt owns one too, but of course his has silver plated hardware, and I'm hardly that extravagant."

A coachman waited silently in the front as a footman hopped down and opened the door. When the footman took Mary's elbow, she again cried out as if in pain.

"I'll help her." I reached and boosted Mary from behind. It was indelicate, but she seemed to flinch at every touch she could see.

Mary slumped into the seat, and I thought she might begin to weep, but I realized she had fainted. It took her longer than I anticipated, and I said a silent prayer of thanks she had not gone into one of her fits and had waited to faint until we were in the carriage.

"I may have smelling salts," Mr. Tarkington supplied.

"No." I shook my head. "Let her sleep. Should I send the carriage back for you once we've arrived?"

"I'm in the banking business, Miss Roberts. Lending, among other things. There are at least ten men here who would give me a ride on their backs, let alone a seat in a wagon."

I bit my bottom lip. I knew Sarah's words indicated that Mr. Tarkington should not ride with us, but he had so far proved to be trustworthy. Though the ride back to Cambria was not a long one, I worried the red-haired man, or someone like him, might follow us or try to overtake the carriage.

"I could ride with you, if you're worried." Mr. Tarkington let his words hang in the air until I nodded in agreement.

In the coach, I sat beside Mary's crumpled figure, and Mr. Tarkington was forced to squeeze in next to us. As we assembled ourselves, our feet accidentally touched, and I shifted quickly, crossing my ankles and angling myself toward Mary.

The horses set off. The carriage jostled sharply, but Mary only lolled against my shoulder like a ragdoll. The moon was bright that night, and the carriage had two lamps—one on either side of the coachman. I looked down on Mary's countenance and put my arm around her shoulder. Even through my gloves and the layers of her dress, I could feel she was feverish. Heat radiated off her body like a potbellied stove.

"How fast can your horse go?" I asked Mr. Tarkington.

"A bit faster," he admitted, but we might find ourselves knocked around a bit.

I made a quick decision. "Ask them, please. Mary's face is flushed, and I fear she has a fever."

"Of course," he put his head out the window and made some motions to the coachman, who snapped his whip twice. The horse jumped into a sharper trot, and we sped toward the Sutherland mansion.

I took off my gloves and used the one with the missing button to wipe the sweat beading on Mary's brow. The rest of the ride was silent, save for the jouncing and bumping of the carriage along the road.

We soon arrived, and we must have made quite the spectacle, for I could see Mrs. Poole, the new housekeeper, ready to meet us at the door.

Mr. Tarkington hopped out of the carriage and extended a hand to me. "Go ahead and prepare things," he said. "My servants and I will carry her in."

I nodded, again grateful for his assistance, and ran to the door. "Mary was attacked," I explained to Mrs. Poole.

"Did someone hit her?" the older woman clasped a hand to her chest.

"No," I reassured her. "A thin, red-haired Irishman I've never seen before tried to cut off a piece of her hair. He grabbed at Mary, and when she tried to get away, she slammed up against the wall. Mr. Tarkington was kind enough to lend us his carriage, so we could bring her home more quickly. She's feverish now, and I worry the fright has sent her into some kind of fit."

"Run in and tell that Agnes. She's only a kitchen girl, but she'll know where the tonic is. I'll help bring Miss Mary in."

Agnes and I rushed through the house, grabbing up whatever elixirs and tonics she remembered. I asked, "Agnes, is there any liniment? The skin on her wrist may be burned as well, or at least blistered."

"I have some of Doctor Scott's foot salve," Agnes said. "It works for skin that's blistered. Frostbitten toes and corns, too."

I wanted to shake the girl. What did I care about frostbite or corns at a time like this? "Get it," I instructed. "I'm going back to Mrs. Poole. Meet us in the vestibule, and go swiftly, if you can." I felt a bit guilty, ordering the girl about so, but there was little time for politeness or niceties.

As I rushed down the stairs, I saw that Mrs. Poole had laid Mary onto the chaise fainting couch that sat in the entry way. The girls typically sat upon the chaise while buttoning their boots before leaving for the day. Until now, I had never seen it used for its intended purpose, and I felt quite ill at the thought of it.

"I've given her the smelling salts," Mrs. Poole said in a matter-of-fact tone. "She's come 'round a bit, but she's moaning in pain, like."

"Thank you, Mrs. Poole." I turned to the door. "And thank you, Mr. Tarkington. I do not know what might have happened if not for your assistance."

Mrs. Poole made a noise of disdain behind me, and I inclined my head back in her direction to see her frowning. She moved over to Mary and cleared her throat in obvious disapproval.

She must believe there was some sort of impropriety between us, I thought. *I shall have to dissuade her of the notion later.* I knew it would not remedy the situation, but I wanted to thank Mr. Tarkington, privately. "I'll see you back to your carriage," I said.

Mrs. Poole sniffed again, but I ignored her this time and took Mr. Tarkington's arm as we ventured back out into the moonlight. "Miss Roberts," he began, "I know you are in the service—"

"I am a companion and tutor," I explained. "Not a common scullery maid." I felt ashamed immediately after making the pronouncement. What would Father think of me placing myself above others? I should be humble and unassuming at all times.

"I know," he said softly. "I was wondering whether you might be allowed a gentleman caller, or whether your employers would forbid you from seeing me again."

"I would have to ask," I paused, blushing, "but I think it would be permissible."

"I shall be out of town next week, but I'll send my valet George to receive your answer. I hope it may be a positive one."

"Thank you again," I said. And before I could say or do anything more, I turned and hurried back to the house.

"I don't mean to be impertinent, Miss," Mrs. Poole started as I came in the door, "but I would not see that young man again if I was you."

"Why shouldn't I see Mr. Tarkington again?" I demanded. "He seems a decent man, and I haven't done anything improper."

"I know, Miss. I haven't been here long, but I can see already the type of woman you are. Still and all, you said that a man with red hair tried to cut Miss Mary's hair this night? And I've seen a man of that description with your Mr. Tarkington before."

"Well, there are quite a number of Irish and Scottish in the area now, aren't there?" I asked. "Surely, they—"

"He feigned the punch to the man's stomach," Mary whispered, sitting up. "And I believe it was Mr. Tarkington who cut my hair before he brought me inside." She held up a large lock of hair, which was clearly cut half way down. I gulped and felt near tears, seeing her beauty marred in that way.

"I was seeing it peekin' out of his breast pocket," Mrs. Poole admitted. "He's a strong fellow. With just us ladies in the house at the moment, I didn't want to accuse him, but..."

She trailed off, and I took her meaning. I thought of Mr. Tarkington's easy way with banter, but also the way he stared at the women after the performance, and the odd way he spoke of actresses on stage. Then, there was the bragging over a carriage in Mary's time of need. Perhaps he sought a date with me only to become closer to the Sutherlands.

"My mother always encouraged me to find a charming, wealthy man," I said, "but my father told me that charming men were the most dangerous kind, and I should look for someone kind and humble, like himself."

Mrs. Poole smiled softly, "That man seems little like your father, Miss"

"Yes. And you shall have to turn his valet away when he comes to call," I decided.

Mary moaned. "Anna," she cried. "Anna! Take me upstairs before I faint again. I feel as if I'm burning and freezing all at once."

Mrs. Poole and I each put ourselves under one of Mary's arms, though she winced and cried out. We brought her up the steps and into her bed chamber. Thankfully, Mary was in her right mind, at least for a moment. Without protest, she drank a bit of the tonic, and Mrs. Poole found her some cocaine drops to soothe her spirits as I rubbed the salve onto her wrist.

"Better," Mary murmured. "Thank you, Mrs. Poole. I think Anna can see to things from here. You'll stay with me, won't you, Anna?"

I smoothed Mary's still feverish brow as if she was a child. "Of course."

As soon as Mrs. Poole left, Mary pulled herself up to sitting and pinned her hair. "My neck and shoulder. Where he pressed me up against the wall of the opera house," she whispered, conspiratorially.

I looked at her neck. Welts and blisters spread out across her pale skin. "My God!" I could not help gasping.

"Don't tell Mrs. Poole," Mary grabbed my wrist with a grip tighter than I would have believed. "The salve seems to be more medicine than snake oil. It's cooling even now."

I looked down and saw what looked to be a thin frost spreading out where I had put the salve on her wrist. Mary noticed my horrified expression. "It is nothing," she said and ran her other hand over the place, brushing the white away and revealing her skin once again.

It was more than nothing, but Mary was so rarely clear in her wishes or speech that I obeyed her request and smoothed Agnes' cream over the expanse of marked skin along her neck and back.

At last, Mary yawned and fell into bed, asleep this time instead of fainting. I slept in much the same way, exhausted from the night's events.

Mr. Tarkington's valet did come, but Mrs. Poole sent him away before he reached the front door. I never heard from him again.

Several years later, the Hodge Opera House burned for a second time. The night of the fire, the weather was so cold that as they extinguished the flames, ashes mixed snow, and water clung to the great edifice in icicles as thick as a woman's waist. Each time I walked past that place, I remembered the frost on Mary's burnt skin, and shuddered.

Part III

Black Crepe & Cinnamon

Pictured: Miss Victoria Sutherland

May, 1885

Thankfully, Mary had no further incidents over the following weeks. Her burns healed quickly and left no scars. As the days grew warmer, I felt the heaviness of the house begin to lift.

Mornings and early afternoons were reserved for giving lessons to Mary and the twins, Naomi and Dora. Mary did sums when she was able. She became upset when writing and struggled in composition, where she often turned in garbled essays I could make little sense of. As a result, I removed these lessons from her schooling. However, I was pleased to see she took well to history lessons. More than once, I found her hiding behind the curtains, her nose buried in Flanagan's *Epochs in American History*.

Though I was loath to admit it, Mary sometimes tired me greatly. I began to instruct her early in the day. Then, I let her work complete her homework as I moved on to lessons with Naomi and Dora. After teaching Mary, working with the twins was like biting into a bright, juicy orange after weeks of eating nothing but dry bread.

Naomi detested studying, but she enjoyed reading literature almost as much as she enjoyed playing pranks. Other than our schoolbooks, my mother and father had only kept the Holy Bible for reading. As a result, though Naomi failed to learn much of science or mathematics from my efforts, I learned a great deal about literature from hers.

In contrast to her sister's propensity for ignoring more sober schoolwork, Dora had bright eyes as sharp as her mind.

With her upturned mouth and pert nose, I had no doubt Dora would soon break the heart of every man she met.

However, as I had seen before the performance at Hodge Opera House, Dora possessed the same business sense as Sarah. She also exceeded at composition and debate, cushioning staunch words and ambitious plans with a flirtatious grace I could not teach. If Sarah ever needed a business partner, Dora would be up to the task.

The parlor, now cleared of the icehouse, was reserved for music, and it was pleasant to hear the dulcet strains lifting up each evening as I moved freely about the house. The songs became so familiar to me, Sarah encouraged me to join in the singing. Soon, I was able to blend my voice with the Sutherland's songs, and even Isabella said I should join them on stage, at least for some of the hymns.

In the meantime, work on the house had begun to pick up speed. Other maids and servants began to arrive to help, as the structure had been completed, and the house was now truly becoming a mansion. Mrs. Poole had her hands full with parlor maids, chamber maids, scullery maids, kitchen staff, and even a laundress. They stuffed mattresses with feathers, placed walnut tables near each door, and filled glass-doored bookcases with picture books and lithographs.

A sturdy fellow by the name of Gorman was to be both coachman and farmhand for the long-neglected field. Though I often caught him staring at Victoria as he went about his work. Worse was a moony-faced lad named Orren Longmate who practically drooled over Isabella each time she glanced his way.

Dora, Naomi, and I first saw this spectacle during one of our lessons. Always ready to distract me from teaching, Naomi leaned whispered, "Orren doesn't need to be here, you know. He has a good position in Lockport as a shopkeeper. He works there during the week and spends his weekends here cleaning out the stables."

"Is that Orren?" I asked. "One of the men at the opera house mentioned his name. Why ever is he here if he has another occupation?" I wondered.

"He saw us perform in Buffalo last year and declared his love for Isabella," Naomi giggled.

"He tried to cut off a lock of her hair to keep as a remembrance," Dora added, refusing to look up from her work. "Not the same way it happened to Mary, of course. Instead, Orren brought a box of chocolates and asked that once Isabella finished the last bite, she place a lock of hair in the box and return it to him."

"It was quite romantic," Naomi said.

"It was quite ridiculous," Dora retorted. "When Orren applied to be the stable hand, he brought six references and a letter he'd written himself stating his intention to work his way into Isabella's affections and make an honest woman of her."

"Well, that part was rather a bit much," Naomi conceded.

"It's offensive," Dora looked up, finally stilling her ever-quick pen. "He came to see her on stage, and then said he needed to rescue her from it. As if she needed rescuing. Isabella doesn't need to be rescued, but she does need something better to do with her time instead of teasing Orren."

"I would not mind spending my afternoons toying with the affections of a young suitor as Isabella does," Naomi said.

Dora considered this. "I don't think I will ever marry," she said at last, "but if I do have a beau, I hope my suitor won't be as mopey as old Orren." Both girls giggled until poor Orren looked over at our little group, which only caused them to laugh even harder.

I joined in their merriment. Then, remembering my kind but stern schoolmistress, I felt a sudden flush of embarrassment. Perhaps I was not doing my duty properly. But then, these girls had never been to a proper school, and we were so close in age, they were more like friends than pupils.

That night, I sat together with Mary on the twin brass beds and sturdy rocking chairs Sarah had procured for the upper room. Each night, after singing, Mary and I retired upstairs, and I read to her from one of Naomi's many books. I enjoyed the stories, and the books helped her fall asleep.

Following the Alice books, Mary chose *Uncle Tom's Cabin*. It surprised me, given Fletcher's political leanings, but Mary had read the book before and confessed to me that she had named her little dog Topsy after her favorite character. After finishing Mrs. Stowe's novel, we made our way through *Little Women* and *Little Men*, and moved on to *The Princess and the Goblin*, a story I loved and knew my mother would have hated.

After finishing a short chapter, I paused to open a new letter from Faith. Mary often enjoyed hearing these letters and had begun to talk of Faith as if they were friends.

That night, though the moon was already in the sky, I could smell cinnamon of bread and muffins as Mrs. Poole baked next morning's breakfast. As I yawned and took out Faith's letter, I marveled at how hard the older woman worked.

"Mother and I are safely arrived," I began to read. "The mountains are so calm and peaceful. It is nice to see the blue mist each morning. Flowers are already in full bloom and the days are warm. Some of the older boys have already left school for the summer because—"

Mary began muttering, "Underwater. Underwater." She repeated this chant over and over. Her caustic alto voice went deeper and deeper, echoing off the walls.

"Mary," I scolded, hoping to cut off the mad fit before it began, "you needn't make such noises just because you don't want to hear Faith's letter. I can keep it to myself."

She threw herself onto the ground, her legs flailing. I thought to go for Grace or Sarah. Then, Mary went stiff. Her limbs seemed paralyzed, but she twitched slightly as if she was trying to break free from whatever demon gripped her. Father had always spoken against the sanitariums which placed the mad in restraints, but I could understand why the alienists had gone to such lengths. If these fits were a regular occurrence, something would have to be done.

Mary's hands turned into claws as she spasmed and shook. One of Father's parishioners in West Virginia had been afflicted with epilepsy, and he had once gone into a fit during our final prayer time. I recalled the importance of ensuring that the distressed did not bite off their tongues. I looked around wildly, trying to find something to put into Mary's mouth.

Her body jerked upwards as if being pulled by an unseen force. Wave after wave of convulsions moved her body back and forth until the rigidity in her limbs was thrust out. Her body went soft, but still twitched, flopping like a ragdoll being thrown about by a toddler. "Dead," Mary moaned. "Dead. Dead. Dead. Under the midnight water."

I'd no idea what it meant, but she went still at last, crumpling into a sobbing mass in her sweat-dampened nightdress.

I carried Mary to one of the beds and laid her upon it, feeling her forehead for signs of fever. Her head was as damp as her dress, but cool to the touch. Satisfied that she was of no harm to herself, I at last ran for help.

No music came from the parlor, so I frantically darted down the long corridor and into the kitchen, where Mrs. Poole and Agnes were sitting quietly behind a large pile of mending. I stopped short trying to catch my breath, "I thought you were baking this evening. Have you seen Grace or Sarah?"

"Wednesday for wash. Thursday for mending. Friday for ironing. Saturday for baking," Mrs. Poole sang, sticking a needle through the sock she was darning to punctuate each word. "Why ever would you think we was busying ourselves with the baking on a Thursday, child?"

"I smelled cinnamon," I said. "Have you seen..."

"Cinnamon?" Grace's usually flutelike voice croaked out behind me. "When?"

"Upstairs with Mary."

"Go back to her," she yanked my arm, causing me to stumble out the door. "I'll call the others."

I ran back through the hallway, now truly panicked. Of all the sisters, Grace was the least emotional. Unlike Victoria's outbursts and Isabella's theatrics, Grace was typically calm and collected. She usually took Mary's fits in stride, like a nurse who has been through battle and knows she must tend to the sick, even when the bullets fly past. Seeing Grace rattled unnerved me.

I rushed back upstairs. Mary's room was still lit by the lamps and sconces that now adorned it, which I took to be a good omen. The scent of cinnamon clung to the air, and I moved to Mary's bed to sit beside her. She wept but did not stir.

Rain began to patter against the windows, first tapping politely, then striking against the pane in ever crueler insistence.

I thought to take out the novel again, or perhaps go to fetch Topsy to comfort Mary. Before I could walk to the bookcase or again descend the stairs, the four older girls crowded into the room.

"What happened?" Sarah asked as Grace took my place beside Mary.

"We were reading as usual and then I, I—" I stammered.

"Did you say something to set her off?" Victoria demanded.

Gulping, I shook my head, "I was reading one of my sister's letters to her, as I often do. Suddenly, she went into a fit. There was no reason for it. None. I promise you."

"And you smelled cinnamon?" Grace asked.

"Yes, can't you?" I turned wildly, not understanding the looks passing between the girls.

"Did she say anything?" Grace smoothed Mary's dark hair and pulled the quilt up around her shoulders.

"Just, 'underwater,'" I said, lifting a hand to my own brow where achy pain was beginning to blossom.

"Underwater?" Victoria snapped.

"Yes. Underwater. She said it over and over again. Then her body went rigid, and she shook as if being yanked up toward the ceiling."

Their eyes all rose up toward the roof of the witch's cap for a moment before sinking back down. Grace and Sarah turned to minister to Mary while Victoria continued to scrutinize me. Isabella was staring at me too, but with a look more mysterious than accusing. I searched out Naomi and Dora for support, but they were standing in the doorway clutching each other and crying softly.

"She seems to be coming back to herself," Sarah shrugged, though just as she said this, thunder clapped outside, and Mary jumped violently.

"Grace, stay here with her. Anna, go to Mrs. Poole and gather all the servants in the ballroom. Make sure everyone is lined up and accounted for."

"And the animals," Grace added, opening *The Princess and the Goblin* to the place I had marked it.

"Yes," Sarah nodded gravely. "Once everyone is present, send Mr. Gorman out to count the animals."

"I'll go with her," Isabella joined me at the stairs.

"Why are we taking a census at twilight?" I asked Isabella as we made our way down to the kitchen.

"You smelled cinnamon," she said.

"Of course. Don't you?"

"No."

"Is this why Mary went mad? Because of the scent of cinnamon?" I was bewildered.

"No one sensed it but you, Anna. But I would wager whatever you smelled wasn't cinnamon. It was incense."

"Incense?"

"Incense and myrrh, no doubt. Their mingled scent is a portent of death."

I stopped and looked at her to see if this was one of her usual jests. Her usually rosy face had gone pale and even her lips were as ashen as parchment. Isabella placed a trembling hand against my back. I thought at first, she was trying to comfort me, but I realized she was actually trying to steady herself.

"There will be a death here tonight, if there hasn't been already," Isabella said, ominously.

I didn't know what to think. She was so often ridiculous and dramatic. But Grace and Sarah had been upset as well. Before I could reply, she called for Mrs. Poole.

Isabella's soprano voice rang through the empty corridor as the lights flickered. The windows' velvet curtains seemed to sway with the power of her breath. Outside, there was another clap of lightning.

***

Three days later, the doors of the mansion were draped in black crepe, and the sisters were robed in the heavy, black dresses of mourning.

Twelve horses were brought out of their stables, their manes braided, and their hooves shod with gold-plated horseshoes. I had no inkling as to where the Sutherlands were able to find such things.

It did strike me that, though the sisters had not dressed in black after the death of their father, they did so on this day. Still,

I remained silent on the matter as Grace and I helped Mary to dress while Sarah readied the funeral procession.

The front cart was small enough for one horse to pull and had been filled with flowers, as had the wagon at the rear of the assemblage. Following the flower cart were seven carriages, one for each of the seven sisters in order of their births. Behind this was a wagon for the staff, in which I planned to sit.

"Give her some morphine," Grace whispered to me as we tightened the strings of Mary's corset. "She'll never make it through otherwise."

I took the needle from its glass case. We'd had to dose Mary every day since the death.

That night, when everyone was accounted for in the ballroom, I thought the danger had passed. Standing in line with the other servants, I wondered if the fuss was perhaps nothing but one of the Sutherland sisters' dramatic displays. I secretly thought they were feeding into Mary's madness rather than trying to cure it.

My own family had been so tranquil, passively showing our emotions through wrinkled brows and disdainful sniffs. Living amongst seven women who were used to the theatrics of the stage was like entering another world, and I was still unused to some of their eccentricities.

However, once the animals were similarly lined up and numbered, Gorman discovered that Mary's beloved dog Topsy was missing. Topsy's small broken body was eventually found the next morning, drowned in a puddle caused by the torrents of rain. Topsy had indeed been "underwater" as Mary had said.

Upon learning this, I wondered whether Mary's affliction was not insanity at all. Perhaps, it was a sensitive clairvoyance tormented by living in a house where death seemed to hide like cobwebs in every corner.

I also wondered why a dog's funeral was cause for so much ornate ceremony when their father had been buried in what seemed almost a pauper's grave in comparison.

As I considered this, I leaned over Mary, gently sliding the needle into her arm. Her head lolled toward me and she whispered, "We are having a splendid funeral because darling Topsy is gone forever, but Father is still with us."

My heart raced in fright and I looked over to Grace, who was pulling Mary's dress over her head. "Is that true?" I asked.

"What?" Grace struggled to get the large puffed sleeves over Mary's now limp arms.

"She said Topsy was gone forever, but your father remains."

Grace pulled me aside for a moment out of her sister's hearing, "Mary is mad, Anna. You mustn't forget that. Don't be seduced by her insane ramblings. We humor her because there's no use arguing, but everything she says is merely fancy."

"But she knew about the death," I argued. "Down to the very detail of the water, and the cinnamon I smelled."

"My sisters are fascinated by the occult," Grace shrugged. "They get caught up in the drama of it all, even Sarah, though she is more dedicated to the Lord than the rest of us."

I was taken aback. How could she stand there denying everything that had happened over the past few days?

***

An hour later, once I was seated in the servants' wagon, I mentioned this conversation to Mrs. Poole. I had said nothing to either her or Agnes about anything else I had seen, and I felt a bit like a proverbial lazy maid—those indiscrete domestics who had nothing to do all day but gossip about their employers.

When I tentatively mentioned what Grace said about the occult, Mrs. Poole shook her head, "I knew they was up to no good. My husband Frank told me. He says, 'Now Shannon, don't ya be going down to that new house with all its flash. They's nothing but loose women over there, no matter how many of the greenbacks they got in the bank."

"I've not seen a man come around the house," I protested. There was enough strangeness about the place without adding false rumors into the mix.

"There's loose and then there's *loose,*" Mrs. Poole said. "What I mean to say is they've got some backward morals."

"Why stay then?" I leaned into the hay bales they had provided for us to sit upon. I knew my own reasons, but I had never inquired into the minds of the others. Surely, they must have had some of the same strange encounters as I'd had.

Mrs. Poole softened. "Well, they may be loose, but I loves 'em all the same. I was working for the Wrights before. That daughter of theirs, Nettie, plagued me something dreadful. I was in the milliner's trying to explain for the third time why a certain hat was not to Miss Nettie's liking when Miss Sarah walked in. She overheard our conversation and declared the hat to be 'Just fine for her tastes.'"

I tried not to show my shock at hearing my old friend Nettie's name. It was the first week of June. I had only been in service for a little over three months. Yet it seemed my former life had vanished like steam rising from a boiling pot, with only a few teardrops of water left as evidence. I gripped the hay tightly, its strands biting into my fists. Mrs. Poole seemed to sense my discomfort, but only paused briefly before continuing her tale.

"I says to her, 'Well, I wish my employer felt the same way, Miss. She's been awfully upset about the way these feathers lay.' Well, Miss Sarah just harrumphed in that way she does. She turned to the shopkeeper and ordered seven of them hats, one for each of the sisters. Then she turned round to me and offered me a job."

"'I'm in need of a housekeeper,' she says, 'and you look smart enough to do the job.'" Well, I was just a ladies' maid and I told her so. I explained I couldn't leave on account of me boy Billy being so sickly and all. The Wrights were some of the finest people in town, least ways in terms of money. I didn't think I'd find a better position elsewhere.

"Miss Sarah says, 'What are they paying you over at that dreadful place?' When I told her, she doubled it, right then and there. She says, 'Go and pack up your things. If you think they've treated you fairly, give your week's notice. If not, I'll see you this afternoon.'"

"And did you go right away?" Agnes cut in, grinning and reveling in the story.

"I cut it by half," Mrs. Poole laughed. "It was a Thursday. I told Mrs. Wright I'd be taking my leave the following Monday. Monday was my usual day off, and I wouldn't want to be packing up my things on the Sabbath."

The wagon continued splashing through the mud as we sat, considering this for a moment. Nothing could be heard but the turning of the wheels and the larks whistling through the windless trees.

From the carriage before us, Mary's sweet alto voice rose into the air. As she sang mournfully, her sisters joined her song, "Amazing grace, how sweet the sound..."

Agnes sat up a little, eyes wide. "It may be wrong, I know," she said, "but even when they take to singing church songs and hymns, I feel as if someone's poured ice water down my neck."

"Then you're afraid too?" I felt more at ease, finally sharing my woes.

"Oh, ever so much," she nodded, then paused, considering, "only not of them, you know. Just of that place." She pointed back to the house.

"Will you leave, then?"

Agnes leaned against the rail of the wagon and gazed out over the road as we neared the cemetery. I looked to Mrs. Poole, thinking perhaps Agnes would not answer me, but the older woman only looked to Agnes, waiting for her reply.

"I had a dalliance with a lad who lived across the way from our farm," Agnes started, still refusing to look at us. "I loved Johnny more than anything in the whole world, but Pa said I was too young to marry and didn't approve me seeing him. Said he didn't seem honest. When it became clear I was in trouble, Johnny promised he would speak to his ma and pa about standing with me before the preacher. Before we could make arrangements, my pa found out and forced me out of the house."

Agnes glanced back to us, eyes filled with tears, "I didn't have nowhere to go but Johnny's. When I went to his door, his ma was surprised to see me. She greeted me so kindly, I knew

Johnny must not have told her anything about our... predicament.

"She took me into the sitting room and said Johnny had gone away earlier that week to homestead out west. 'He's been planning the trip for almost a year,' she explained. 'We thought he'd leave at the end of the summer, but yesterday morning, he declared it was time to move on. Something about the weather. I do wish he had time to tell his good friends and neighbors goodbye.'" Agnes paused. "I couldn't do anything but give her my thanks and take leave."

"Didn't you tell her?" I asked. "Surely, they could have followed him and brought him back."

"I was so stunned, I didn't know what to say. I suppose I should have told her right then what had happened, but the idea of marrying a man who so clearly didn't love me..." Agnes shook her head. "No. I'd rather be in the poorhouse than trapped in a loveless marriage. And if he ran once, he'd be sure to run again."

"How did you come to us, dear?" Mrs. Poole's voice was soft. I was glad of it, for I had feared she'd accuse Agnes of being a harlot.

"I lost the baby," Agnes whispered as the sister's song of grief faded. "I couldn't eat hardly anything, for my heart was broken and the poor thing just...." she trailed of, wiping away her tears.

"I stood outside the "Ladies' Relief Society and Home for the Friendless, willing myself to go in, thinking perhaps it might not be so bad. I thought maybe a few other girls in my situation would be there, and we could give comfort to one another.

"Then, as I looked up at the big stone building, Miss Grace came up beside me and asked me why I was crying. No one had ever inquired as to my situation. Usually, they turned their heads away when they saw I was growing large without a husband by my side. Miss Grace was so kind."

Agnes paused and smiled sadly with just the corners of her lips tilting upward. "When I looked into her blue eyes, I couldn't help but tell her all about Johnny and the baby and my pa. I thought she'd sneer at me. Instead, she took me by the arm and said, 'You shall come and work for me, Agnes. We're building a grand house, and we're much in need of people to fill it. Come work for us. If you find the situation not to your liking, I promise to send you off with a good set of references in your hands.'"

We came toward the cemetery gate as Agnes snuffled again. Mrs. Poole reached over and handed her a handkerchief. "So, I agreed, and I've been relatively happy these past few weeks, though the house seems filled to the brim with ghosts and ghouls." She paused, considering. "Funny thing though. I never remembered giving her my name."

As she said this, the wagon jolted over a rut in the road. Gorman was driving us. He pulled tight on the reins, but the horses followed the quickening procession and refused to stop. Agnes, who had been sitting up by the rail was nearly tossed out of the cart. Mrs. Poole cried out. I don't know how, but I kept my wits about me and grabbed onto the girl's sleeve and pulled her back in.

"She was nearly crushed beneath the wheels!" I exclaimed.

Agnes rested on the floor of the wagon a moment laughing in near hysterics at the near miss. "That's what I get for being filled with such melancholy over Johnny," she said. "I can hardly think when I remember him. I must remember to give thanks for what I have now instead of crying for what's gone before."

"You must remember to sit safely when in a moving wagon," Mrs. Poole said.

The horses finally slowed their gait and nothing more was said. I cannot say what thoughts filled their minds, but for myself, I could not help but think of the timing of Agnes' fall. Nothing had happened when we spoke of the sisters' kindness or even their eccentric peculiarities, but whenever anyone spoke of their mysterious and unexplained clairvoyance, misfortune seemed to follow.

Like the funeral procession, Topsy's memorial service was more appropriate for a gentleman of stature than a dog. A newspaperman stood just outside our group, furiously scribbling notes on everything he saw. And I noticed a small gaggle of boys from the neighborhood hiding behind some bushes just past Topsy's gravesite. They had followed our procession for a lack of any other excitement in their day. I saw one boy sneak out and snatch up one of the golden horseshoes, which a horse from Grace's carriage had thrown off.

He ran back to the bushes with his prize—a souvenir of the most flagrant display of wealth and eccentricity he would likely ever see. I had no doubt that between the boys' tales and the journalist's odd obituary, the gossip in town would reach a fever pitch.

Of further interest to me was the fact that a minister had been called in. I was shocked that a man of the cloth had agreed to read scripture and say words over the body of an animal, who certainly did not possess a soul.

"We begin our service with a passage from the book of Job," the bearded preacher began.

Sarah stepped forward and opened her ever-present Bible. "Ask now the beasts, and they shall teach thee; and the fowls of the air, and they shall tell thee," she read. "Or speak to the earth, and it shall teach thee: and the fishes of the sea shall declare unto thee. Who knoweth not in all these that the hand of the Lord hath wrought this? In whose hand is the soul of every living thing, and the breath of all mankind."

She closed the book and moved back to her place in line with her sisters. The minister cleared his throat. "These words of the Spirit-inspired, inerrant Bible serve as a clear testament that the animals of the earth praise the Lord just as we do," he said.

"The birds of the air, the fish of the sea, and the very earth itself have a pure love for God we may never be able to attain. Where we may have doubts from time to time, Topsy, your beloved dog, had none. Where we may stumble into sin, Topsy was pure of spirit. Where we may seek out dark spirits, Topsy spoke only to the Spirit of the Lord, who rules over the entire earth," the minister paused, clearing his throat again.

So, he knows, then, I thought. *He knows about the Spiritualism, and yet he agreed to speak at the funeral today. Or, more likely, he agreed to speak today because of the Spiritualism.* I had to admire the man, if this was the case. He took an opportunity to both show his Christian charity and reprimand the family for their behavior.

His words on this had little effect, however. Victoria rolled her eyes, Isabella yawned, Sarah crossed her arms, and Naomi and Dora exchanged a knowing look and smirked at each other. Mary and Grace seemed too consumed with grief to notice his admonishment.

After taking a moment, the minister continued, "Chapter Twelve of the book of Proverbs further tells us, 'A righteous man regardeth the life of his beast.' Again, life has confirmed the words of our Lord. The righteous care for their animals. Those who are wicked show nothing but cruelty to the beasts placed in their charge.

"Topsy was well-cared for. She was beloved by her entire family, pampered and petted almost as if she were a child. Indeed, her care is proof of the righteousness of her family. Mary Sutherland, in particular, was like a loving mother to Topsy.

"The dog's life on this earth shall not go in vain. For her life is a testament to the love of the Sutherland household. Topsy may be gone, but the love that is in all your hearts remains. May you love each other as you loved Topsy." Here, he stopped and nodded to Sarah.

She stepped forward, turned to her sisters, and began to sing, "All things bright and beautiful. All creatures, great and small. All things wise and wonderful. The Lord God made them all."

The other sisters joined in, and I was nearly moved to tears. I did not mourn for Topsy, but I did agree with the minister. The Sutherlands were odd. They argued and threw tantrums when they did not get their way. They had fits and strange encounters with spirits that could not be explained. And yet, there was love in their home. They loved each other with a ferocity evidenced by the way they had treated Topsy, by the way they had hired Agnes in her time of need, and by the way they had offered me friendship as well as a reputable occupation.

Behind me, I heard a sob. I turned, thinking to see Agnes. Instead, I saw Mrs. Poole, tears streaming down her face as she joined the Sutherlands in their song.

***

That night, after we returned from the funeral, Sarah declared that the family would be departing earlier than expected for the circus.

"I wanted to go to the first parties of the season," Victoria pouted. "Maisie VanDusen had her coming out this April, and I've been invited to ~~her~~ Calpurnia Merrill's wedding in July."

"We must leave as soon as we are able," Sarah insisted.

I was sitting with Mary as she slathered a foul-smelling salve onto her hair. I had not been a part of this nighttime ritual often, and I was unsure I'd ever grow used to it. The girls gathered at least once every week to unloose their tresses and rub the mixture on their scalps and through their hair.

"I don't have any objections to the eggs being put into the mix, but do they have to be *rotten* eggs?" Isabella complained as Grace handed her the bucket of brew which stank like sulfur.

"I know," Grace admitted, "it is most vexing, but you've only been able to grow five feet of hair, Isabella. Don't you want your hair to be like Victoria's? Her hair is over seven feet long now."

Isabella seemed to ponder this a moment, "Victoria's tresses are, by far, the longest of all of us, and Naomi's the thickest, but I think your locks are loveliest, Grace."

Victoria bristled at this, and I knew Isabella was only trying to start up trouble, though I secretly agreed with her. Victoria's hair was a rich chocolate and fell in long waves down her back, but Grace's curls were as warm as gingerbread and reached nearly to the floor. When she brushed it out earlier that evening, it shimmered a rosy gold in the fading light of the sunset. My own red hair seemed dull in comparison.

"My hair has hints of auburn, but it will never be as smooth and lovely as Grace's. When the light hits me, it only reveals tangles and snares," Dora said, wrinkling her nose as she rubbed the tincture on her scalp.

"I *do* want hair as long as Vicky's, but is it necessary to go about smelling like a chicken coop all day?" Isabella frowned.

Grace stopped her ministrations for a moment and said, "There was a time, not too long ago, when we did smell of chickens. Chickens and dung and stables with nothing to wear but burlap sacks and no shoes for our feet. Just be glad that those days are over."

She took another glop of the thick mixture and offered it to me. I blushed, feeling pleased that I was included in what had seemed an act reserved only for the family. I untied my braid and rubbed it through the ends of my hair.

"Besides," Grace continued, "we can at least be pleased that Sarah talked Papa into adding rose water to the mixture. It's not quite so bad as it once was."

She assured me, "We changed it a few years ago, Anna. But it still seems to work. Our hair grows longer than our legs. The tincture has only a few simple ingredients— Borax, salt, quinine, cantharides, bay rum, glycerin, rose water, alcohol, and soap."

"And rotten eggs," Dora laughed.

"And rotten eggs," Grace agreed.

"Well, I'd have liked to take the eggs out of it myself if I could help it," Sarah wiped soiled hands on an apron.

"Then why don't you," I asked, taking more of the mixture from the bucket.

Sarah gave a shrug. "If it weren't for the eggs, it might not work properly." She stood. "And now, I must to bed," she declared, hastily wrapping up her own four feet of hair. "We'll have to pack our things in the morning. The new costumes are in the lower attic. Anna, I'll be needing your help getting them. Try not to tarry too long tonight. You will need your rest come tomorrow."

I nodded, and Grace handed me a long rag to wrap my own head with. "So it doesn't stain the pillow," she said.

Mary had been silent throughout the evening, and when I rose to leave, she walked beside me. Before turning into her room, she whispered, "She daren't change the mixture, for Father and Mother wouldn't like it." I shuddered and tried not to think of what might happen if Fletcher and his wife were thus disturbed.

***

I was the only servant to accompany the Sutherlands on their journey. Lessons with Dora and Naomi were left off for the summer. Sarah told me, "When we travel, your sole job is to keep Mary sane. The Chilly Billy's Colossal Show was overwhelming enough, but Mr. Barnum's circus is the biggest, grandest show on earth. He will expect several shows a day, and I fear Mary may fall apart. Given her fragile state, I might not have agreed to go... but he offered us more money than he tried to pay for the Cardiff Giant."

I tried not to show my shock. The hoax of the Cardiff Giant had taken place in Syracuse years ago, but P.T. Barnum had so famously offered up $50,000 for the giant, nearly everyone still recalled the story. The idea that he was paying the Sutherland family so exorbitant a fee was incredible.

Sarah's broad face broke into a wide grin, "Our little home shall be a palace by the time we return." My mouth opened in surprise again, for I could not imagine the mansion being any more luxurious than it already was.

"I know," Sarah acknowledged my surprise. "It is already a grand house. But I don't take much stock in saving my pennies. We have had so little all our lives, we want to savor every cent we make. As the Good Book says, 'You can't take it with you!'"

Sarah rose to leave, but paused, placing a hand on my shoulder and fingering the material of my dress. "I would have you change out of your mourning weeds for good," she sighed. "I know it is proper to wear them at least a year in honor of your late father, but we are unable to wear our own black and gray dresses for Fletcher. And then there is the fact of the circus. Everyone wears their finest and brightest. Even the servants."

My lips thinned. Would I forever be I be asked to give up so much of myself, even my melancholy? Such an impertinent question could not be expressed, so I merely sighed, "I expected that. I understand, Miss Sutherland." I kept my voice clipped. "I will change into my Sunday dress as soon as I am able."

She must have heard both my words and my tone, for her voice softened like an open palm offering a gift of thanks. "Anna, your single Sunday frock will not be suitable, either, I'm afraid. Traveling on the rails wears a dress thin faster than anything I know, except perhaps farm work But I'll have Victoria buy some new things for you. She is the fashion plate of the family and I know she will enjoy the task." I smiled, grateful for this small gesture.

The first morning of our journey, I tried not to fawn too much over my new wardrobe. Each of the sisters was bedecked in a seal skin coat and hat, chosen by Victoria. They were heavy for such a summer day, but Victoria declared, "These cost over a thousand dollars each. We shall be as regal as queens when we depart."

Then she added with a dismissive sneer, "If you must change out of them, you may do so once we are safely in our private car. For my part, I intend to stay this way all day, no matter the heat."

She was foolish to say this, of course, and as glowing with sweat as the rest of them. So, it was no surprise when Victoria stepped into the train car and unceremoniously tossed the coat to the floor, revealing a light organza dress underneath. I smirked when I saw the dress had the same puffed sleeves as the coat, but none of the smothering heat. Her sisters said not a word, but I made sure to put the coat away neatly once Victoria's back was turned. If it were ruined, she would certainly want to place blame on anyone but herself.

The Pullman cars were covered with ornate walnut panels. Silk shades covered each small window, giving the train the feel of a sitting in an opulent study. Chandeliers hung at intervals, their teardrop crystals tinkling as the train rushed over the tracks. The Sutherland's had secured a private car for the journey, with velvet green sleeping berths, though the trip would only last twelve hours, and they were hardly the types who would sit still for long.

As the older girls roamed around the train, Mary, Naomi, Dora, and I walked to the lounge car where tables had been comfortably arranged around seats with plush curtains. A serving girl brought us plates filled with sliced tomatoes, oysters and dainty finger sandwiches, along with drinking water which had come straight from a fountain inside of the train. It was cool and clear, and I never thought to see such a marvel.

This was a far cry from the plain passenger train we had taken up from West Virginia. When we moved, the journey took two days, but we could not afford to stay in a sleeping car. Faith and I fell against each other in our hard, wooden seats.

The sisters were beginning to take luxuries for granted, and I noticed that both Isabella and Victoria were becoming more insistent in their demands as we drew closer to New York.

However, I also noticed Mary's demeanor changed almost as soon as we boarded the train. Sarah needn't have worried about her sister's delicate temperament, for she seemed cheerful and more like a normal girl than ever.

As I sat with Mary, Naomi, and Dora, Mary practically bounced up and down in here seat. "Tell Anna the story of Father and the poisoning," Mary squeezed my arm. I smiled at this gesture of friendship. We were nearing Rochester. The silvery haze covering her eyes was dissipating, and I could now see that Mary's eyes were nearly violet, not the charcoal black they appeared when she was shut up in her room.

"In truth, it is a good yarn, if one has never heard it before," Naomi began.

"And if one did not know father well enough to realize that it contained mostly embellishments," Dora added.

"That's true, too." Naomi nodded her curly head. "The first time I heard this tale, its original version, was at the supper table when I was six or seven. Father's position was not a popular one. As I'm sure you know, Anna, he was reviled for being in favor of states' rights, particularly after so many families lost sons and brothers in the Civil War."

Dora broke in, "I'm surprised he wasn't ousted from his position as minister sooner, but he made such fervent speeches, people seemed to forgive him his politics."

"Do you think Father believed anything he said about the Bible?" Naomi asked her twin.

Dora put a gloved finger to her lips, "I don't know. He liked an audience, and when he drank, which was often, he enjoyed riling people up. He almost fed off their anger and hatred of him. In the pulpit, it was just the same. Only then, he fed off their admiration."

Mary fidgeted beside me but said nothing. Naomi eyed her and said, "All right, I'll get on with the story, then."

Naomi turned back to me, "Father's orations both in the church and on the street caught the attention of first the governor and then President Buchanan, who himself was a Doughface and Copperhead and appreciated both Father's politics and his passionate addresses."

"Doughface?" I wondered.

"A Yankee not opposed to slavery," Mary whispered.

Naomi grew animated as she continued the tale, "With the help of President Buchanan, Father saw his situation much altered. Mother and Aunt Martha replaced their rough muslin garments with soft dresses of fawn and blue and pink. There was money for bonnets and corsets and shoes with little buttons all up the sides. Father purchased himself white duck trousers, broadcloth coats, and even a beaver hat. There was new china, and white sugar was always set out on the table."

"Not that we ever saw any of it," Dora added in. "Sarah remembers, of course, but by the time Naomi and I came along, those days were long gone."

Naomi was too enthralled with her own words to be put off by her sister's bitter sarcasm. "Father left for Washington to attend Buchanan's inaugural address," she said.

"Truly?" I was surprised. In all the stories about Fletcher Sutherland, a few things had been noted about his ties to a president, but I surmised he was a local campaign worker or some such.

Everyone in town said he was a miserable loafer, and his family would have been better off without him. It was true that Fletcher had helped to promote the sister's singing act for the past few years, but most of their recent success was placed at the feet of Sarah's business sense rather than her father's staged publicity. It surprised me Fletcher was regarded well enough by President Buchanan to be invited to such a prestigious event.

"Oh, yes," Dora assured me. "Mother told us there was even talk of Father running for office or joining the president's staff. Mother and Aunt Martha were planning the move to Washington... but then, the incident occurred."

"Before the inauguration, Father left a robust young man. When he returned only a few weeks later, he was much altered. His eyes were sunken, and his chest was nearly as thin as a bird's. Martha said she could hardly look at Father's graying skin and dark eyes without wanting to weep," Naomi said.

Naomi took a sip of water, and I knew she was giving a dramatic pause to keep my interest piqued. It worked. I was on the edge of my seat as she continued. "They were poisoned!" her bass voice boomed. "There were fifty of them in the president's party. They stayed the night at the National Hotel. After dining there, they all fell ill. Four men died, including the president's nephew, who had been acting as his secretary. The rest, including Father and President Buchanan, were taken to the infirmary."

"Poisoned?" I gasped.

"Yes," Dora broke in. "Father said it was likely because of the slavery question. There were people who wanted war and people who didn't want war and people on both sides were upset about the Dred Scott decision. Even the people who agreed with the Supreme Court didn't think the president should have interfered, especially before he formally took the office."

Naomi interrupted, "After the poisoning, President Buchanan recovered and was robust as ever. Father wanted to stay by his side, but he was weakened from the event. The president suggested he return home."

"Unfortunately, once he came home, the country began to turn against Buchanan as war became inevitable. Father's political ambitions were finished. And he was too sick and weak to seek other work at first. Aunt Martha came to the house to help, but Mother needed more help than Father because..." Naomi paused, looking worried.

"Because she was ill," Mary whispered. "We share the same affliction, you see."

Dora interrupted once more, trying to change the subject away from Mary's difficulties. "So, we were poor for quite some time, as you know, Anna. And it all started with the poisoning."

"I doubted the group had been poisoned at all," Naomi admitted. "Father was such a storyteller. I thought he made the whole thing up."

"Me, too," Dora said. "But I never said anything about my doubts. "Once, when Father told this story, Victoria asked, 'Did they do really do it on purpose, Father? I heard in town that the poisoning was nothing more than a serving of clams gone wrong.'"

"Even then Victoria was contrary," Naomi giggled.

Dora nodded and continued, "Father told us they found rats in the water tanks! It was possible that someone had set out rat poison to get rid of the vermin. Then, after ingesting the poison, the rats found their way into the water tanks, died there, and tainted the water supply. But Father said it was more likely that someone was trying to assassinate President Buchanan without getting caught. They poisoned the water, and the rats drank the water and got poisoned too."

Naomi laughed again. "It was a thrilling tale in and of itself, but later, Father would claim he tried to thwart the poisoners. He said he saw a group of men dumping arsenic into the water and tried to chase them down. Already poisoned, it was too late, and he was too weak to attack them. Even so, he warned President Buchanan, and they were able to make it out alive."

"I heard that version. It was like something out of *The Three Musketeers*," Dora laughed. "As if Father was a swashbuckling adventurer risking his life for the good of his country."

"The story hardly made him any friends," Naomi said. "And I should say, Anna, that none of us agreed with Father's politics."

"Absolutely not," Mary said, more forcefully than I had heard her say anything. "Naomi read me *Uncle Tom's Cabin* and *Oroonoko* and Frederick Douglass. Slavery was an abomination, and I'm glad it's over."

"Well, that is certainly true," Dora said. "And Sarah worked just as hard for abolition as Father worked against it."

Naomi said, "Not in Cambria, of course. They wouldn't have her. But up in Buffalo where no one knew or cared who her father was."

They all nodded, and we sat in silence for a moment until Dora stirred. "Now, let's have no more dour talk. Come along with me, Mary. I want to walk to the caboose and watch the track as it fades behind us."

Mary looked as if she would rather stay in the safety of our warm dining car than venture out among the strangers lining the rest of the train, but she agreed and went with Dora.

Once they were gone, Naomi asked, "Anna, have you shared a bedchamber with Mary before?"

I shrugged. "A few times when I fell asleep reading, and a few others when I needed to calm her from her fits."

"After we board the circus train, you'll be sleeping in the same car as Mary." Naomi set down her water glass. "I must warn you to be on your guard."

"She seems improved." I said. I did not want to comment on Mary's affliction and offend Naomi. After all, I would not want people talking about Faith behind her back, no matter what troubles she might have. That was the way of sisters. Our loyalty was a knot that could not be untied.

"She *seems* so," Naomi's bass voice dipped even lower, "but Mary becomes restless. She is prone to somnambulism when we travel."

"Mary is a sleepwalker?" I dropped my fork. I had heard tales of people committing horrifying crimes as they slept— completely unaware of any wrongdoing their bodies enacted while their minds were elsewhere. Some thought them to be ill or mad. Others believed them to be possessed by spirits... or worse.

Once at a family gathering in West Virginia, my mother's cousin Eleanor tried to delight, and frighten, us children with such a story. She told us of a man named Fain who had been sleepwalking and had shot a hotel porter before waking up in grief.

But the story which made me feel as if I'd sat on a broken needle was of Albert Tirrell. "Albert Tirrell murdered a street woman," Eleanor said, not pausing for an instant when my mother tried to interrupt her.

I didn't know what a street woman was, but I leaned forward eagerly as Eleanor's voice tickled my ears. "He slit her throat and as her head fell from her body, he set fire to the house. When the thick smoke began to fill Albert's lungs, his spirit returned to his body. He was roused at once. Realizing what he had done, fled all the way to New Orleans."

I wanted to know what happened next, but Mother broke in, "What utter nonsense. Everyone knows that man was full of lies. He was perfectly in control of his faculties. I believe he had just been reading that dreadful *Edgar Huntly* book. That's what gave him the idea. The book was fifty years old at the time, but still doing horrible damage to the morality of any who dared to open its filthy pages. That's why I only keep the Good Book in the house. No one's life ever twisted off the path by reading the Bible."

Eleanor looked as if she had a word or two to say about that, but Father stepped in, "I'm not so sure, Ida. I have been to the asylums. The mad often wander about as if in a dream in the daylight. I see no reason others might not have similar infirmities when the moon rises."

Mother demurred slightly. "You may be right, William. Only the good Lord knows what truth lies in the deepest recesses of our hearts. It seems a pretty convenient excuse, if you ask me, but I'm not one to judge."

She crossed her arms, "I'm also not one to let my girls hear stories that oughtn't to be told until long after they're in bed and sleeping too deeply to hear them."

I was perhaps eight at the time, and like the somnambulists, my mind seemed to wander as I lay in bed. I could not sleep for fear I would harm someone without realizing it. To lose control of my senses was my worst fear.

"All I can say is that you must be vigilant, even when you rest your head upon the pillow... or I may be doomed."

"Whatever will she do to you?" my hand rose to the lace at my throat, thinking of Albert Tirrell and his gruesome deeds.

Naomi's deep voice boomed in laugher. "This monstrosity atop my head!" She ran two hands through her frizzled mop. "Last season on Chilly Billy Cole's train, we were forced to share rooms. The third night out, Mary cut off a whole section of my hair as I slept, as if she was Delilah and I was Samson. I woke when she was part way through the job. Her eyes were glazed unnaturally and she hardly blinked. I knew she did not know what she was doing"

"I did wonder why you fashioned your hair in that manner," I admitted, smiling.

"Just be sure to lock the door at night," Naomi said, "and keep your hair tightly braided."

I could not help but laughing at this. Naomi, like the other Sutherlands, had a way of making the unnatural seem normal. I wanted to say more. Mary was only thirteen. If she cut her sister's hair last year, would her spells grow worse?

"Come on," Naomi held out an arm, "let's go find Dora. She says she won't marry, but if we let her wander around the train much longer, she will probably fall in love with the first man she meets!"

I relaxed. Talk of madness was over, and our easy friendship was restored. In truth, Both Dora and Naomi would fall for the first young men they met. For now, they ran down the length of the train with Mary in tow, laughing, and living in the last blushes of girlhood I myself had been forced to leave behind.

Part IV

A Memory on Fire

Miss Grace Sutherland.

Pictured: Miss Grace Sutherland

June, 1885

I didn't know which was more overwhelming—the buildings, which reached higher than any tree I'd ever seen, or the stench of the street, which was a stomach-churning combination of soot, sweat, and sewage.

Though I'd seen Mary faint more times than I cared to recall, I'd only done so once myself, the night I'd seen Fletcher in the so-called "ice house." I was not sickly either as a child or as a young woman, and due to my station in life, I was never afforded the opportunity to be a wilting flower, who collapsed at every whim, demanding smelling salts.

Upon inhaling the air in New York City, I thought all that might change and clutched my stomach, turning back to the railcar, and trying not to retch.

"It takes a few moments to get used to," said Grace as she stepped out of the train. She lay her hand on my back, stroking my hair. She whispered, "Breathe through your mouth and keep your eyes level; the skyline can be dizzying."

I did as Grace instructed and attempted to collect myself. "Farm air is so clean, even with the stench of livestock," I tried to explain.

"I know," Grace agreed. "When we go home, and you look back up into the sky, it will seem as if you can smell the stars, everything is so clear. In the city, everything seems a bit muddled. The first time we came here was for the opening of the Broadway Museum, and it took me nearly an hour to stop... well, I don't wish to be indelicate, or to vex you further."

Grace had a gentle, motherly manner about her, but I rarely spent time with her. As the middle of the seven girls, her role was unclear.

I listened to Sarah as if she were my mother and treated Mary as if she were my child. Dora and Naomi were friends, and Victoria and Isabella like the older girls at the schoolhouse—sometimes generous, sometimes demanding, but ultimately, caught up in their own world, uninterested in associating too frequently with us younger girls.

In that moment, I decided to look at Grace like an older sister—more caring than Victoria and Isabella, but not so demanding as Sarah. I thought to tell her my thanks for helping me off the train, but a pair of horses pulling an omnibus trotted past and my senses were immediately assaulted again as the mingled sweaty smell of horse and man wafted by.

"Oh!" Isabella cried, stepping off the railcar. "How perfectly dreadful!" She dramatically and swept past us, lifting up her skirts as high as she dared.

"Sarah," Isabella called, "there is muck everywhere, and I simply won't stand for it."

"Lie in it then," her eldest sister called back through the window, laughing.

Isabella harrumphed and walked on tip-toe to the station door.

"Victoria will feel much the same, I expect," Grace sighed. "But then, they'll be going back to the hotel directly for some rest. I dozed a bit on the train, though. I was wondering whether you might not like to tour the city for a few hours? We can watch the train being unloaded."

I turned back to the train, skeptically. "Not that train," Grace laughed. "You must excuse my vagueness, Anna. I meant the circus train. They'll be unloading it today and tomorrow to ready for the parade. It's not far from here, but if you would like a bit of a tour, we can travel to Battery Park first. The French steamer Isère brought in the Statue of Liberty only last week, and I should like to see her construction."

I agreed at once and was excited when Grace said we'd get to ride the omnibus. We set off as the others made arrangements to be taken to the hotel.

"There are living quarters at the circus for all the members of Barnum and Bailey's company, but we're being paid a hundred and fifty a week... each," Grace whispered. "So, we'll be staying in the best hotels all season."

It always struck me as odd the way the Sutherlands spoke of money. My mother had drilled into me the idea that one should only discuss money among family, and even then, only in the most dire of circumstances.

I merely smiled and asked, "But wouldn't it be more fun to quarter with the rest of the circus folk?"

Grace shook her head. "You might think so, but you never know who might join the circus, and some of the crew can be quite rough. Unfortunately, we may have the need to stay with the company when traveling through some of the smaller towns where no hotels can be found."

As the omnibus clattered along, Grace pointed out the sights as we passed. More passengers seemed to squeeze in at every stop, and I pushed against the sides of the omnibus, closing my eyes every now and then when the mass of bodies overwhelmed me.

"Look!" Grace grabbed my shoulder.

We had turned from Ewen Street, and I stretched my neck up to see the spire of Trinity Church. "We'll pass the new Brooklyn Bridge later," Grace said. "Except for the bridge, Trinity is the tallest building in New York."

I looked up, wondering how all those bricks and stones could be stacked so high one upon the other without crumbling down in a heap.

"They only finished the interior of the new chapel inside a year ago, though the original edifice was there for decades," Grace explained. "There's said to be a marble altar and bells that way nearly three tons!"

"Three tons?" I echoed.

"Wait until we see the statue," she said, grinning like a child. Away from her sisters, Grace was sprightly and buoyant. I realized that she spent so much of her time playing nursemaid and peacekeeper, she had little time for diversions. The truth was, Grace was still young, and she wanted to have as much fun as Dora and Naomi.

"Is it the statue that remarkable?" I asked. I'd heard little about it, but felt caught up in Grace's enthusiasm.

"The bust was on display at the Champ de Mars at the World's Fair in Paris," Grace explained. "I saw a tintype of her last summer. Then, when Cole's circus came through New York, I went to see the base they'd prepared for her arrival. Men were still finishing the construction, and one told me it would be nearly as tall as the statue herself—over one hundred fifty feet tall."

"That's more than the lengths of twenty-five men lying end to end!" I exclaimed.

"Everything is big here," Grace laughed. "New York is exactly like the circus. Larger than life!"

"Seven wonders of the world with seven feet of hair each," I did a bombastic impersonation of Mr. Barnum.

"They do tend to use a bit of hyperbole," Grace admitted. "You know, Anna, your hair is longer than Sarah's now, though it may not be as thick."

"That can't be," I raised a hand to my head.

"She curls it because it's shorter. But it isn't Sarah's fault, you know. Once she turned thirty, her hair became brittle. Now that she's forty, it tends to break at the ends. She thinks the curling helps, but I think the heat does nothing but dry it out further."

"Is Sarah that much older?" I marveled. I wondered, but did not dare ask how old the rest of them were. I was under the impression that their ages ranged nearer from thirteen to thirty, but in this, I had clearly been mistaken.

Grace gave me a pointed look. "She was sixteen when the war began. Her beau died the second year— Ezra Hobbs. He was the only man she ever cared for, and she hasn't courted anyone since. Sarah changes her age for the show and tells everyone she's only thirty. She says it's because younger performers are more popular, but I think it's because she doesn't want to talk about the war. Professing you were merely six rather than sixteen means you can pretend you don't remember any of it. And she never has to speak or think of Ezra with anyone."

"Sarah had a beau? She seems so..." I trailed off. The word I wanted to say was "mannish," but before I could think of a suitable substitute, Grace grabbed my sleeve.

"We're here!" she said. "Get off quickly, or we may be forced to exit at the next stop."

We hopped off the omnibus just as it began to pull away. Battery Park was the only spot of green I'd seen in the city, and it calmed me greatly. People strolled through the park as they would through the countryside. Some were alone, but most were couples walking arm-in-arm. A pleasant sea air breezed in from the Upper Bay, and sailboats drifted along with it. This was a place for leisure, away from the bustle of the city surrounding it. I felt more at home than I had since stepping onto the train.

Two men on high-wheeled velocipedes rode toward us. "Watch," Grace said, with the same glint in her eyes I had seen before in Naomi's.

At home, Grace was level-headed and much more mature than the younger girls. But when the gentlemen rode nearer, one raised his hat in greeting. In response, Grace whipped the central pin from her hair. Her long auburn locks blew out behind her.

Grace threw back her head and arms, and in the wind from the harbor, she looked for all the world like a Valkyrie, readying for battle.

The young man gaped in astonishment, and fell over the front of his handle bars, tumbling onto the path with a crash. His friend nearly collided into him and yanked his bicycle to the left. Then, jolting onto the grass, he found himself in a similar state of affairs, falling to the ground with a loud grunt.

My instinct was to go to them and inquire whether they needed assistance, but Grace laughed like a demon and ran in the opposite direction, hiking up her skirts and petticoats to gain greater speed.

When I at last caught up with GRACE, she was out of breath with laughter and shaking so badly in her mirth she could not pin her hair back into its original, modest state. "Let me help," I said. Grace smiled at me, conspiratorially, as we did up her nearly unmanageable curls, which had tangled in the wind.

"I have caused a mess, haven't I?" Grace said, remembering herself. "Only I have so few opportunities to cause messes of my own. I could not fail but to control the impulse. I do hope they're not injured."

"Only a bit startled," I reassured her. "And you probably shouldn't have done it. But when I think of that man's face..." I spread my lips like a large-mouth bass in imitation. We both burst into another fit of giggles.

Coming to the edge of the park, we saw glinting masses and folds of copper glittered through piles of wooden scaffolding. I had always loved holding a shiny new penny in the palm of my hand, but looking at the portions of statue scattered throughout the park was like gazing into the blazing center of the sun by comparison.

We moved toward the scene in silence, watching the men at their labors. Some were unpacking boxes, with one man on top and another man below, both working furiously with heavy hammers and thick crowbars. Others stood gazing up, scratching their heads or hooking thumbs into their suspenders, as if wondering how they were ever going to assemble this beautiful monstrosity.

"Man by the name of Eiffel designed her," one of the idle workmen called to us. "Same guy what did that big tower up in gay Paree." He pronounced the word Paris with a joking French accent, though his voice was far from French—nasal, with words which seemed to run together.

Grace ignored his attentions, though I knew she was taking in every word. "You want I should walk ya over and show ya her face?" he asked.

"Oh my, yes!" The words jumped from my mouth before I could stop them.

"Anna," Grace admonished, and I reminded myself once again that the Sutherland moods were as ephemeral as a moth in the wind. Merriment had left her, and propriety had returned.

"Ain't no trouble," the man continued, wiping greasy calloused hands over already-dirty trousers.

I looked to Grace with both hands clasped to my chest as if pleading for my soul. She shrugged. "Very well then. I am curious myself, I must admit."

The visage of the statue stood nearly three times my height. Hanging between two frameworks of scaffolding, she swung in the wind like a great copper bell.

"The finest belle of any ball," Grace murmured, as if reading my thoughts.

"That she is," the workman said. "Showed to her my mother once. She said the lady had a lovely Roman nose finer than any painting she'd seen back in the old country."

I knew the nose was what would be called Grecian, rather than Roman, but nodded in agreement, not wanting to be rude. Instead of replying, I stared at her carved eyes and lips, wondering at how such a lovely creation could ever have been rendered so perfectly.

"'Keep, ancient lands, your storied pomp!' cries she with silent lips. 'Give me your tired, your poor, your huddled masses yearning to breathe free,'" Grace said, eyes closed in reverie.

My lips parted in surprise, but Grace opened her eyes and turned to me. "Those are lines from the poem by Emma Lazarus. She sold it a few years ago to raise money for the statue's base."

"Yep," the worker assented. "A hundred thousand people contributed to the fund, but I'd wager Miss Lazarus paid the most. I could only spare eighty cents myself, but they says to me, Charlie, they says, 'Ya know that every little bit helps.' And I agree."

We all stood there a few moments more until Charlie cleared his throat. "Apologies ladies, but I gotta get back down to the shipping crates now, if you don't mind."

Grace nodded in her usual gracious manner, and we walked back to the omnibus, which I thought might be less crowded now that most had concluded their business for the day. Unfortunately, I was mistaken. It seemed business in New York was never concluded, and once we had taken our leave of the park, the rush of bodies surrounded us once again.

At last, we reached Madison Square Garden. A large white building, which lacked a roof. What I thought would be a large garden looked more like a castle with square turrets at each corner and giant fortress-like towers out in front.

When we came around the bend to see Barnum and Bailey's train, my mouth fell open in surprise. "I never anticipated this," I said.

"No one ever does." Grace shook her head. "The posters and paintings don't do it justice."

She was correct. There was not one line of cars, as I had anticipated. Instead, there were lines of trains up and down the stretch of land for what seemed to go on for miles. I stared at the crisscross of silver cars, glittering in the day's waning light.

Still, one thing bothered me. "They are pretty," I started, "but... I did think they would be more colorful."

Grace turned to me, "Colorful?" Her mouth quirked to the side, and I recognized in her face the same puzzled look Naomi had when trying to do sums. After a second, her lips settled back into their usual benevolent smile. "Oh, you must be thinking of the wagons. The wagons are inside the larger cars. We're a bit late, but we may be able to see the men unloading one. They'll be used in the parade tomorrow and—"

"Look out!" I grabbed the back of Grace's dress and pulled her back as a horde of wild-looking horses flew past.

"Good Lord!" Grace exclaimed, then covered her mouth as if remembering herself.

A tall, mustachioed man called out to us. "Are you hurt, Miss?" He sprinted over.

"She is unharmed, I think," I called back.

He reached us quickly, and, seeing we were unharmed, he took a handkerchief from his pocket and wiped beads of sweat from his brow.

"Begging your pardon, ladies," he panted. "We thought we'd seen the last of our visitors today, and I told young Jimmy he could take the horses for a run—get their legs back in working order after the long ride. I don't like keeping animals cooped up for so long without a bit of exercise."

"It is nothing." Grace smiled. "Thankfully, my companion had the sense to pull us out of harm's way."

"Why if it isn't Miss Grace Sutherland!" the man exclaimed. He used the handkerchief to wipe his hands, and stuck one out in front of her. It was still encrusted with dirt and grease, but I appreciated the effort.

Grace shook his hand tentatively. "Forgive me. Do we know each other?"

"Ah, I am sorry again," the stranger said. "I forget myself. I know you from your cabinet card, of course... though the photograph hardly does you justice. And I've followed you and your sisters in the papers, so I feel as if we have known each other for quite some time. And yet, you know nothing of me. My name is Joseph Henry Bailey, but my friends call me Harry."

"Bailey? Any relation to Barnum's latest business partner?" Grace asked. Her mouth quirked again. This time it looked as though she were thoroughly amused, though I could not say why.

"Of course!" Harry tilted his head toward me and winked.

For a moment, I thought of Edgar, that laughing young boy who had made the same bold move when we were young. Then, my mind went to Mr. Tarkington and the night of Mary's attack, and I did not know whether I should accept or distrust this dashing young man.

I thought we might say goodbye and take our leave, but Harry's deep voice boomed out again, "Now, I know you and you know me! Yet, I am afraid I do not recognize your lovely friend."

"This is our companion, Miss Anna Louise Roberts. She is often with my sister Mary, but I thought she might enjoy seeing a bit of the city and the circus before the show."

"Mary, of course," Harry nodded as if he knew everything about Mary's afflictions.

"Well," he considered, hooking his thumbs into his suspenders, "I'm afraid there is not much left to see tonight, as the animals are all inside the Garden. As I said, we had quite the number of spectators earlier this afternoon—at least two hundred—so we made sure to unload the menagerie first."

"Did you really have such a crowd?" I asked.

"Absolutely. It's all part of the scheme," Harry laughed. "Some of the other circuses don't allow gawkers at the trains, and some don't even have a parade! 'Why work for free?' they ask. They don't realize, as Mr. Barnum does, that a few days' free work pays more in the end."

"How?" I wondered.

"Have you ever eaten ice cream?"

"Once." I blushed. "At a party."

"When you tasted it for the first time, didn't you want more?"

"Yes," I admitted.

"You see!" Harry exclaimed. "It's the same with the circus. Once people get a little taste, they want more. Give them a peek at the elephants' tails as they exit the trains, and they'll come to the parade."

"Get them to the parade," Grace picked up, "and they'll see the lions, the tigers, the Siamese twins—"

"And the lovely Sutherlands," Harry added.

"And the *lovely* Sutherlands," Grace laughed.

"But only for a moment," Harry said. "Only for a second before the next act passes them, and the next, and the next, and the next. And after all those strings of moments, they'll want more than a taste. They'll want to see the show."

"And with Mr. Barnum's shows, there's always more to see," said Grace. "They come on Friday and they'll stay until Monday when the train packs back up for the next stop on the tour."

"Especially this year," Harry hinted.

"Now why would that be, Mr. Bailey?" Grace raised an eyebrow in question.

Harry's jovial attitude changed suddenly. He ran his thumb and forefinger over his thick blond mustache, as if considering how to form his next words.

"A few weeks ago," he began, "there was an incident on the new Brooklyn Bridge. It was Memorial Day. A woman's heel got caught in the planks of the pedestrian promenade. When she started screaming, the crowd around her apparently thought the bridge was about to collapse. It caused a complete panic, and twelve people were caught in the melee."

"Injured?" Grace asked.

"Dead, I'm afraid," Harry grimaced. "But, Mr. Barnum had inquired about a parade across the bridge last year when it was completed. The mayor wouldn't allow it at the time, but after the tragedy..." Harry paused and shrugged.

"They're allowing the parade to prove the bridge is safe?" she guessed.

He nodded. "We were given the new route yesterday."

My stomach turned. The Sutherlands had nothing but good things to say about the great showman PT Barnum, and I had seen his magic for myself at the Opera House, even if only for a moment. I knew Barnum was famous for his stunts, but would he use such a tragedy—the death of a dozen people—for his own gain? The thought of it made me sick.

"Would you like to see the circus wagons being unloaded?" Harry changed the subject. "As I said, the animals are away for the night, but the rest of us will be working for a few more hours yet."

Grace looked to me before answering. I knew she wanted a clear answer as to my wishes, but I could only think of the twelve dead, and the families who would still be in mourning as circus elephants tramped across the bridge where these poor souls lost their lives. Any profit gained from the exploit would be nothing but blood money.

I attempted to smile. Misperceiving my demeanor, Grace believed I had no objection to seeing the men's work. "It is interesting," she promised as we walked down the tracks.

"The big top isn't the only place we perform death-defying feats of strength," Harry said, pointing to a group of men carrying long poles. "There are nearly eighty cars altogether. About twelve years ago, they converted the horse-drawn wagons to iron horse flat cars. They only had sixty cars back then, but it took them nearly twelve hours to load up. We can do it in about half that time now." He grinned proudly.

"The poles are for the tents," Grace explained. "We won't have a tent in New York City, but no other city in the world has a venue like Madison Square Garden."

"Unfortunately," Harry added. "Now, I work as the assistant to the Equestrian Director, but when I first started, I was a canvas man. Spent nearly every day driving stakes into the ground. You have no idea how many stakes must be pounded in— not just for the big top where we hold the main show, but the sideshow tent, the menagerie, and the museum tent, too. After the stakes, we raise the poles with pulleys. And only after those are secure do we roll out the canvas. They're trying to train the elephants to help with that. It's heavy work."

"I can imagine," I said. "But if the tents aren't going up today, why are the men carrying the poles?"

"The tent poles serve a dual purpose." Harry pointed to the work in front of us. "We need the poles to help take the circus wagons out of the train. The ends of two poles go onto the train bed. Once they're set in place, the men gently roll each wagon down to the ground."

"What about the boys running between them?" I wondered.

"They're checking for stones," Grace said.

"You're absolutely correct, Miss Sutherland," Harry boomed. "You see, Miss Roberts, the wagons are extremely heavy, particularly the band wagon they're taking down now. It will be pulled by the horses you saw earlier. It takes all forty of them to drag it through the streets."

"Though some of that is for show," Grace could not help but add.

"Yes," Harry admitted, "but the bandwagon weighs over eight tons, and even a pebble on those great poles can upset the process. I've seen a man nearly lose his leg because the left pole became slippery with mud. The man up top lost control of the wagon, and the man below had to leap out of the way before he was crushed to death. The left wheel went over his leg and broke it in two places."

I gasped. The more Harry said, the more I was beginning to feel the circus was a dark, violent place.

Harry swiped nervously at his thick mustache. "I don't mean to upset you. That was several years ago. No one has been hurt since, I promise."

We watched as the magnificent wagon was lowered to the ground. The red carriage was ornamented in gilt scrolls. The Five Graces—representing charm, beauty, nature, creativity, and fertility—were carved into the side and covered in dazzling gold paint.

"Creativity is my favorite," Grace said, pointing to the central figure, "though she looks nearly as dour as the others. I don't know why anyone would carve them with such sour looks on their faces."

"The bandwagon leads the parade. Bailey— um, that is my *uncle*," he emphasized the last word, "believes the Graces give a sense of gravity and class to the spectacle. So, the circus can be compared to the great Greek hippodromes, where people came for miles to see the great chariot races. Or the Colosseum, where spectators flocked to watch gladiators face off in armed combat."

And even more came to see Christians murdered for sport, I thought, but did not dare to say. My father and mother had taught me all about this dark period of history. According to them, the Romans were savages who cared for nothing but filling their bellies and lining their pockets. As much as I was dazzled by the extravaganza before me, I could not help but wonder if the circus purveyors were much the same.

"The light is dying," Grace said, placing her arm through mine. "We should take our leave."

"I hope you enjoyed your brief tour, Miss Sutherland," Harry smiled. "And will we be seeing you in the parade tomorrow, Miss Roberts?"

"No," I demurred. "I'm hardly a performer. The ladies have obtained rooms at a hotel. It's along the route, and I expect I'll watch from the window. The city is a bit overwhelming. I cannot imagine what it would be like once all this added in."

Later, as Grace and I rode home on the now nearly-empty trolley, I leaned over to her and whispered, "Mr. Bailey seemed nice enough, but I don't care for the way he winked at me."

"He winked at you?" Grace looked puzzled, but not alarmed, as I imagined Sarah might be at hearing such a thing. "When?"

"When he gave us his name," I said.

To my surprise, she laughed. "Oh, that. He wasn't winking at you."

"He most certainly was." I bristled. "I may not be as sophisticated or well-traveled as you, but I know when a man is winking at me."

"Calm down, Anna. I only meant he was winking in your direction, but I doubt it was flirting. He was hinting about his name."

"His name?"

"*Bailey*." Grace shrugged, as if to say that one word would explain everything.

Seeing my confusion, she continued, "I suppose you're not used to people changing their names, but it's quite common among performers. I suspect the wink meant that either he changed his name to Bailey, or that his original surname is in fact Bailey, but his claims of any relation to Barnum's partner Mr. James Anthony Bailey are entirely false."

"Why should he want to pretend such?" I wondered. "Surely Mr. James Bailey would know it was nothing but deception."

Grace stared at the city lights, considering this. "He is ambitious," she said. "If he was truly a canvas man, he's not afraid of hard work, and now he's been promoted and is managing a few of the other workers. That's not an easy feat for one so young. Harry is one to keep an eye on."

I could not imagine changing my name, and very identity, for mere ambition, but we were weary from our travels, so I said no more.

***

The sisters had reserved an entire hallway of nine rooms—one for each of them, one for me, and one for their costumes. I thought this last to be overly extravagant, but could not object, particularly when they were being overgenerous in arranging my own quarters.

I slept soundly that night, though I had not expected to, given some of the ferocious images that came to mind whenever I thought of the circus. I supposed the city, with all its sights and sounds, had quite worn me out, for I was asleep as soon as my head rested upon my pillow.

A few hours later, I awoke to piercing screams coming from the hall. Forgetting I was still in my nightdress, I ran out to see if I could help. All seven sisters were clumped together. Each was still wearing a nightdress, and each had her hair fashioned into a single braid, hanging to the floor. Their personalities erased, and they seemed much less like seven girls than seven long-haired angels, or a single mind sharing seven bodies.

This thought disappeared as soon as Mary began screaming again. "I won't go! I won't!" she shouted.

When she at last caught my eye, she shrieked, "Anna! You're here to protect me. Don't let them take me! I can't go! I can't!"

Sarah grabbed my arm and pulled me into the group. "Talk some sense to her," she hissed.

"Mary," I tried to soothe her. "Where are they asking you to go?"

"The parade. And I know about the bridge. It nearly collapsed last month. They can't make me walk across it. I'll fall right into the river. I know I will!"

I couldn't blame her for protesting. Plenty of native New Yorkers avoided the bridge, fearing the same fate.

"Look at the newspaper, you silly girl," Victoria held up a newspaper, which I now noticed had been folded at each of the hotel's doors.

"Barnum plans to take Jumbo and twenty other elephants besides. Not to mention seven camels, ten dromedaries, and all the rest of us." She read, "It will be as if Noah's Ark is emptying itself onto the island. If successful, Jumbo's arrival in Brooklyn will be Barnum's greatest triumph."

"*If* successful," Mary cried. "But it won't be. It will be a disaster that ends with all of us drowned at the bottom of the river.

Drowned like Topsy—wet and cold and alone, even though we're together. I shan't go!"

She tore away from us and fled back to her room, slamming the door behind her.

"It won't do to have six of us in the parade," Victoria said, looking pointedly at Sarah.

"I know it," Sarah lifted her square chin. "And at our first appearance with Barnum and Bailey, too. Every single performer is required to be there. The whole company is expected."

"The whole company except Mary," Victoria said.

"Surely, he'll understand," Grace broke in. "He knows of Mary's troubles."

"Yes, but I assured him they wouldn't interfere with any major performance," Sarah said. "A promise I clearly should not have made. But, she's usually better once she's away from the house."

"The longer we're away, the better she seems," Grace agreed.

"Until she becomes exhausted from the work," Naomi said.

"Or throws a fit for no reason," Victoria scoffed.

Or for a very good reason, I thought, thinking of Mary's last two spells, one of which signaled the death of her beloved dog, and the other, which resulted in burns on her arms and her precious hair being cut for a man's twisted pleasure.

Yet, I could see why they would not heed their sister's warnings this time. She was screaming in protest, but her eyes remained clear, and she wasn't biting, scratching, or even

156

rocking, as she had in other times. Perhaps this was less a premonition and more the irrational fears of a young girl.

"We have three options," Dora said, and I noticed Sarah look at her sharply, as if surprised her younger sister was going to take charge of the situation.

"We can all stay here and join the circus at the Garden tomorrow," Dora continued. "We can go without Mary. Or...." she paused for a moment, "we can ask Anna to go in her place."

Six nearly-identical heads turned to stare at me. I shifted under their gaze. "Me?" I gulped.

"How long is your hair?" Sarah demanded.

My hand flew to my head. "I... I don't know," I stammered.

"Nearly three and a half feet," Dora supplied.

"Not so long as Mary's then," Sarah nodded, "but almost as long as mine."

As Grace had told me earlier, Sarah had the shortest hair of the family, but it was thick and wavy, and I did not believe mine to be comparable. Then there was the parade itself to contend with. I was used to cows and horses, postmistresses whose names I knew, and shops of only one or two stories. I did not like the bustle of the city, with its buildings towering like Goliath over the masses of people scuttling about below. And I thanked the Good Lord we would only be in New York a few days more before moving on to New Jersey, which was sure to be more peaceful.

"You can pile it up on your head." Sarah held my face, turning it first to the left and then to the right.

"Your hair isn't thick yet," Isabella chimed in, "but we can braid it, wind it around your head, and hide a foundation piece in the center. My hair is thin too, so I carry a few pieces with me for appearances like this."

Before I could protest, I was hustled back to bed. The next morning, I found myself riding the trolley surrounded by six girls who would, at least ~~of~~ for the day, count me as one of their sisters.

***

Whenever I think back on that first parade, it is a memory on fire.

I walked past so many odd personages—the twins who could not leave each other's side, the Aztecs, the bearded lady, the skeleton man, the Japanese dancers, the lady equestrians, the aerialists... on and on they went, each more peculiar than the last. At first, I tried not to stare, and then I could not, for they all became a blur.

Eventually, we came to our spot, the procession commenced, and I was overtaken by a crushing cacophony which seemed to press in on every side—the bandwagon with its forty horses before us, the calliope behind, the shrieks and giggles of children in the streets, and the gasps and whispers of their astonished parents. It seemed as if the eyes of the entire city were staring at me.

Billowing like smoke, the scents of the circus were just as crushing as the restless spectators. The dung from the elephants wafted past as they tramped through the streets. The damp fur of the rest of the menagerie combined with the sweat from acrobats, who tumbled past us, grinning. And of course, the crowd, whose stench had been bad enough the night before, when they were not pressed in together.

A conflagration of color overwhelming me. My eyes again felt unable to fix upon any one spot. I turned to see the brown tent-like dress worn by the fat lady; the pink and blue tights of the trapeze artists; the pale purple worn by the Lilliputian singers; the rainbow balls of the jugglers. I blinked and turned back, only to see the flags of crimson, burnt orange, and umber flapping like flames in the breeze. If there were smelling salts to be had, I surely would have asked for them.

Instead, I stopped dead in the middle of the street and might have stayed there had Naomi not grabbed me by one arm and Dora by the other.

"It can feel like you're under siege," Dora shouted into my ear, though I could barely hear her above the fray. "You can see why Mary didn't want to come. New York is the largest city in the country. Nearly a million and a half people live here, and half the town is out today! The rest of the tour is tame in comparison."

"Just walk with us and stare at the back of Sarah's head when you feel overcome," Naomi advised. "That's what I do. When it's too much, just paste on a smile and stare straight ahead. No one cares, as long as you keep waving."

I nodded, feeling comforted now I was no longer walking alone.

We continued, arm-in-arm, for a few blocks before I felt capable of taking my eyes from Sarah's braid long enough to look at the people gazing out at us. Once my mind became used to the throng of people, my eyes were able to make out individual faces.

Children hung out of windows, waving at the scene below. I noticed one pigtailed girl blowing kisses, and I blew her one back, not knowing whether she would see me—one long-haired girl walking quietly amongst the most remarkable humans and animals on earth.

I noticed that many of the people clustered around us were pale and freckled-faced with hair in shocking shades of red. In truth, they looked almost like walking carrots. I turned to Naomi, a question forming on my lips.

"The Irish section," she rasped in my ear. "After this, you'll see the blond Germans, the darker Italians, then the Russians, and then the Jews. There are nearly a hundred thousand living in the city now."

I gasped and might have run away, had I been in any landscape I could recognize.

"It's alright," Dora said into my other ear. "They're perfectly harmless. Most are here as refugees. A few years ago, the emperor of Russia was assassinated. The Jews were blamed, and many had their homes and businesses destroyed."

"They're just like the rest of us," Naomi added. "And as Mr. Barnum says, 'The circus is for everyone.' Young or old, Christian or Jew, man or woman, rich or poor. Everyone loves the circus."

I shook my head and stared again at Sarah a few feet ahead of us. I had heard tales of Jews from both my parents. My father told me that during the war between the states, Jews sold food and other goods to both armies. "They were nothing but greedy war profiteers," he said. "Drove honest, hard-working Christians out of business and violated every trade regulation imaginable."

My mother said they were, "Dirty bloodthirsty heathens." But, she had also once called my employers' first home, "A sinking ship filled with rats." So, I could not very well find import in her words.

Instead, I tried to believe Naomi and Dora, who had only lied to me when playing pranks. *The war was a different time,* I reasoned. *And it ended nearly two decades ago, long before these immigrants even arrived on our shores.*

Still, I felt myself shrinking against the sisters as we proceeded into the ghetto. I could not help but lose the plastered-on smile as I glanced around at the women in their faded, ragged kerchiefs and the men, leering and stroking their thick black beards.

Then, I saw a young girl break through the crowd and run over to tiger's wagon, which was just ahead of Sarah. The tiger was caged, but I knew the trainer could not see the child, and she might stick her hand between the bars to pet the beast. Worse, she might find herself falling beneath the heavy wheels of the cart, which could not stop quickly enough, no matter how the coachman might pull on the horses' reins.

Ahead of us, Sarah and Grace were talking to each other while Isabella and Victoria continued to wave to the crowd. In an instant, I could see that no one else saw the girl. I tried to scream, but only Dora could hear me above the roaring crowd. As Dora turned toward me, I grabbed Naomi's shoulder and pointed at the girl, who was now within feet of the cage. The twins' eyes grew wide and they acted at once.

Together, we three picked up our skirts and ran toward the girl, whose blue threadbare dress was at least a size too large and trailed in the mud behind her.

Naomi reached the child first and snatched her up just as she grabbed hold of the tiger's cage. The great striped cat gave out a terrifying roar, though I would guess it was as startled as the girl, who was now sobbing, in Naomi's arms.

A woman in a torn gray skirt and stained apron ran up to us. She was crying and screaming in what Dora later told me was

Yiddish—a language which mixed German with Hebrew. The girl held out her arms toward her mother, and Naomi proffered up the child.

We stood outside the parade for a moment as the woman hugged and kissed all three of us, while her daughter squirmed and whimpered. After a few moments, it became quite the ridiculous scene as most in the parade remained unaware of the near tragedy and continued walking ahead. Not wanting to be left behind, Dora, Naomi, and I lifted our skirts once again and jogged back to our place.

For the first time, the applause and shouts of praise which reached us felt justified. We had saved a child, and was that not an act worthy of applause?

I felt my anxieties slowly give way to a rush of exhilaration. As we continued the parade without incident, I thought back to a time before my father died when I was still in the good graces of the other children at school. During recess one afternoon, I found Edgar sitting under a tree reading *The Adventures of Tom Sawyer*.

When I asked whether the book was any good, he said, "Some of the adventures are dull. Who cares about painting a fence or giving a cat pain killer? The really good bits happen when Injun Joe comes around. He's a dastardly, murderous fellow, and Tom's terrified of him. A fellow must be afraid to have a *real* adventure. Otherwise, there's no excitement."

Edgar was right. At times, nearly everything about the Sutherlands and the mad world they lived in scared me half to death, but each episode was more thrilling than the last. I wondered what other thrills I might allow myself if I ignored my panic and let go of petty concerns.

In any case, seeing the Jewish mother and her child had made me more sympathetic toward them. The woman reacted the same as any Irish, Italian, or German mother. She behaved much the same as my own mother might, though I laughed aloud at that notion. Mother would never have let me see the parade, let alone run into it.

Mary's fears had been as baseless as mine, for when we at last reached the newly-built Brooklyn Bridge, the company came to a halt. I knew PT Barnum was up front with the bandwagon, but we could not hear his speech.

It must have been brief, however, because the dromedaries, camels, and elephants, which had been at the tail of the parade, now came forward to the front. Meanwhile, the rest of the performers in the parade blended into the crowd to watch the final procession.

They say that a dog who smells anger will bite, and horses who sense fear will whinny and throw their riders. In the same way, the dromedaries must have felt the anxieties of the crowd, for they faltered at the first stones and refused to cross the bridge that had taken fourteen years to build.

I knew, as everyone else did, that if the animals did not traverse the great expanse, no one else would either, and the cost of building the bridge would be wasted.

Along with everyone else, I held my breath as the trainers snapped their whips and prodded at the gentle beasts with bull hooks—long canes ending in metal hooks at the end. After a few moments of urging, the dromedaries at last walked across the bridge. The camels were next, but still no one seemed to breathe. At last, the crowd let out a collective sigh of relief as the first of the elephants set his large feet upon the stones.

"That's the dwarf elephant, Tom Thumb." Dora squeezed my hand. Naomi was on my other side and I glanced behind to see the four older girls craning their necks to see the show.

"I thought Tom Thumb was the smallest man in the world," I said, not taking my eyes off the elephants.

"General Tom died last year," Dora said, and her voice dropped in a way that showed she felt the loss deeply. "They bought the elephant a few months ago and named him in memory of Tom."

I nodded, not wanting to talk for a moment. As the next elephants came to the bridge, my eyes traveled upward to the thick cables above. I could not know whether it was genuine or some trick of my imagination, but the bridge seemed to sway in the wind. I felt unsteady watching it.

When the crowd broke into applause, I pulled my gaze back to the road. Jumbo, the thirteen-foot, seven-ton elephant, now had all four of his giant, heavy feet on the Brooklyn Bridge.

The procession moved forward until the great elephant reached the center. Then, one by one, the animals each turned in a small circle where they stood. At last, it was Jumbo's turn. The applause stopped, and the air went silent.

Nothing could be heard except the crack of the trainer's whip in the air, which echoed down the long thoroughfare. Then, Jumbo raised up on his hind legs, showing his full height. He blew his trumpet like a king announcing his triumphant return to the castle.

The crowd went wild.

"We won't see anything else exciting today," Sarah's voice sounded behind us. She pushed her way through the mass of bodies and stood arms akimbo, so no one could come within three feet of her. "That beast blew his horn in a declaration of victory. It was the climax Barnum hoped for and will assure every one of these fine men and women will pay tomorrow to see more."

The band struck up its next tune, and the rest of the performers reassembled themselves to continue the loop around the city.

"Let's find a cab and retire to the hotel," Isabella said, coming up beside her older sister. "Most of the performers will follow the parade route, but we all know the show is done, and my legs are weary."

In the growing heat of the day, no one disagreed. We walked a few blocks before coming upon a Hansom Cab Company, where Sarah paid a whole dollar and a half for us girls to ride only a few miles. When I saw her hand over the money, I gaped, though I should not have been surprised. I was learning to accept the Sutherland's lavish lifestyle and found the cab ride much more pleasant than the trolley.

When we arrived at the hotel, Sarah declared she would keep one of the taxis to, "Do a bit of shopping," and Victoria went with her. In Sarah's usual sense of generosity, I was invited to come along.

For a moment, I considered going. A voice deep inside me whispered, *Perhaps Victoria will find you another lovely gown to wear*. Feeling sinful, I refused the offer, blushing in shame for my wicked, greedy thoughts.

As soon as we entered the hotel, I went upstairs to check on Mary. To my surprise, she was lounging in her bedroom, reading a book bound in green cloth with silver gilt letters embossed on the cover. "I picked it up in the shop next door," she said coolly, not lifting her eyes from the page.

"*The Country Doctor*," I read the title along the spine. "That doesn't sound like a book you would enjoy, Mary."

"Oh no, it's quite fascinating," she insisted. "Nan is a young woman who would rather become a doctor than marry and have children. Can you imagine?"

"I can." Dora appeared in the doorway. "I remember Mother and Martha running around after all of us with no time for rest or leisure. Set the fire for breakfast. Clean the breakfast dishes. Boil water for the wash. Wash the clothes. Hang them to dry. Set the fire again for supper. Clean the dishes all over again. Not to mention the pain of bearing eight children for a man who... well, perhaps that part is best left unsaid. In any case, motherhood is a punishment I don't wish to receive."

I must admit I almost broke in to remind Dora I was not truly one of her sisters, and there were still but seven of them. Thankfully, as I opened my mouth, I recalled their now-deceased brother Charles and saved myself the embarrassment.

"I don't know that motherhood should be called a punishment," Naomi said, stepping in the room. "You must remember, Kitty, the drudgery of cooking and cleaning was back when we had naught but two coins to scrape together. We have a girl for the cooking now, and the laundry too. And nursemaids could be hired—one for each child, if you wished it."

"I'd rather use my head for business and make more money for the family," Dora replied.

"More money?" Naomi asked. "What more could we possibly need?"

"A laundress for each of us?" Mary asked, giggling.

"No," I said. "A camel for each of you to ride upon so you no longer need to walk in any parade."

"And a bandwagon to announce our arrival each time we return home," Naomi laughed.

"Laugh all you want." Dora tipped her upturned nose even higher into the air. "Anna's shown me I'm good at sums, and I want to use my brains for something more than knowing how often to change a diaper."

"Every two to three hours," Naomi said automatically, "unless it's wet."

"You see." Dora pointed at her sister. "Not even a thought to it. You're a smart girl, Naomi. Don't you want to use your mind?"

"I think child rearing is quite important, thank you very much," Naomi snipped. "Father said that motherhood was the most significant occupation a woman could have. It is God's divine mission given to women alone. A mother must give her children wisdom and moral fortitude, and she must sow the seeds of truth, wisdom, joy and peace. At the end of her life, if she has done the job well, she shall see a spiritual harvest, bearing fruit in her children and grandchildren."

Dora rolled her eyes. "Father hardly lived by such a lofty moral code, and I never understood why he should preach such when every action he took prepared us more for the stage than the nursery. You needn't quote his sermons at me."

"And you needn't quote those ridiculous suffragettes who believe women should vote like men and act like them besides," Naomi huffed.

167

"I think it's fine to do both or neither, if one wants," Mary whispered from her bed. The two girls looked over at her, stunned she had any thoughts on the subject.

Mary closed her book and changed the subject. "But how was the parade? Did Anna perform marvelously? Was Gittel alright?"

"Oh, Mary, I was nearly overcome by the noise of the teeming crowd," I admitted. "I can see why you refused to go."

"That's not why I refused to go," Mary plucked a chocolate from the box on her bedside table and popped it into her mouth.

The three of us stared at her, and I wondered whether she would become cryptic again and decline to say anything more.

"Well?" Dora tapped her foot impatiently.

Mary shrugged and waited until she had finished her chocolate. "I wanted Anna to have a turn. I thought she'd have fun. And I was worried I wouldn't see Gittel in time. The wheels of the cart move so quickly, you know."

"Mary, you keep saying the word 'Gittel,' but I don't know what it means," Naomi sat at the foot of her sister's bed.

"Isn't Gittel the funny little monkey that keeps time with the organ grinder?" Dora asked.

"No," Mary said. "The girl. The one with the blue dress. She was unharmed, wasn't she? I asked Father, and he said I would never be able to reach her in time, not with all the crowd packed in around me, but he thought you would, Anna. And, I knew you'd like the performance, once you got used to all those eyes on you. And you did save her, didn't you? And you enjoyed yourself, too. I can tell."

My mouth went dry and I stumbled for words. At last, I managed, "I did... I saved her in time."

Mary nodded. "She's going to work in the garment district someday. I don't quite know what that means. Only I know she'll make and wear finer dresses than the one she had today. Poor little thing. She reminded Father of me at that age—when I used to run in the weeds wearing nothing but an old sack."

"And look at us now," Dora broke in, trying to ease the tension of the room. "Dreaming of having dozens of babies or dozens of cooks or whatever else we might desire."

"Hmm," Mary murmured in vague assent and picked her book back off the bed. There was nothing more for me to do than stare and wonder at the mystery.

It seemed like an age passed before we heard Isabella calling from the hallway, "Girls, Grace and I are dressing for supper. I told Sarah I wanted to dine at Delmonico's tonight, and she promised to reserve us a table."

She poked her head into the room, "Mark Twain dines there, and Abraham Lincoln himself once said the steak was the best in the country. Can you imagine? I've heard the desserts are just to die for, and I plan on ordering one of every single item on the menu!"

"And that," Dora looked pointedly at Naomi, "is why I want to go into business." She grinned and skipped out of the room. Naomi shrugged at me and followed Dora out.

"I don't want to go." Mary turned another page in her book. "I have plenty of chocolates to eat."

169

"Mary," I laughed, "you cannot have chocolates for dinner. Be reasonable. You have to perform tomorrow. Chocolates will give you nothing but a bellyache for your trouble."

She sighed, setting down her novel once again. "You know the songs well enough. And everyone saw you in the parade today. Just be me until we're out of New York. I hate this dreadful place."

A bird seemed to flutter in my chest. "I can't be you, Mary."

"No, of course not." She sat up at last and slid her feet onto the floor. "You have to be Naomi..." she yawned and stretched her arms above her head as if waking for the first time that day, "or is it Isabella? There are so very many of us. I can never remember."

"Stop talking nonsense and get dressed," I snapped. She wasn't vexing me, but after the talk of Gittel in her blue dress, I was anxious and did not feel like going to a famed restaurant with a sour stomach.

So, I hustled Mary to dress and refused to hesitate, even to protest when she insisted I wear an old frock of Dora's for the evening, though it was a shade of yellow so offensively bright, it nearly burned my eyes to look upon.

Part V

Between the Rows of Freaks

Pictured: Miss Naomi Sutherland

June, 1885

"The actual circus is much more orderly than the parade," Sarah explained as we rode in yet another handsome cab back to Madison Square Garden.

[handwritten: we]
[handwritten: Hansom]

This time, we were alone. The others had split into two other cabs and Sarah had requested I ride with her.

I wrinkled my brow. "I thought it would be even more of a chaotic display than yesterday."

"It can seem so, if one fails to understand the grand scheme," she explained. "The main program is under the big top. Inside the tent are three rings, each with a separate act. The show begins with a procession, followed by the performing stallions and the tumbling tournament."

"At the same time?"

"Of course! That way, there is always something new, and the audience is never bored. Have you ever seen the insides of a watch?"

I nodded, and Sarah continued, "It works much the same— the rings are like gears that interlock with one another. Each seems to tick along without getting in the others' way."

She listed things off, closing her eyes as if to remember, "After the tumblers come the other physical acts—barrel dancing, parallel bars, and roller-skating feats. After that are the equestrian acts and gladiatorial contests."

"Like the Romans?" My mind flew back to images of Christians facing lions and winning only to be boiled in oil.

Sarah must have detected the anxiety in my voice, for she laughed and said, "Not quite. It has less to do with sword play and more to do with feats of strength—men picking things up and showing off. I find it quite silly."

"Oh." I breathed a sigh and relaxed into my seat.

Sarah cleared her throat. "The height acts come next— flying rings, high wire acts, and the trapeze. Those are quite the performers, though I must say I cannot quite approve of the costumes the trapeze girls wear."

"Is that how the show ends?"

"The show never ends," she laughed again, "or at least that's how it seems. The horses trot out again, and the bareback riders go round the rings. Then there are animal acts—the trained doves, goats, even geese, if you can believe it. Then the clowns perform, and then the elephants. He always ends with the elephants."

"But where will you be?" I could not picture seven sisters singing in the midst of girls whizzing overhead on the trapeze and men zooming past on roller skates.

"We will be performing in the sideshow tent. The sideshow is what they call a ten-in-one. Ten acts are performed. Usually, they have an eleventh act lined up as a surprise encore for the audience. Then, when the show is over, it starts all over again."

"It sounds exhausting," I said.

"It can be a bit tiring, particularly on our voices, but we have time to rest while the other acts perform, and there are breaks for mealtimes as well. As long as we don't strain when singing, we manage fine."

"Even Mary?" I could not help but ask.

"Even Mary," she smiled kindly, and I could see Sarah was pleased I had thought of the welfare of her youngest sister.

"In addition to the big top and the sideshow tent, there are the menagerie where animals are housed when not in the main show; the hippodrome, where races are held throughout the day; and the museum, which contains the curiosities. The Hindoos are there, as well as the Burmese dwarf, the Nubians, the Guatemalans, and JoJo."

I wanted to inquire about JoJo, the dog-faced boy, but Sarah was trying to educate me, and I did not want to divert her attention too far from her theme.

"There are over six hundred performers," she continued. "And when they're not under the tents, they'll be in the backyard."

"The backyard?" I echoed.

"The back lot, some call it," she explained. "it's a large area, restricted from the public. The backyard is everything. Rest area, the cook house, the doctor's wagon, the tailor, the blacksmith, dressing rooms..." she trailed off and waved a hand as if to say, "everything means everything, Anna."

We were able to hear the show before it came into view. The noises from the surging masses mingled with men shouting for spectators to turn their heads this way and that.

"Ignore the barkers," Sarah motioned to men outside each tent. "And take a Bible with you. Hold it to your chest wherever you go."

She thrust a heavy book into my hands. "Whatever for—" I started to ask, but Sarah cut me off.

"It has nothing to do with religion, and everything to do with keeping away the wrong sort. *Men* who prey upon any pretty

175

young lady who passes by. You may be in service, for now, but you are still a lady, Anna. You're not the type of girl who associates with ruffians. Most carney folk are disreputable. The Bible keeps them away. All of us carry them."

Sarah got out of the carriage in one large, manly step, and I thought how interesting it was that she should work at the circus, yet think herself above it, particularly after how she had started her now-prodigious career. The same woman who ridiculed Nettie's pretentions seemed to have developed some of her own.

It was hard to ignore the barkers as Sarah had instructed. The first caught my ear as soon as I exited the cab.

"Step right up folks," he waved his purple top hat high above his balding head. "Step right up. Here before you stand Jack Spratt and his wife. The thinnest man in the world married to the fattest woman on earth. Jack Spratt can eat no fat. His wife can eat no lean. And so, between the two of them, they lick the platter clean! You've never seen such a marvel in your life."

"A marvel, but what a marvel," a voice to our left cried. "JoJo the Dog Faced Boy. Be he man, or be he beast? Is he half-dog or half-boy? Is he—?"

Another barker broke in, "Is he as magnificent as Myrtle Corbin, the Four-Legged Girl from Texas? A true oddity if ever you saw one."

The yelling continued, and I looked to Sarah, who strode over to meet her sisters.

Mary, who had shrunk back into herself, was huddled next to Grace. I grasped Mary's trembling hand, and tried to joke with her. "Now, isn't this much more exciting than sitting alone reading *Nan, the Country Doctor*?"

She giggled and squeezed my hand in return. "Yes, and I would guess the confectionary here is better than the chocolates I had yesterday." She stood a bit taller, and Grace smiled at me in approval.

As we stood in front of the Garden, I doubted Sarah's story that the circus was like a clock. From what she said, I expected everything to be housed under tents, but the street was filled with wonders.

A sword swallower was few feet away, while another man beyond him seemed to breathe fire. Further down the row were three women performing tricks on bicycles. Another barker shouted out for us to come inside the sideshow tent where the show would start in an hour. "See the living skeleton and the Elastic Skin Wonder!" he yelled.

Meanwhile, I was thankful that instead of the stench of sweat, which seemed to assault me the previous afternoon during the parade, I now perceived the scent of roasting meat mingled with the sweetness of pulled taffy and the salt of popcorn. My mouth watered.

"Must we always perform between the rows of freaks?" Victoria sighed.

"They are all out today, aren't they?" Sarah glanced around and motioned for us to move to the side of the building, away from the barkers and ticket sellers.

"Most of them aren't with us. They're unofficially auditioning, trying to get a spot with Barnum's show," Isabella smirked. "I suppose the old humbug is wandering about, checking out prospective candidates."

"Is it always like this?" I stared as an exotic looking woman sauntered past in a puffed skirt the length of a boy's short pants.

"Only in New York," Isabella and Victoria said together.

A white-haired man in a cobalt blue suit sidled up to us, "My, my, my, if it isn't the seven most pleasing wonders of the world."

It was shocking to see a celebrated figure like Mr. Barnum up close. Though I had seen him from afar twice, I still thought of him like a phantom or specter, whose spirit drifted onto the stage only when the applause of the audience called for him.

"Uncle Phineas," Dora cried, throwing her arms about his neck.

"Ah, my little Kitty," he patted her head gently. "And how are my other girls?" He turned and received similar hugs from Naomi and Mary, while the older girls waited for Mr. Barnum to press his lips to their gloved hands.

Sarah was last, shaking his hand in a gentlemanly manner. For his part, Barnum accepted her broad hand with a serious nod, though he did look as if he were holding in a great bellyful of laughter.

"And who is this eighth wonder of the world, might I ask?" he twinkled at me.

I blushed. Though he was many years older than I, Mr. Barnum lived up to his reputation. The humbug was flirting with me. "No one, sir," I stammered, "only a servant."

"Nonsense," Mary cried. "Anna Louise is my very best friend, and one of the most beautiful and loyal people I know."

She stomped her foot as Barnum laughed, "Well now, my little mousy one, outside your songs, I think those are the most words I've ever heard come out of your mouth."

He turned to me, "You must be a great asset to the family, Miss Anna, if Mary speaks of you so. Be sure to continue taking care of them."

He paused a moment and stroked his chin, "You were in the parade yesterday, were you not?"

I looked to Sarah before answering, but for once, she looked as nervous as I felt. I knew she did not want to lose the generous income Mr. Barnum was giving them.

"Yes, sir," I gulped. "Mary was... ill. We did not think the crowd would mind if I stood in her place."

He touched a hand to the braid winding around my head. "Your hair must be fairly long as well."

"Yes, sir," I said again, though it was a statement and not a question.

"Put the tincture on it as the sisters do," he declared. "If one falls ill or loses her voice as happened last season, you can fill in as a substitute."

"Would you be amenable to such a thing, Anna?" Sarah eyed me as if sizing up my abilities in a single glance. "Performing was not part of the duties I described when you were first hired. Stage life is not suitable for everyone. I would not want you to feel forced into it."

"I don't know," I stammered. "I never considered it before. My hair could grow, of course, but I do not know whether my singing—"

Mr. Barnum cut me off, bursting into a fit of laughter. "My dear, the public doesn't come to a circus for the singing! They come for the show. The theatrics. No one will mind if you hit a sour note here or there as long as you drop those lovely locks in a most dramatic way at the end of it. That's what they'll remember—the waves of hair flowing over the stage like water over Niagara Falls."

"And your singing is perfectly acceptable," Sarah assured me. "Your tone is clear and lovely. You don't have much of a range, but we can practice scales and other exercises to improve it. You'll never be as good as Naomi, but few of us in this world are. I believe you could do as well as Mary or Isabella, given enough time."

I saw Isabella frown at this. Before I could reply, Barnum straightened his crooked satin tie, and motioned to Sarah to walk with him, as the rest of us trailed behind. "I'm considering bringing on the Pinhead, but I have not yet decided," Barnum told her, confidentially.

"Hmm," Sarah considered. "That book of Darwin's is all the rage now. You might be able to advertise the Pinhead as the missing link."

"Just the thing," he clapped her on the shoulder. "The churchgoing public will eat it up. Is it real? Are Darwin's theories correct? Is his work complete hogwash? They'll love the Pinhead more than the Aztecs. You have the head of a businessman, Miss Sutherland."

He motioned back to the rest of us, "Speaking of business, you might think of something to do with yourselves beyond our show. You're not quite like the rest of the rabble, you know. Ladies of quality don't last long in the circus, no matter how pleasant their company may be."

Without explaining quite what he meant, Barnum pulled a watch from his vest pocket. "My word! Ladies, it is time to take your places. The tickets are sold, the gates are opening, and the people demand a show!" With that, he clicked his heels and sprinted away.

"Alright, girls. You heard the man." Sarah took charge. "We're seventh in the sideshow program. Go get into your costumes."

The six Sutherlands moved as one toward the tent while Sarah turned to me. "It wasn't just talk, Anna, what Barnum said. I do not know how you feel, but I would like you to consider it."

I opened my mouth to reply. "Don't answer now," she held up a hand to stop me. "Come to the sideshow today and spend time in the backlot. Tomorrow, I would like you to see the menagerie and museum tents. Then, the day after, you're to go to the big top. Once you've seen everything several times over, we will have a family meeting and discuss the situation."

"That would be agreeable," I said as feelings of both dread and exhilaration fluttered in my belly.

"As I said before, our lifestyle is not one that most people would choose," she paused, "but there will be time for talk of that later. For now, I must run, and you must take a seat in the front row."

She bustled away, I assumed to the backyard. As the crowd swelled through the Garden's gates, I made my way into the tent.

The bombastic lecturer, Professor Harold Everett, announced the Punch and Judy show first. Before long, I found myself laughing at the ridiculous puppet show. However, as the story continued, there seemed to be something grotesque in the violent way Mr. Punch hit his wife with his bat to the beat of the drum played behind the small wooden stage.

My discomfort turned to revulsion when Miss Ida Jeffries was announced. The woman had African features, but pale, powdery skin and a shock of blond hair that sat like a freshly-picked puff of cotton atop her head. She wore an odd, homemade dress that came only to her knees and was covered in clumsily-sewn cloth flowers, though I knew all the performers were paid generously for their talents.

Ida's appearance was somewhat off-putting, but what truly alarmed me was the thick emerald and gold snake wrapped around her shoulders like a shawl.

She set the slithering monster on a small carpet before her. It coiled into a heap and lay still until she took out an odd-looking horn and began to play one squawking, toneless note after another.

At the same time, she moved her hips and undulated her belly. Her dance was almost seductive, and I wanted to turn away in disgust, but my eyes locked upon the snake, whose poisonous head was lifting up from its pile of slimy skin.

The snake seemed as mesmerized as the audience. It curled and twisted in time to the music. At last, Ida's notes began to change to lower, more melodic tones, and the snake twisted back down toward the floor. It lay its head upon its great belly, as if asleep.

In the crowd, we moved to applaud, but the show's announcer motioned us to be quiet, as to not awaken the lethal serpent from its charmed rest.

When Ida left the stage, I felt the spell lift and wondered whether this was one of Barnum's famous humbugs—a trick the audience could both perceive and appreciate all at once. The other members of the audience must have felt the same. A tall woman next to me asked her husband, "Gerald, was that snake charmed, or do you think she trained it the way you might train a puppy?"

"I can't rightly say," Gerald replied.

As the whispers and titters continued through the tent, a much more respectable man came in Ida's place. Professor Everett pronounced, "Ladies and gentlemen, I must assist our next performer, but only a touch, for this is Charles Tripp, the Armless Marvel! He can perform more feats with his ten toes than you can your ten fingers."

The professor bent to remove Charles' shoes and socks. He placed paper, pen, and an inkwell before the Marvel. "Come closer," he beckoned to the audience. "Notice his gentlemanly penmanship. See the way he signs his name with a flourish."

I leaned close to the stage, and indeed, Charles wrote almost as neatly as a woman, or at least with cleaner strokes of the pen than the boys I had known in my school days.

His lack of arms did not stop him from cutting paper, painting part of a landscape, and, for his finale, riding a tandem bicycle in circles around the stage, pedaling in the back as Professor Everett steered from the front.

They rode off backstage before the professor came bouncing back to the front. "And now for some prestidigitation," he announced. "Prepare yourselves for the greatest illusionist of all time!"

With that, he held up an empty hand and, without warning, a coin appeared in his palm. "You there, ma'am," he pointed to a woman seated two rows behind me.

"Me?" she looked around, embarrassed.

"Yes, you. Would you mind joining me on stage for my next bit of magic?"

"I suppose," she laughed and made her way to the front.

The professor helped her onto the stage. He was handed a bedsheet from someone behind the stage and asked the woman to stand still. When she complied, he covered her with the sheet. A moment later, he whipped the sheet off to reveal—nothing!

We all uttered squeals of delight and clapped until I thought my hands might be rubbed raw.

The woman appeared at the back of the tent, another marvelous feat, and she bowed demurely, clearly unprepared for the attention, and then took her original seat.

Professor Everett held up both his hands to stem the applause. "A taste. A taste only. Much more to come, folks, much more to come. Now, please greet our next act, the famed hirsute lady of great renown, Miss Annie Jones!"

The crowd again went wild, and I clapped along with the rest, though I had never heard of the "famed lady." To my shock, she was the bearded woman I had seen at the parade.

Annie was a slim, buxom woman. She wore a low-cut dress with no sleeves, and her hair was piled atop her head like a turban. She turned this way and that, displaying a beard longer than that of St. Nicholas. Then, Professor Everett provided her a stool, where she sat and told us her story.

"I was born an infant Esau," she began, "and I have performed for hundreds of thousands of people such as this fine audience since before I could walk. When I was not yet three years old, a phrenologist kidnapped me from Mr. P.T. Barnum's benevolent care. Thankfully, I was reunited with my circus family, with whom I have stayed for over twenty-five years."

She brought out an accordion and began singing "Camp Town Races," which was followed by more songs by Mr. Foster, including "Jeanie with the Light Brown Hair," "Old Black Joe," and "Oh! Susanna." By the end of her performance, we were all singing along and clapping in time to the jolly tunes.

James Maurice, the Elastic Skin Wonder, was announced next, though I aimed my gaze at the floor, for I could not bear to look at the man, nor John Darrington, the Living Skeleton who came after.

Thankfully, their appearances were quick and followed by Professor Everett, who completed a few card tricks, none of which was as impressive as the disappearing act with the woman from the third row.

"And now," the professor boomed, "those seven wonders, the Seven Sutherland Sisters."

A few men in the back hooted and whistled in a way they had not for Miss Annie Jones, or even Miss Ida Jeffries, despite their having more womanly figures and scanty costumes.

I had seen the Sutherlands rehearse and perform shows before, but this performance was of a different sort. It seemed a bit more vulgar, more aggressive than the performance at Hodge Opera House. Though I could not quite explain how.

Perhaps it was not the lack of hymns, but the venue itself that gave me such an impression. When the Sutherlands finished, letting down their hair seemed more an act of shocking defiance than a display of beauty.

I clapped as the audience howled and stomped their feet. Gerald and his wife, who had been seated behind me, left the tent. "How brazen!" she exclaimed.

"Such a lurid display," Gerald agreed, but I caught him leering back when his wife wasn't looking.

I followed them out. I did not wish to ~~not~~ sit through the last three, or possibly four, acts. I felt tired and thought a walk around the grounds might allow me some time to breathe and ponder my situation.

I should have known better than to think of the world outside the tent walls as a calm garden where I could take a stroll. But I was able to make my way around the far perimeter of the great white castle without being pushed or prodded by too many of the patrons.

After I had been at my paces for nearly a quarter of an hour, a familiar voice behind me inquired, "Am I mistaken, or shouldn't you be finding your rest in the backyard?"

I turned to see Harry Bailey. I almost failed to recognize him as he was wearing a bowler hat, roguishly tipped to one side, which matched his dapper, black suit. No thumbs in the suspenders or bare shirt today.

"You are not mistaken, Mr. Bailey," I smiled. "I most likely should go to the back lot as my employer requested. I only thought..."

I stammered, unable to describe my thoughts at this moment. Mr. Barnum's proposal and Sarah's affirmation of his grand plan raced in between thoughts of *no it is too much* and *perhaps I could make enough money to send my sister Faith, so she might be more comfortable.* Then there was the notion of fame—something which seemed both great and terrible.

"I can escort you," he offered an elbow.

"Thank you," I said. "But I should tell you I am not allowed gentlemen callers, nor do I want any."

I wanted to be firm on this point, though the first part was a lie. I was allowed callers, as long as Sarah approved. However, after my last brief flirtation, I was not interested in courting or marrying a man. At least, not at the moment. I was not ready to declare myself to be forever like a nun or Nan, the country doctor, quite yet.

I thought putting off Harry might be rude, but Harry Bailey was prepared to be even more discourteous than me. He let out a great guffaw of laughter and held his belly until tears came to the corners of his eyes.

"I suppose I shall take my leave, since you seem to find me so amusing," I huffed.

"No, please don't," he said. "I should have realized that my offer of friendship might have seemed like something more. In truth, I am enamored with your employers, though not in the way you have just intimated."

"No?"

"Truly. I find them fascinating."

"Moreso than the rest of the freaks and wonders here at the circus?" I tentatively took his still-proffered elbow, and we began to walk.

"They are unique in their own way," he said. "Not the daring women who stand on the backs of horses or tumble through the air without nets, but not like the Aztecs or the Phantom Lady, either."

"Their hair," I began.

"Yes, but their hair is a thing of beauty. So many of the performers here are things to be examined and wondered over. Why does Annie Jones have a beard? Did her mother see a bearded man, who frightened her just before she gave birth? Do the Siamese twins communicate to each other without speaking? What does the Skeleton Man eat?"

"How did a man with no arms learn to write with such pristine penmanship?" I supplied.

"Precisely. Your Sutherlands seem more suited to the stage shows of Vaudeville than they do the circus."

"They have performed at a variety of venues," I said. "You have to understand, Mr. Bailey—"

"Harry, please," he insisted.

"Hmm," I uttered, not wanting to take such a liberty. "You have to understand that in our hometown, the Sutherlands are considered oddities. Some of the crueler townsfolk call them freaks."

He nodded, "And here, they are in a sideshow, so they feel as if they fit in."

"No." I shook my head. "Here, they are thought of as well-bred young ladies whose talents might be too good for the circus. Here, they are treated to seven maids who comb their hair and help them dress. Here, they are applauded instead of ridiculed. Celebrated instead of reviled."

"So, this is their true home?" he stroked his thick mustache, considering the idea.

I thought of Sutherland Mansion, its rooms crowded with the ghosts of memories, and perhaps real spirits besides. "I do not know," I began, slowly. "I would not go quite so far as to say it is home. But I would say that this is where they can be themselves under the right sort of scrutiny."

We said no more and entered the backyard, where one of the chefs was raising the flag to signal the first meal break.

"Right on time," Harry grinned. "There will be a break after the ten-in-one finishes its second run. You should be able to find them in the meal tent."

Naomi was the only one I could see inside. She stood in line, waiting to be served a heaping pile of meatloaf covered with mashed potatoes.

Harry and I walked over to her. "Anna!" she exclaimed. "We worried you'd left for the day when we didn't see you at the second show. Did you not enjoy it?"

"It was quite—" I started and was thankful she cut me off.

"Quite fun and exciting, isn't it? But who is this handsome looking fellow you're walking with? Is he the one who distracted your attentions from the show?"

I blushed and began stammering, but Harry only laughed. "No. I'm afraid Miss Roberts has made it quite clear she has no interest in me, or anyone else, for that matter."

"Is that so?" Naomi's mischievous eyes twinkled. "Well, all the better for me then."

Both she and Harry laughed, but I could only stare at her boldness. I had not seen Naomi flirt with a man before. Her flirtations were unlike Isabella and Victoria, who coquetted with nearly every man they met, if he were handsome or wealthy enough. Naomi did not put on false airs. She spoke like her usual jovial self, except with a bit more vivacity than she might have if I was the only member of her audience.

"Miss Naomi, you are more delightful in person than you are in pictures," Harry said.

"Are you the young man who gave my sister a tour a few nights ago? The collector of cabinet photographs?"

"I see my reputation proceeds me." He gathered a plate of food and handed a second to me.

"I must admit it is only because you knew Grace on sight." Naomi led us through the lines of performers to take our seats at one of the long tables.

"I have been praised a bit for my singing," she said, humbly, "and Isabella for her theatrics. Dora and Victoria are so pretty, and everyone knows Sarah, she is so gregarious. Yet, Mary and Grace always seem to be forgotten. Mary is delicate, you know, and hardly cares for fame or adoration, but I cannot help but wonder about Grace."

"She is often retiring and motherly, but she can be spirited and daring when she wants," I said, thinking of our wild walk through the park. "I think she would seek out accolades if she truly wanted them."

"That is well-observed, Miss Roberts," Harry said. He turned to Naomi to add, "But I think all the women in your family are lovely and worthy of praise."

Naomi smiled sweetly, but she could not comment further before two ladies with broad faces and identical faded green dresses joined us. I felt a sense of familiarity but could not place where I had seen them before.

"Hallo." They spoke together in thick accents before sitting down, one on either side of the table.

"Hello," Naomi smiled. "Olga, Gretchen, this is my friend Anna. And you most likely know Mr. Bailey, the world-famous assistant manager who can tame horses with a single look."

They giggled demurely and again, I could not help but feel I had met them before. "Were you ladies at the parade yesterday?" I asked.

"No," Olga said. "On the days before the shows, we work in the kitchen, helping to prepare food for the canvas men. Also, our performance is not one we like to advertise ahead of time."

"Why not?" I wondered.

Both women looked at me with amused looks on their faces. "You saw us, did you not?"

"I did, but I can't place where."

"The sideshow tent," Gretchen explained. "I went under the sheet and... zoop!" She bent down low toward the table.

"And I bounce up in the back... zaaa!" Olga exclaimed.

They grinned, and I smiled back, yet I felt a touch of sadness that the magic of the professor's show was now lost to me. "So, it is nothing but a trick?"

"A trick of the eyes, maybe," Olga said. "A humbug for sure and for certain. Only staying show after show see the truth."

"And they revel at the deception," Harry assured me. "They believe they are amongst the few who have discovered the secret."

"You should come. Watch the rest." Gretchen shoveled food into her mouth.

"Yes. Come, watch. Watch more than once. Two, three, four times even," Olga agreed. Then, she ate in a manner similar to her sister, and the two said a hasty goodbye before rushing back to the sideshow tent.

"I suppose you must return as well?" Harry asked Naomi.

"In a few moments," she said, "though I don't feel the need to act as though I were a barn animal at the feeding trough before I do so."

"Naomi," I scolded.

"It is quite alright," Harry chuckled.

"Where are the others?" I looked around. "I don't see them here."

"Sarah wanted to use the time to practice a duet with Grace. Then, Mary declared she would eat nothing but fudge, taffy, and candy corn, and Dora went off with her to do the same." She paused shaking her head. "Candy for supper. Can you imagine? Those girls can be such children sometimes."

"What about Victoria and Isabella?" I wondered.

"Off to play games and buy trinkets," she said. "Or at least, to watch men play games and allow men to purchase trinkets for them."

"Such children," Harry quipped.

"Indeed," Naomi laughed and stood to leave.

I stood along with her, "Mr. Bailey, thank you for your company. I am sure you must return to your duties now."

"The races do call my name." Harry nodded. "Thank you for allowing me to eat with you, Miss Roberts."

Then, he turned to Naomi and asked, "Miss Sutherland, would you mind permitting me a quick word?"

"I suppose not," Naomi said, "as long as you are brief."

I made the awkward excuse to leave and exited the cookhouse only to stumble into a woman hanging costumes on a line. A red coat trimmed in gold ribbon fell to the ground.

"And after I just laundered it," the woman barked.

I apologized, turned, and bumped into a man in white makeup and a tall scarlet hat. He was carrying a wooden crate of white geese, which squawked and hissed like great ivory harpies. "Don't upset the birds," the clown admonished in a similarly hissing voice.

Embarrassed at my apparent lack of grace, I dashed back to the sideshow tent.

Much as I felt out of place among the performers, I did not know whether I belonged with the audience either. Watching the show through, I saw there was a rhythm to it, as Sarah had said.

When I arrived, James Maurice, the Elastic Skin Wonder, was in the middle of his performance. I forced myself to look upon him this time as he stretched the skin at his face and chest. The act was repellant, but I considered that he had most likely been eating with the rest of us only a few minutes before and would perhaps go home to a wife at the end of the day.

I felt warmer toward the man... until he pulled the skin at his neck a full eighteen inches away from his body! The professor held a measuring stick and counted off each horrible inch. And then, James Maurice stretched the skin right over his face, as if pulling a shirt up over his head! I thought I might become ill.

John Darrington, the Living Skeleton was next, his arms and legs thinner than those of a small child. When he moved, his knees and elbows stuck out like jagged boulders set upon sticks.

I closed my eyes for a moment, and when I opened them again, I kept my gaze upon his face, which looked like that of a normal man, though the rest of him did not.

Professor Everett performed the trick of the disappearing woman again, and I noticed that it was now Olga who went up to the stage and Gretchen who appeared behind. I wondered how the professor performed his other feats, and laughed out loud, for it finally struck me that he was likely not a professor at all.

The Sutherlands strode onto the stage with confidence, and I could not help but laugh, for I knew that Mary's bright smile had nothing to do with a desire to entertain the audience before her, and everything to do with the candy she'd been eating all day.

In the audience, I applauded when the Sutherlands let down their tresses, but this time, I stayed for the rest of the show, which ended, as Sarah promised it would, with a surprise eleventh act.

After the curtain call, everyone left the stage except for the professor. He bowed dramatically and pronounced, "Ladies and gentlemen, may I present... Mademoiselle Etta! You have seen her daring feats under the big top on the high wire. Now, prepare to be amazed as she plays the part of human contortionist!"

The young lady came forward and flipped to stand on her hands. Facing the audience, Etta bent her legs forward so that her feet touched the tip of her nose. Then, she dropped her legs to the floor and scuttled them around her body. It was as if her bottom half worked completely independent from her top half.

"Years ago, they might have called her demon possessed," a man behind me whispered to his friend. *I might do so even now,* I wanted to reply.

Etta clutched her feet with both hands and slowly rose to her full height. I thought the exhibition done, but she pulled one of her terrible legs up over her head while Professor Everett emerged from backstage, wheeling out a glass box, which sat atop a wooden frame.

We all gasped in horrified amazement as the girl folded herself up into the box. Once tucked into the box, Etta reached up one hand and waved goodbye. The professor set up a puff of smoke, and swiftly wheeled her off the stage.

I thought of the ice box that had become Fletcher's home. I heard what sounded like a roaring river and realized it must be the blood rushing through my ears, as I had often heard others describe the sensation.

Fortunately, I was sitting, and able to hold my head in my hands until my senses returned. A woman at the back of the audience, however, was not so lucky, and the barker outside was called in to assist her as her husband fanned her face with his wide-brimmed hat.

Is this woman's fainting nothing more than another humbug? I wondered. *Is she a display to distract us as the stage is cleared for the next show? Or an act to prove the shocking nature of the sideshow tent? Will people go back to their friends and family at home and say "You must see the sideshow. A woman fainted this afternoon, it was so outrageous!"*

I could not say, but as I sat through the sideshow twice more, I saw other women overcome. None were dressed the same as the first.

As the hours passed, some of the feats and wonders became less appalling to my eyes. I enjoyed Annie's singing, and after her third performance, I was able to ignore her beard. I noticed Ida, the charmer, danced however she pleased, but her snake always rose with the high notes of her horn and settled back down with the lower.

The Punch and Judy show became dull after a second viewing, but I did enjoy Mr. Giacomo Galleti and his performing birds, though both the man and his birds had hissed at me earlier.

At last, the show was done. I stood outside the tent and stared at the setting sun, whose colors I did not think could ever be rivaled... until I had come to the circus.

Naomi rushed over to me, breaking through my reverie. "I must speak to you before the others finish changing from their costumes," she breathed. "Harry... that is to say, Mr. Bailey, has asked whether I will accompany him to dinner this evening at Keens' Chophouse. Lavinia Warren has rented out the banquet hall and invited a number of guests from the circus. Apparently, Harry is a favorite of hers."

She looked at me expectantly, as if expecting me to say something in reply. "Well that sounds like a lovely prospect, Naomi," I said.

"Yes, he seems a nice man, but one can never be certain, and I don't want to be out with a man I barely know at night in the middle of a city I have but a passing acquaintance with."

"That is wise—" I started.

"So, I asked Harry that you might come as chaperone." She bit her bottom lip. "I hope you don't mind. I have had men ask for my time or attention, but I have never yet accepted their invitations..." It was rare for Naomi to blush, but in the waning light, I saw her cheeks turn as crimson as the sun.

"Of course, I will come," I assured her. "Where are your sisters? Should I ask Sarah to make sure I am not needed?"

"I asked her. Not having a mother, I felt I should ask someone for permission, though Sarah is more like a father than a mother sometimes." She laughed, embarrassed at this admission. "Don't tell her I said so."

"But you did not want the others to know about the outing?"

"Dora and Mary would merely tease me. Isabella and Victoria are prone to jealousy already..." she trailed off again.

"I understand," I said. "Will they retire to the hotel, then?"

She shook her head, "I don't know all their plans, but Sarah said she will be going shopping first and then back to Delmonico's for dinner. Sarah insisted they buy steaks to send back home for the servants and the animals."

"From the restaurant?" I gaped at her.

"She's done it before," Naomi shrugged. "When we were here with Cole's circus last year, Sarah and Mary sent steaks back to Topsy. The old housekeeper did complain the meat was rotten and covered in maggots by the time it reached the house. Sarah said the woman was absurd, and that a dog like Topsy could eat anything, particularly a steak from one of the finest restaurants in the country."

"We'll have to see whether Mrs. Poole feels the same," I said. "Now, we cannot be late for your first night on the town with a gentleman caller. Is your dress in backyard?"

"I left it in the costume tent. Do you think it will be fine enough?"

"I think that Mr. Bailey would enjoy your company even if you wore a dress of burlap."

"Though perhaps not a snake for a scarf," she laughed, gesturing to Ida, who walked past, unaware of our stares.

I hoped, for Naomi's sake, that we might escape without question from the others, but Isabella was still in the wardrobe tent, looking over costumes.

"Why aren't you with the others?" Isabella looked Naomi up and down.

Her younger sister sighed. "I've been invited to a dinner party, and Anna is accompanying me."

"With whom are you having dinner?" Isabella's eyes narrowed into slits.

"Lavinia." Naomi smiled mischievously, though I was not sure why.

"Pooh, that dreadful woman!" Isabella turned back to the racks of costumes."

"It was your own fault," Naomi laughed.

"It most certainly was not," Isabella retorted, refusing to look at us.

"What happened?" I dared to ask.

"She bit me," Isabella snapped.

"Bit you?" I echoed.

"Lavinia is the Christian name of Mrs. Tom Thumb," Naomi explained. "She is a true lady, no matter what her size, but my sister thought she would be much more like a child."

"I had never met a dwarf before!" Isabella protested. "She is so small. How was I to know she wasn't like a baby doll? She looks so much like one."

"Isabella declared, 'Why she is the most darling little creature I ever laid eyes upon!' Then, she picked Lavinia up and rocked her like a baby!" Naomi had tears streaming down her cheeks as she laughed at the memory.

"Lavinia cried out, 'Put me down, you witchy girl!' but Isabella refused, or at least she was unable to comply quickly enough. So, Lavinia bit her finger."

I let out a burst of laughter.

"I still have the scar," Isabella admitted. "Now, hurry up and be gone, both of you. I've met a man this afternoon, and he's promised to show me the sights of New York."

"Unchaperoned?" her sister gasped.

Isabella rolled her eyes. "Father is gone, and Mother has been dead for years. We work in a circus among the freaks and itinerants. And at home, they whisper and call us sluts. Why should I bother with the burden of a chaperone? I am old enough now to see whatever man I chose and accompany him wherever he might take me."

"Isabella, you don't have to play the role people have cast you in," I said and immediately clapped a hand over my mouth for my impertinence.

She turned her thin face toward me. "I play whatever role I want."

"She's right, Isabella," Naomi said, clasping my hand in hers.

Isabella's voice was cold. "Morality is for children," she spat. "If I wish to live a life of diversion or decadence or hedonism, I will do so. And I don't need two little girls, who know nothing about men, telling me what to do. Go to your *little* dinner party and get out of my sight."

Naomi grabbed up her dress and went into the changing room, emerging a few moments later. As Isabella stared us down, we ran from the tent to the entrance of the Garden, where Harry was waiting for us with a handsome cab.

"I have heard about ladies being fashionably late," he smiled, "but never had the pleasure of observing such behavior until today."

"I am sorry," Naomi said as Harry took my hand to assist me into the cab. "One of my sisters was behaving in a most shocking manner."

"Was it Miss Dora?" he asked, helping Naomi up the small steps.

"No!" Naomi said in surprise.

"Why should you suspect Dora of impropriety?" I asked, once we were all seated. Then, I remembered myself. This was their date, after all. I should remain a more silent observer, acting as I had done as a child and not speaking until spoken to.

"I did not mean to alarm either of you. Only, this afternoon between your appearances in the tent, I saw Dora conversing with a young man who was dressed in the most flamboyant suit I've seen outside the big top."

"I do not think I have much to worry over regarding Dora," Naomi said. "Kitty and I are the best of friends, and just the other day, she proclaimed she cared more for money than for men."

Naomi paused, then gave a small giggle, "But this does sound like a juicy bit of gossip, and I shall have to tease her with it later."

"Oh, please don't," Harry said. "I should not have spoken out of turn in such a way. I am sure your sister is a paragon of virtue."

"Well, one of my sisters," Naomi laughed. "I cannot speak so highly of all of them."

"Now you tease me with your own gossip," Harry replied.

I sat silently, listening as Naomi and Harry chatted. They spoke so easily with one another, as if they had known each other for years and were beginning a courtship years after a long, rich friendship. My heart panged with a bittersweet envy—happiness for my friend, melancholy for myself.

At last, we arrived at the restaurant, and I wondered whether a hand would be offered to help me out of the carriage, or whether the two companions had forgotten about me entirely.

Happily, Harry remembered my presence long enough to offer an arm as I stepped from the carriage. Naomi had gone ahead of us into the restaurant, and he whispered, "Thank you for agreeing to come, Miss Roberts. Your friend is the most delightful creature I've ever met, and I am grateful for the pleasure of her company this evening."

I squeezed his elbow. "She is a dear," I said. "Mind you to treat her well. Others... the townspeople where we come from, have not, and because of the stage, Naomi has grown into womanhood being beloved of everyone and no one."

He nodded but could say no more as Naomi was frantically motioning to us to hurry into Keens'.

The restaurant was dim and narrow with dark walnut wood lining the walls. It was a bit like walking into a tunnel, and I wished the party had chosen Delmonico's for their event. Its spacious dining room and sparkling chandeliers seemed much more welcoming.

"Keen opened this place a few months ago," Harry told Naomi. "It's been all the rage since. He managed the theatrical and literary society called the Lamb's Club. He was such a popular host, he decided to start up his self-named restaurant just next door."

"How fascinating," Naomi said. "I have always wanted to host a literary salon. Wouldn't it be so amusing to talk over literature, philosophy, music, art, perhaps even politics?"

"Miss Naomi," Harry smiled, "if you hosted a salon, I do believe it would be the most delightful gathering I should ever have the pleasure of attending."

"Well, it would be a particularly *exclusive* salon, so if I were you, I would not presume an invitation," Naomi joked.

"I shall have to prove myself tonight then," Harry twinkled at her, "and perhaps my invitation will be forthcoming."

Harry spoke to the maître d'hôtel, who led us back to the banquet room, where were greeted by Miss Lavinia Warren, or Mrs. Tom Thumb, as she was billed at the circus. She was even tinier than I had imagined, and though I would not behave as Isabella had, I could understand the impulse some people might have to treat her like a doll.

"Welcome, Mr. Bailey!" she cried. "And have you brought guests with you this evening?"

"Hello, Lavinia," Naomi bent to shake her hand.

"Naomi," the petite woman said, coolly. "I hope your impertinent sister Isabella is not with you."

"No. None of my sisters have come tonight. And I do hope you will allow me to apologize once again for Isabella. She vexes my own patience on a regular basis, and her manners are appalling."

"Thank you. It is nice to see your manners are not the same, and I look forward to speaking with you further. I am sure we have enough in common to become good friends," Lavinia smiled, and I appreciated the good grace with which she accepted Naomi into her circle.

We took our seats around the long table, which held a mixture of dwarves, regular-sized people such as ourselves, and one woman who seemed nearly twice my height.

I shall not stare, I uttered silently to myself over and over, trying my best to be polite. These people were oddities under the big top, but their salaries from Barnum and other venues determined their place among high society as well. It was a bizarre combination, and being rather normal in both appearance and station, I did not know how I should proceed.

"This is Miss Anna Louise Roberts," Harry introduced me, and I bent down as Naomi did, to shake Lavinia's small hand.

"Are you a performer as well?" she asked.

It was, of course, the very question I had been asking myself the entire day, and I was unsure how to answer it.

"Anna is our companion," Naomi answered for me. She spoke quickly, giving me a sidelong glance. I realized she worried I would reveal myself to be her tutor as well as her friend. I would never have done so, particularly when she was trying to impress the dashing Mr. Bailey.

"Anna has not performed with us yet," Naomi continued, "but she was able to take my sister Mary's place in the parade this week. Mary is sometimes unwell. Anna assists Mary in her more troubled times."

"I have heard about Mary," Lavinia said. "My prayers will be with her tonight, and I will ask the Lord to heal her. However, have you considered that all eight feet of that heavy hair may be affecting her brain?"

"Several doctors suggested the same," Naomi admitted. "We have been discussing cutting it off. Though Mary would no longer be able to perform with us, she may fair better."

"No," I broke in. "I am sorry, ladies. I do not mean to intrude on your conversation. However, I saw Mary once when someone tried to cut but a lock of her hair. She reacted violently and fainted dead away."

Naomi's mouth turned into a thin line, and I hoped I had not given away too many of the family secrets. At times, I forgot I was a servant, and in that role, I should keep the mysteries and enigmas of the Sutherland sisters to myself.

If Naomi was displeased, she did not show it. Rather, she bobbed her head and graciously changed the subject. "Lavinia, Anna has never heard the story of how you came to the circus."

"I have been told I have an interesting history." Lavinia turned her small, ringleted head up to me.

"It was really owing to Charles. You knew him by his stage name, General Tom Thumb. I would not have performed had it not been for Charles. Phineas Taylor Barnum had a reputation of exploitation, and I did not want to work with him, at first," Lavinia said.

"Just look at what happened to Joice Heth," the similarly small man beside her added.

Lavinia nodded sagely. "Joice Heth was a slave and belonged to a man named Lindsay, who put her on display as the childhood nurse of George Washington. Barnum bought Joice and continued the charade. It was more than one of his usual humbugs... though I do not approve of those small trickeries, either."

"She was blind and almost completely paralyzed," the man continued the tale, "and yet, he earned fifteen hundred dollars a week from her appearances."

"And never gave Joice her freedom, so far as I know," Lavinia concluded. "Not when the good Christian ministers of Rhode Island protested, and not even when the papers of New York turned against him. In the North, slavery had been banished ten years before her exhibition, but that fact didn't stop Mr. P.T. Barnum from keeping Joice a slave as he showed her off."

She shook her head, frowning. "So, you can see why I was hesitant to work for the man," Lavinia said. "However, Charles convinced me Barnum had changed. Charles said that the episode with Joice happened nearly thirty years before the war, and much had changed since then, including the hearts of men."

"And you found Mr. Barnum agreeable?" I asked.

"He has his faults," she said. "But he once told me, 'Lavinia, the noblest art is that of making others happy.' And I must say I agree. Some actresses live for the applause of the audience. They want to feel admired."

"But you do not?" I said.

"I don't mind the admiration." Lavinia patted her curls. "But being on stage is a luxury. It's a gift. The Lord has gifted me with talent. Sharing that talent with others and making them happy is an opportunity few are blessed with."

I wanted to inquire about her life further, but the waiters came with our meals, and the smell of roast mutton filled the room. I did not realize how ravenous I was until that moment. I had to hold myself back from devouring the meat, which was a far departure from the gravy-covered slop we had been given at lunchtime.

The talk turned to events of the day, and I saw that Silvia, the giantess at the end of the table, had two plates of food for every course. I wondered at her appetite. Naomi told me later that Silvia was nearly eight feet tall and often appeared beside Lavinia to further exaggerate the differences in their bodies. While working together, the tallest woman in the world and the smallest had become the best of friends.

After we were served, Naomi and Harry engaged in intimate conversation with each other, as if no one else was in the room. I continued talking with our host, and learned that the man beside Lavinia was, in fact, her fiancé, Count Primo Magri, and the man to his left was his brother, Giuseppe.

"They have been such comforts to me, since my dear Charles departed," Lavinia told me as our desserts arrived. "There was a fire in Milwaukee. I did not think we would make it through the flames. Charles helped me escape. I was fine, but Charles suffered greatly from the smoke. He made it through the night, and I thought it would be fine, but he suffered a stroke later."

"How dreadful," was all I could think to say.

"I missed Charles so much, I did not think I would ever return to the stage again. But after his death, I met Primo, and we formed the Lilliputian chorus," she gestured around the room. "A wealth of friends to perform Mr. Swift's *Gulliver's Travels* and more acts besides. My sister and Charles may be gone, but I have found joy in my new life."

When the meal was complete, after-dinner drinks were served, and the men retired to the gentlemen's only section, where they were to become part of the Pipe Club.

"The restaurant owners bought over fifty thousand clay pipes from the Netherlands for patrons to enjoy," Naomi explained. "But women are not allowed to partake, for obvious reasons."

Naomi excused herself to the powder room, and as soon as she disappeared around the corner, Lavinia beckoned me to lean closer to her, "I think you would make an amazing performer, Miss Roberts. You are sparkling company, and that is the key to success in the circus. Charisma is more important than singing or long hair, or even a small stature."

Before I could reply, Naomi returned. "Lavinia, you never did tell us your whole story!"

"I know," the small woman pouted. "It went clear out of my mind when we began speaking of Joice. We shall have to get together again some evening. I will tell you my story, and you can tell me yours!"

The men came returned, and I promised Lavinia we would dine with her another time. When we all took our leave, I again thanked Lavinia for her kindness and generosity.

She thanked us all for coming, but held my hand a little longer in her goodbye, whispering in earnest, "Remember what I said. You would make a marvelous actress!"

***

The next day, Naomi, Dora, Mary, and I squeezed into one carriage, while Grace, Victoria, and Sarah got into another. Isabella had not come home until sunrise, and declared she would not come, "Until after I've been properly bathed and fed."

"Properly bathed," Naomi spat as soon as we got into the taxi, "as if we didn't go weeks without washing when we were younger."

"We were not part of society then," Dora said. "There isn't enough toilet water in the world to cover up a week without washing. Though I do wonder what activities Isabella has been partaking in that she would need one this morning."

"And what activities have you been up to, Miss Kitty?" Naomi asked. "A little birdie told me you were spotted yesterday talking intimately with a dashing young man."

"I talked to several young men yesterday. Some young ladies, too. A grandmother even," Dora said, looking out the carriage window instead of at her sister.

"And after declaring you would never take a husband," Naomi clucked, teasingly. "What a shame your moral fortitude crumbled so easily."

"I was at the hotel last night, reading *The Prince and the Pauper* and playing dominoes with Mary," Dora retorted, sticking her already upturned nose higher into the air. "Where were you, miss? Out, galivanting around town with Anna, having a fine time with a man I haven't even met!"

I couldn't tell whether she was envious of me, Naomi, or Harry. Did Dora wish to be courted like Naomi, or did she wish for more of her sister's attentions?

I put myself in Dora's place. I did not know what I would do if a young man came and took Faith from me... but then it struck me that I had been much inattentive to my own little sister since adopting seven more. I promised myself I would write to her that afternoon.

"You will meet Harry soon enough, Kitty. Now, don't pout. I was only teasing about your own young man, and besides, I have other news before we reach our destination."

"What is it?" Mary's timid voice sounded out.

"It is that Mr. Barnum and our dear sister Sarah have asked Anna whether she will work with us!"

"Oh, goody!" Dora exclaimed, just as Mary cried, "Oh, no!"

"I have not yet given her my answer." I felt color rising in my cheeks. "I would be a substitute only, if Mary felt ill as she did during the parade, or if one of you had a fever."

"You must do it," Dora said. "You simply must. It would be ever so much fun, and we could teach you all sorts of things, the way you taught us. It would truly be as if you were one of the family."

"No," Mary squeaked. She cleared her throat and sat up straight, as if delivering an important address. "No. If Anna performs, she won't be my Anna anymore."

"She's not *your* Anna, anyway," Dora said. "She all of ours now, and why would you not want her to have such fun with us and make a few dollars besides?"

"Too many people stare and laugh," Mary said.

"Which is why you don't like it," Dora answered, "but I don't care about the laughter, and most who stare enjoy the show. Right now, Anna only makes us happy, but if she begins to entertain, she can make whole crowds happy."

They were both correct. I found myself unable to respond to either argument.

Mercifully, I did not need to, for we had come to the circus at last, and Sarah, whose carriage had arrived first, was motioning furiously to us.

"Harold just asked me if we could go on early. Seems the Armless Wonder tried to ride one of the clown's new one-wheeled velocipedes."

"Did he fall?" Mary asked.

"No," Victoria giggled viciously. "He did quite well until the clown caught up to him. Tipped the Armless Wonder right off onto his backside and gave him a black eye to boot!"

"He's in the infirmary tent and will probably be there until after the cooks raise the first flag." Sarah had a grim look on her face. "This is why we need a substitute—Anna, or someone else, if she chooses not to perform. I cannot believe I let Isabella stay in the hotel this morning. If she isn't here by the second showing, I don't know what I'll do."

"We can all do separate acts," Dora said. "Victoria has a dramatic reading. We can follow that with Naomi's comical piece. A duet between with Mary and Grace after that, and then another with you and me. If we drag it out a bit, Isabella may still have time to come for the finale."

I wanted to help. The Sutherlands were new to Barnum's Circus, and I knew they did not want to fail their first week. I gulped and stepped forward. "If she doesn't make it in time... I can jump in line and untie my hair as you do."

Dora clapped while Naomi and Sarah beamed at me. Victoria rolled her eyes at Dora's exuberance, as I expected her to. Neither Grace nor Mary said a word, but both eyed me, dubiously, as if they were unsure this was the correct decision, no matter how dire the situation.

In the end, it did not matter, for Isabella came in with a flourish in the midst of Mary and Grace's duet, adding her voice to theirs as if a trio had always been planned.

When they finished, Mary and Grace moved to the back of the stage, making room for Sarah and Dora, but Isabella took a step forward and began singing "Sweet Violets," from the new play *Fritz Among the Gypsies*.

I imagined they would be angry, but Isabella sang the tune in such a clear sweet soprano, which belied the words and gave the song the most comical turn, I could see that the Sutherlands were as delighted with the performance as the audience.

They came forward as one to join her in the chorus, "Sweet violets, sweeter than all the roses, laden with fragrance, and sparkling with dew."

The audience applauded, and at the apex of their applause, the Sutherlands turned in one accord and let their hair shimmer down their backs.

The applause turned to shouts of "encore, encore," and I realized what had been missing from their first performances. Magic.

The magic of the Sutherlands was inherent in the way they worked and moved together like watches with their clicking wheels, cogs, and pins, which interlocked to keep the hands turning.

When things were overly-planned out, when things went almost too well, they were more like an hour glass, which was merely tipped until the sand moved from one side to the other. The Sutherland magic lay inside their disorder and disarray— when they worked from instinct rather than a set program. Then, the stakes were raised. They invested their hearts into their music. They would bleed to make it work, to keep the audience happy, to hear shouts of praise and acclimation.

I did not know whether I could do the same. Could I have the same passionate fire in my belly? The same drive to succeed day after day and night after night? I did not know if I had the heart.

I *did* know that, however desperately I now wanted to be a part of their family, I would never fit in. I would always be the substitute. An ancillary wheel, fused atop the others, unable to move to their rhythm.

Silently, I made my way through the crowd to visit the menagerie tent, as Sarah had originally instructed.

Under the tent was a cavalcade of cars where the caged animals were held between performances under the big top. The elephants were nowhere to be seen, so I supposed they were out for a performance and decided to view the tiger first.

The beast lay on his side like a great striped cat, and when he stretched his mighty paws, I could see that he had no claws. He did not roar or growl in his repose, but I guessed he had no teeth, either.

Camels, dromedaries, and zebras separated the tigers from the lions. These, more gentle creatures, were housed in a pen that ran along the side of the tent where children could purchase small handfuls of food to feed them.

"You're a friend of Harry's, ain't ya?" a smiling, broad-faced boy asked.

"Mr. Bailey is a friend of my employer, Miss Sutherland," I said cautiously.

"But I saw him talkin' with ya," the boy insisted.

"He is an acquaintance of mine, yes," I replied.

"I'm Georgie." He held out his hand and I shook it. "Mr. Bailey told me if any of you nice young ladies was to come in, I should give you some of the food for free—that is the kind we be sellin' for the animals here."

"Alright," I paused, feeling there was yet more.

"And he told me, 'Georgie, you give them girls a ride on one of the camels, if they wants it.' Because we be giving rides often, Miss, only we don't usually do it in New York where it be so crowded." He grinned at me.

"A ride?" I looked at the camel, who I feared might spit at any moment, as I had heard they were want to do.

"Yah, Miss! Would you be wantin' to ride? I got me a saddle here and anything else ya might be needin' for."

It was like the parade all over again. This time, I was determined not to trade excitement and adventure for fear, no matter how peaceful it might be to remain with my feet fixed firmly on the ground.

"I would love a ride, Mr. Georgie," I said in my firmest tone, trying to convince myself it would be fun.

"That's fine, Miss. I'll take ya out of the tent, and we can do a right fine walk around the grounds. Drums up business, ya know, so the bosses don't mind, specially not with ya bein' a friend of Mr. Bailey's an' all."

He dragged a saddle and a pile of blankets out from within the folds of the tent, and I reminded myself to look in corners and keep my eyes open, for the circus held more secret crevices and compartments than a European castle.

A red oriental blanket went on the camel's back first, followed by the large saddle, which spanned its humps. "Hold here like this, see?" Georgie placed my hand on the black bar at the front of the saddle.

"Then, ya grip your legs tight to his belly like this," he said, bunching his arms up in demonstration.

I was too frightened to say anything. Georgie pulled a small set of steps from next to the paddock where the rest of the animals stood, munching their handfuls of food while the rest of the circus patrons ceased petting them to stare at me as I shakily took my first ride.

I ascended the steps, only to have Georgie, and more than a handful of spectators, laugh uproariously as I attempted to sit side saddle upon the beast's broad back.

"I told ya, Miss," Georgie slapped his thighs in laughter, "ya gotta throw your leg over and grip him. You'll fall right over onto your backside if ya try to be a proper lady 'bout it."

I grit my teeth, hiked my skirts up a few inches, and threw my leg over the camel's back, as Georgie commanded. *At least this will make a fantastic letter to Faith.* The thought came quickly followed by another: *If I don't fall off and break my neck.*

I did not fall, so Georgie grasped the camel's bridle and led us out of the tent.

The animal's humps moved up and down like waves, and before we had gone a hundred feet, I felt as if I was being tossed about by a great ship. Still, the sensation was not entirely unpleasant. Eventually, I became used to the rhythm of it.

As more people began to gather around, Georgie whistled to me. When I looked down at him, he said in a harsh whisper. "Wave and smile, Miss We're not givin' no rides to anyone else what asks today, so they've gotta think it's part of the show!"

So now, I must perform on top of it all, I thought. *Though a bit of waving is nothing compared to the trapeze artists who must smile while flipping through the air. However do they manage it?*

I slowly lifted my right hand and began waving to the crowd, keeping my left hand firmly around the saddle's bar, while gripping my legs as tightly as possible around the beast's midsection.

Georgie looked up at me, and I thought he would be pleased, though I knew my waves must have seemed timid and half-hearted. "Smile," he hissed through closed teeth and upturned lips.

I shined the brightest smile I could muster and waved again, this time, aiming my gaze at a family with four young children who walked by us.

"Mother," I heard one girl say, "Look at that lady up there. Isn't she grand? When I grow up, I want to wear my hair in a braid around my head just like her."

A small thrill went through me, and I felt a warmth in my breast that seemed to spread as more families watched, laughing and waving and cheering for me, though I was doing nothing but waving back. I began to blow kisses to the crowd, feeling as though I should give more of myself to them.

When we circled back to the tent and the undulating beast came to a stop, Georgie helped me down the small steps. "You did well, Miss. Gave the people quite the show! We could do that a few times a day, if Mr. Bailey would approve of it. Might bring more people in the menagerie tent and away from the sideshow. But, perhaps your other young lady friends might not like that too good?"

"I don't think they would mind," I said. "And I don't think I would either. I shall take you up on your offer, Mr. Georgie, but only if your boss permits it."

The warm feeling of pride in my chest did not dissipate as I took my time looking at the other animals. As I fed a handful of corn to one of the zebras and allowed his velvety lips to snuffle over my open palm, I realized I had not felt the emotion since my father died, and quite possibly not for quite some time prior to that event. It felt good, and I looked forward to feeling it again.

My mother always said, "Pride cometh before the fall," but I did not know whether I agreed with her completely. Surely arrogance and vanity were to be avoided, but was there not some sweet simplicity in the satisfaction of a job well-done or even more so, in a day well-lived?

I considered this carefully as I walked past the lions and the spotted leopards, disappointed to see that they were sleeping just as the tiger had been.

My disinterest in the resting animals did not last long as the six trained panthers were active enough to make up for the rest. Stalking about their cages, they looked ready to pounce on whatever delectable child wandered in.

Drawn by their sleek, black coats, I ventured to their cages, wanting to see whether their claws were also removed. But as I approached, one of the ebony creatures lunged toward the bars of his cage, pawing at the bars, and screaming. The next turned and screamed too, and the next.

A trio of trainers rushed in. They raised their voices and snapped their whips, but to no avail. The panthers' piercing shrieks sounded for all the world like a family of women being murdered.

Their high-pitched wails roused the previously-sleeping tiger, the lions, and the leopards. Though all the cats were caged, I feared for my life. Yet, I found I could not move. I stood, gaping as if asking the terrible beasts to end my life and devour me right there and then.

"It must be the smell of camel on ya," Georgie shouted above the screams. "Get out now, Miss! The other men and women have grabbed up their kiddies and we'll have no more visitors if you don't be leavin' now!"

He grabbed me by the arm and pulled me from the tent. As soon as I stepped outside, the noise within ceased. I had expected to hear the commotion slowly die down, but the change was immediate, and I could see that young Georgie was as shocked as I.

"Maybe you better be stayin' away then?" he asked, not unkindly.

"I think that would be for the best." I nodded, tears stinging the corners of my eyes. "Thank you for your assistance, Mr. Georgie, though I do not suppose we shall see much of each other from now on."

"Aw, I wouldn't say that, Miss," he shook his head. "Ya do got a way with animals... though maybe not them big cats. And ya got a way of charmin' the public it seems, too. Ya ought to think about learning a trade. Do like a horse act or somethin'."

I promised to think about it and moved to take my rest in the backlot before heading to the museum, which Sarah had also wanted me to see.

As I turned, I saw a trail of Sutherlands heading into the cook tent, where the flag had just been raised for the afternoon meal break. When I went to follow, I noticed Dora had not gone with them.

Instead, she was walking swiftly over to a corner of the Garden's long, castle-like wall. When she reached the turret, with its high citrine flags, she stopped and looked around furtively.

As I watched her, curious, a young man came up to Dora, embraced her by the waist, and kissed her firmly on the mouth. I let out a small gasp of surprise, both intrigued and ashamed of watching the intimate scene.

The man must have been the same personage whom Harry had referred to the other night, for though he was not dressed in any particularly loud fashion, there seemed something flamboyant about him. He was slim and imperially arrayed in a black jacket, pinched in at the waist in the French style, rather than the broader overcoats favored by Americans and the British.

His bowler hat was much the fashion, however. He took off his hat while speaking with Dora, and even in the distance I could see the wavy brown hair, which splendidly complemented his thick mustache. He was quite handsome, and for a moment, I was jealous of Dora for receiving his attentions.

He bent to kiss her again just as I felt a sharp tug on my wrist. "I've been sent to get you," Isabella said, grimacing. "Mary is having a small fit. She seems in her right mind, but she's being stubborn and says she won't go back on stage today."

Isabella saw where I was looking and seemed to become more agitated. "That girl," she snarled.

I merely shrugged my shoulders, as if Dora's indiscretion was meaningless. Isabella herself had found companionship in New York, but she never was one to endure being upstaged, and I knew Dora would have hell to pay for kissing such a dashing young man. I only prayed Isabella would not tell Victoria about it. The two could be terribly spiteful when they teamed up.

I started, "She is flirting, just as we all do, I am sure it's—" and was cut off as the man took Dora into a passionate embrace, planting his mouth upon hers as if he could not breathe without her.

Infuriated, Isabella clenched her jaw, grabbed onto my arm, and dragged me back to the cookhouse tent.

Part VI

A Propensity Toward Imitation

Pictured: Miss Dora "Kitty" Sutherland

August, 1885

The day I spied Dora kissing her mystery man, I was able to soothe Mary from her tantrum. Still, her fits of stubbornness and crocodile tears lasted the rest of the week we sojourned in New York, but she seemed to return to herself as we entered New Jersey, and by the time we traveled to Connecticut, she was in her right mind. In truth, I was secretly saddened at this, for the more Mary found confidence, the more independent she grew. By midsummer, she had little need for my help.

My hours away from the family were hollow. When the sisters performed, I sat in the cook tent, staring at the performers as they entered and exited the backlot. If the family was engaged in the evening, I sat in my bedchamber like a lighthouse keeper, staring out the window, awaiting their return.

In my youth, I felt solitude as a tranquil breeze, allowing me to breathe into myself for a short time before returning to the world again. I was rarely alone, so those moments were brief and welcome. Now, solitude became a foul brute, gnawing slowly at my mind, though I was never fully devoured.

My isolation at last abated when Mary fell in and out of new tumultuous tempers throughout the next weeks—as we traveled on the tracks from Connecticut to Rhode Island and into Massachusetts. As a result of our mutual moods, I grew passionate about my work and focused all my attentions on my friend. As nursemaid and companion, I stayed backstage in the sideshow, encouraging Mary and walking with her on breaks between performances.

Because of my bouts of lethargy and melancholy, I walked through the museum tent once or twice, but did not have the energy or inclination to see the entire big top show until after we entered Boston.

Outside of my mood, I could not say why I refused to go and pushed the thought away each time it bubbled up amongst my thoughts. Except that I did not yet wish to speak with Sarah about performing, and I felt going to see the "big show" would mean I was ready to discuss the matter with her. The thought tired me, and as to the actual show itself, I believed it would be more of the same—comparable to what I had already seen in the sideshow.

By then, I had grown used to oddities and freaks, for JoJo the Dog-Faced Boy, the Armless Wonder, the Burmese Dwarf, the Afghan Warriors, and the Hindoo Dancing Girls all ate with us under the same cookhouse tent. When they shared stories with me, I felt I had been accepted into their motley family, and yet, I was still set apart, often found myself lapsing into silence amongst their chatter.

Though the meals from hotels and restaurants wearied me and made me ache for a night of homemade cooking, I did enjoy the travel. I shared this pleasure with Grace. She and I stole away for more than one tour of cities and towns. I liked each town more than I had New York, where I could never quite get over the smell.

For those few months, I tried to be more faithful in writing to my own sister. I told Faith the animals, the people, the towns, and the Sutherland's shows, which improved greatly as they performed for audience after audience, day and night. Faith was able to send some replies, in care of the circus, which was always found by the mail carriers.

But miles of railroad tracks separated us, and Faith's tales of schoolhouse woes seemed both insignificant and foreign to me. At last, I received a letter which read:

Dearest Anna,

I am writing to tell you of mother's joy—and of mine also. She has become friends with a man she courted before meeting father. He is William Fenn, a kindly man who owns and manages several coal mines, though he does not work in them himself.

They plan to marry soon! I hope once the nuptials are complete, you can at last rejoin our happy family. Mr. Fenn, or Father, as Mother says I must call him now, has considerable wealth, though of course, we are not to speak of it to others so plainly.

I know they will want you to come back home. You could finish school and become a teacher or obtain a position in one of the shops in town... or perhaps, you could meet a nice, young man of your own. There is a boy at school with bright blue eyes I know you would like!

I dropped the letter on the ground, unable to read further. My father was hardly cold in his grave, and while she should have been wearing mourning weeds, my mother was galivanting around town with a man who was, most likely, the wealthiest prospect she could find.

A wave of disgust washed through me as I thought of my mother's greedy hypocrisy. I would not live with her again. Nor would I be content to stay in a sleepy town where my only prospects were teaching school or selling dresses I couldn't afford to snippy girls with gaudy tastes and vulgar demands.

Though it might hurt my sister for the moment, I decided I could not write to Faith again until the circus season was over. It hurt my heart to read her letters, and I was sure that, for Faith, the letters only served as painful reminders of my absence. She would grow accustomed to the silence and would miss me less once my messages ceased to arrive.

The letter disappeared from my floor the next day. I assumed a maid had disposed of it, or that one of the Sutherland girls had appropriated it. It was of little significance to me, as I had considered burning it to spite my mother.

I had lovingly read each of Faith's letters at least once a week. The Sutherlands were out for the evening, and I refused to go with them. Instead, sitting alone in a hotel in Massachusetts, I read my sister's words one last time. Then, I tied all her letters with a red ribbon and buried them in a hidden pocket of my trunk.

The action did feel like a true burial. It felt as if I were laying to rest the remnants of my childhood. I swore to unearth them when the circus ended, but secretly, I wondered whether I would be able to honor that promise.

A few nights later, when the train made its last leg toward Boston, I sat listlessly looking out the window. Mary came over and patted my hand, as if she were my caretaker. "You ought to see the circus today, Anna Louise," she said in a patient, motherly way, as if she was reminding me to wash my face before supper.

"I see the circus every day," I insisted, thinking of the effort it would take to leave my usual seat at the sideshow.

"Not really. The sideshow doesn't compare to the big top, and it has been too long since you began playing nursemaid to me. I have been in my right mind, you know. Other times, as when we are at home, it seems to me I almost float away. It isn't the same here."

"How is it then?" I wondered. Because I could see the difference, but I could not tell how to help.

"Performing is an exhaustion," she said. "My body is like a weight. I cannot go on and waving my arms like a scarecrow in the wind. All I want to do is sleep. Sleep and dream and talk to Father and Mother again."

It was talk like this that frightened me, for I never knew whether Mary understood that her parents had passed, or whether they were with her still in a real, almost corporeal form. If she actually saw them in her hypnotic, dreamlike states, I could not be sure. Though remembering the burns on her skin and her talk of the Jewish child Gittel, I thought I could guess.

In all our long days traveling, there had been no more talk of my singing alongside the Sutherlands, and I was unsure how to broach the subject with Sarah. I wondered whether she was waiting until Mary was more herself and less the cowering child she melted into between shows. It could be, too, that Sarah wanted me to show some gumption and ask her about it directly. But unlike Victoria, I had never been known for my gumption, and did not feel I could be so forward, even with a woman I had come to know as a friend.

After Mary's assurance she would be able to work throughout the day without any assistance, I spoke to Naomi.

"Would it be agreeable if I asked your Harry to accompany me to the big top show today? I know Sunday is his day off from the Hippodrome, as there are no races on the Lord's Day, and I thought it would be nice to have a companion for the circus."

"Of course, I do not mind," Naomi hesitated. "But I do think he might spoil it for you."

"Spoil it? Why should he do such a thing?"

"It would not be on purpose," Naomi explained. "He knows all the tricks. He's seen the trap doors beneath the stage. The wires above the crowd."

"So have I," I said, thinking of the first time I met Olga and Gretchen.

"It isn't the same." She shook her head. "You want to see the circus like a child. When you go, you open your eyes in wonder at the great, whirling spectacle before you, and it seems like..." she trailed off.

"Like magic," I finished the thought.

"Precisely."

"Except there is no magic really to be found." I could not say why, but this made my chest feel numb.

"Absolutely untrue," Naomi cried. "There is! Which is why you should not see it with someone who has watched it over and over again for six years. For Harry, the circus is like living beside Niagara Falls. At first, the waters seem miraculous. After a year, they are merely lovely. After two years, the rushing water becomes part of the general scenery—as unnoticed as a cloud in the sky or a blade of grass under your feet."

I wanted to ask again whether she was not saying this out of some strange jealousy, but Naomi chuckled as if reading my thoughts. "Take him with you if you still want, Anna. I'll ask him to hold his tongue. And do not fret about being seen with him. I trust you, and Harry loves me. If I feared he would be unfaithful, I would not continue to see him. I have no desire to marry or court a man like my father."

"And I would never be so disloyal," I said.

"I know." She hugged me around the waist. "That's why I didn't mention it."

In the end, I took Naomi's advice, and was glad of it later when Harry asked, "Did you see Miss Nella Venoa on her mount, Jennie? The horse threw a shoe partway through the routine, but I do not believe the audience noticed. Did you?"

"No," I replied, a bit too coolly. "I was too busy watching her jump through a ring of fire to notice a missing horseshoe."

"You see?" Naomi chuckled. "He would have spoiled the whole thing!"

Indeed, I had been too preoccupied to notice that, or any other mistake Harry would have called attention to.

The circus tent was dim until the show began with a crash of cymbals and a blare of horns. As the band started its triumphant tune, the ring master appeared in the center ring. The lights lifted, throwing the man's long shadow out behind him, giving the impression he was seven feet tall. He wore a velvet suit as red as a freshly-picked apple and a tall top hat to match. Both the jacket and hat were lined in gold—the buttons and trim gleaming up into the stands.

As the first acts appeared, I realized his attire was necessary. One could still see him through the spangled, sequined swirls of color that soon flooded through the tent.

I was delighted to see Lavinia and Count Primo's Lilliputian Chorus and clapped in time with the music as the diminutive dancers dipped, jumped, and twirled. The music softened as the singing began, and I could see why the company was first in the program, for they were simply enchanting.

The dancing bears were next—just as fantastic, but in a more loud and obvious way. I feared the panthers with their horrendous screams, but they were well-trained and performed their tricks admirably.

Coming in on their heels were a series of Japanese girls on one-wheeled velocipedes the ringmaster called "unicycles." They placed plates on their heads and began spinning, flipping, and throwing the plates, catching them on their toes as they balanced, one-footed, and we held our breaths, hoping they would not fall.

As the three rings filled with more wonders than I could count, my eyes were drawn upward to the men and women who began flying overhead. They hung from thin bars, gliding back and forth. Without warning, one would let go, spin, flip, and grab the hands or feet of another. I felt my palms beginning to sweat and my heart seemed to flutter in my chest.

Just when I thought I could not grow more worried for a person's safety, the wire acts began. Holding a long bar, a sparkling girl in pink walked across the high wire. After crossing, she lay the bar down and walked carefully back to the center of the wire where she bounced. I thought she might fall. Instead, she cartwheeled back to the other end where she had begun. It was thrilling. No humbug or false hocus-pocus could have explained her grace and skill.

Below the wire act, the acrobats began their tumbling routine, and my heart slowed to its regular pace, only to thump wildly again when the ringmaster announced, "Ladies and gentlemen, please turn your eyes to Young Nicholas and his Iron Jaw!"

One of the thin trapeze bars was lowered, and a clown attached a mouthpiece as a young boy, of no more than thirteen, approached the apparatus. When he bit down on the mouthpiece, the clowns moved to the side and began pulling on ropes attached to pulleys, slowly lifting Young Nicholas into the air.

The boy did not merely hang on to the bar. He began spinning wildly, throwing his arms out to each side like a wide-winged albatross, unbound by gravity. Exhilarated, I clenched my fists so tightly, my nails caused little indents along my palms.

I relaxed when the equestrian acts were brought forth, though it was thrilling to see them jump over fences and through rings of fire.

At last, the elephants appeared, and I knew, as Sarah had told me, that the show was at its close. I noticed that Jumbo seemed to have lost bits of his trunk since the last time I had seen him perform, but the parade of animals was nearly as stirring as it had been the day they walked across Brooklyn Bridge.

Mind reeling, I sat in my seat until the tent was cleared. When I finally exited, I wondered at Naomi's statement that this awe-inspiring, breathtaking spectacle could ever become mere background noise. I knew, even if that was true, the circus was enthralling, and I wanted to be a part of it.

Dora was waiting for me when I came out. "We're done for the evening," she said. "The others were tired, but I wanted to go see the gypsies tonight."

I looked to the caravans of travelers who had attached themselves to the circus. "To have your fortune read?" I joked.

"Perhaps to find out the fate of the mysterious young man you still refuse to speak of?"

"Perhaps." Dora twinkled. "Perhaps he has sent me a telegram and may be returning from Canada soon. Perhaps, he has asked to meet with me in a few weeks' time… and perhaps I would like to know whether I should invest more time in him or cut ties altogether."

"I do wish you would tell me more about him," I said.

"Come with me, and I shall," Dora promised.

I hesitated. "Dora, I do not wish to commune with spirits." I bit my lower lip. "I do not have time to worship as I should, and I have lost much of my faith…." I hesitated. I meant to make feeble excuses, but this was true. Though I still had my children's Bible, and Sarah had given me a regular Bible besides, both sat unread next to my pillow each night, and I had ceased carrying Sarah's gift around with me during the day.

"Nevertheless," I continued, "I do not believe I could comfortably play at speaking with the dead."

Dora considered this for a moment, and I thought she might begin pouting and insisting I go despite my concerns. Instead, her bright, sharp eyes grew wide as if an idea had struck her. "We'll go to the phrenologist!" she exclaimed. "I saw her wagon— a violet one with lime trim. She has a placard which reads 'Gypsy Queen—Phrenologist and Mentalist.'"

"I have seen it," I admitted, still hesitant.

"They say phrenology is a science," Dora insisted. "And mentalists read your deepest thoughts. There is no listening to spirits or asking them for answers from beyond the grave."

I could not fault this argument, and we made our way to the edge of the circus, where the caravan of wagons lined the dirt road. I felt quite shy, but Dora was a bold girl, and ran her hands over the carvings of each cart as we passed.

We ignored the calls of various women selling their wares and walked straight to the purple and green wagon, where the Gypsy Queen held out her hand for a few coins before bidding us inside. "Come into my Vardo." She crooked a finger, beckoning us forward.

"Vardo?" Dora asked, stepping across the threshold.

"My cart. Most unusual here in America, no?" she smiled, and I saw she was missing two teeth. "In Europe, not so much."

"I am Natalia, the Gypsy Queen!" The gray-haired woman dramatically shook her wide sleeves back, jangling the gold and silver bracelets lining her arms.

Like the other travelers, she was wearing a kerchief, layers of broadcloth skirts, and a thick striped blanket like a belt around her waist. Half of her cart was hidden behind a silk screen, and I imagined that held the wagon's sleeping quarters, while the front had been decorated with phrenology charts hanging from the walls and a set of highbacked chairs in the center.

She motioned for Dora to sit first. Dora took her place and leaned her head back into the woman's dark hands. "Your reasoning senses are quite developed," Natalia said, feeling along Dora's brow ridge. I noticed her accent had disappeared and conjectured that the accent might be hokum, like the girls who disappeared from the stage and reappeared in the audience.

Then, the mentalist closed her eyes and moaned as she slipped her fingers through Dora's thick hair to feel the top of her skull, "You have courage, but not so much prudence or cautiousness as you might. You have wit and friendship, but here, along the back, where your motherly instincts should be, there is nothing."

"Nothing?" Dora echoed.

"Nothing," Natalia repeated. "I do not think you shall be a mother, or if you are, it will not be well for your poor children."

Natalia closed her eyes. "This is why it is good to be a mentalist also," she said. "For I can see that you wish for love, but to be a mother is not your greatest desire. This is a happy thing for me because I do not offend or sadden you by my words."

"Your parental love is lacking, but you are a good friend. Because you do not have much caution, you must be wary of men who whisper pretty things in your ear."

Dora started, and the woman continued, "I see you have already met such a man, but you have kept him a secret—hidden from your family and friends. Bring him out into the light. Let them judge. Your eyes are heavy-lidded with love and blind to his true nature. I do not know if he is true or faithful, but hiding in the shadows will do you no good."

"Last, you have ambition. Self-perfecting, I think. This will help you improve your life. I see another man who will help you meet your ambition, but I cannot say who he is or what he might be to you. Like your father, I think, but not in all ways." Natalia loosed her hands from Dora's head and slumped forward. Clearly, the reading was done.

I stepped forward next, though I felt timid and thought she might be exhausted from the first effort. Upon receiving a second coin for her purse, she roused quickly.

Rather than moving directly behind me as she had done with Dora, Natalia first stood in front of me, holding my head between her hands. She gently turned my head first left, then right. "You are most unbalanced," she pronounced.

Natalia bent my head toward her and felt along the top, moving her fingers over the center ridge of my scalp. "Just as I suspect," she pronounced. "You have a high propensity toward imitation. More than I have ever seen or felt in anyone."

I cleared my throat, unsure whether this required a response.

"Do you perform in the circus? Impressions or some such?"

"No," I dragged out the word.

I sensed her fingers feeling out the bumps and dips of my head. "On the right, charity, benevolence, and self-reflection. On the left, these are missing, but you have greater secretiveness and self-destruction. Idealism on the right, ambition on the left. A sense of hope and wonder on both sides."

She paused and pressed her fingers into the top of my skull. "Oh!" she exclaimed. "Here I see a spirituality that is still being developed. Much potential. If you throw off religion and its rules and embrace mysticism, as I have, there may be..."

Natalia trailed off, moving around to my front again. "I admit, I do not know what to make of this. She ran her fingers down my brow to the ridge of my nose. "A strange series of bumps where there should be individuality. And your sense of time and locality is absent on both sides."

"What does this mean?" I wondered.

"Imitation comes from reproducing what is seen. You are a great observer, but your sense of self is displaced. You may keep secrets, which could lead to your destruction...or possibly to your gain. I cannot tell which, and I cannot read your thoughts because those of your sister are intruding upon me."

Natalia sat down in the chair opposite me and turned to Dora. "You must leave. Go down to Alesky's vardo. He speaks with the spirits, and I know that is what you seek this evening. Your sister... no, I am mistaken. Your friend may stay a few minutes longer."

Dora smirked as if it made no difference to her and exited the wagon.

"Now the air has cleared," Natalia held my hands between her own and closed her eyes.

"No wonder I could not see before," she said. "Your friend has two thoughts—money and men." She shrugged. "It is the same with most young girls. Love and riches. That is all they care for."

She squeezed my hands. "You are different. You have many thoughts all at once, crisscrossing each other and muddled in the middle."

Like acrobats in the circus I thought.

"Yes," Natalia crowed. "Acrobatics in your mind. They reach dazzling heights and humble depths. Now, you must concentrate on a single question."

I shut my eyes and asked the silent question.

"There," she said. "There it is. The question is the answer. Which path to take. The left or the right. To be an unassuming servant, perhaps leaving to take a customary position as..." she paused, "tutor or governess, in a house without... without ghosts?"

I gave a sharp intake of breath, astounded she could see things so clearly. *Yes,* my mind screamed. *A house without spirits which leave fingerprints in dusty corners and whisper their fearsome poetry through the pink lips of children.*

Natalia moaned. "And yet, there is ambition, and you fight fear. Not the fears you think. You believe you fear eyes upon you, people inspecting you and finding you wanting. This is a falsehood. A lie your mind concocted to protect you from the truth."

"Which is?" I leaned forward in anticipation.

"You fear what you might become. You will push the boundaries of your experience and transform into a creature you cannot recognize. And you are right to think such things. You could be great—greater than those you seek to imitate. Despite this, you could lose yourself in the process."

She laughed, "I see. You think you have nothing to lose. Your family has gone. Your friends have gone. You have no home. You are correct. I did not know these things at first."

At last, Natalia dropped my hands back in my lap. "Can you satisfy your ambition without ~~must ask~~ losing your compassion? This, you must answer. It may be a battle. You have hope on both sides, as I said. This can help you. Though I cannot tell you what to do, I feel you have made up your mind. Am I right in this?"

I gave a small smile of assent, and she continued, "You have been imitating your friends already and desire to transform yourself into one of them. Just so. What will be will be. I can only give you a word of caution. Do you want it?"

As she said, my mind was made up. Did I need to hear any more? Curiosity overcame me, and I nodded eagerly.

"Those who seek to walk in the steps of others leave no footprints. You journey will be a lengthy one, but you cannot run from yourself forever. Embrace your gifts. Once you truly know yourself and your desires, you may perhaps be content. Though perhaps not. Happiness is ephemeral." Natalia tucked a strand of silvery hair back underneath her rose-embroidered kerchief.

"I tell you more because you do not come looking for simple, cheerful answers like your friend. Your head says you want truth. I give you truth," she said, slipping back into her false, thick accent. "That is all. The sun is tired. I tire too. You go now."

"Thank you," I whispered. I curtsied to Natalia before leaving, though I could hardly say why.

I knew she had feigned her accent and most likely purchased the bangled bracelets and kerchief to seem exotic. However, I thought her mixture of mentalism and phrenology entrancing. Her insights were well worth the small price of a single coin.

I had gone in hoping to see smoke and mirrors, but Natalia reminded me very much of the Sutherlands, seeming to read the corners of my mind and tease out truths I had been too afraid to admit before. And Dora, too. She had no way of knowing Dora had been keeping secrets regarding her young man.

""I tell you truth,'" I mumbled to myself, imitating Natalia's fabricated accent. I shivered at my own words as the traveler's voice seemed to emanate from my lips. She had been correct in her estimation of my abilities to imitate. Perhaps I could use that odd talent in performance.

My thoughts were cut off as I saw Dora standing outside another wagon, shaking violently. I rushed to her. "Dora? Dora, what is it?" She was so much like Mary in this moment, it terrified me. Trying not to show fear, I held her shoulders and deliberately slowed my breathing.

"That man, Alesky. He told me things. Horrible, horrible things," Dora cried.

"What did he tell you?" A flash of fever seemed to pass through me. I knew that Dora was going to say she had heard Fletcher.

"He said, 'Your father wishes to come forward.' Then, his eyes rolled back in his head," she sobbed. "He began shaking all over. It wasn't pretense; I know it wasn't. Alesky's son was there, and he became so afraid, he ran from the cart to find his mother."

"And did you follow?" I asked.

"I couldn't," Dora moaned. "Alesky grabbed my wrist so tightly, I couldn't move." She held her hand away from her face to show me. Even with the fading sunset behind us, I could see red impressions upon her fair skin.

"Come, let us go to the backlot where you can sit and rest a moment." I put my arm around her waist, gently guiding her away. "I will have one of the boys hail a carriage for us and we can return to the hotel."

"He spoke of death," she said. "But the voice I heard wasn't Alesky's. It was Father's. Father's voice came from his lips. He said, 'Kitty, a death is coming. A considerable death. Be wary of the trains. The locomotive is powerful, even for the strongest of us.'"

Dora paused, breathing heavily. "Then he asked for you," she said. "He said, 'Bring me Anna Louise. I would speak with her.'"

A strange sensation pulled at my navel, and my head went hazy, as if I had imbibed a tumblerful of whiskey. Unaware of my intentions, my feet moved toward Alesky's gypsy cart.

"Anna!" Dora said sharply, bringing me back to myself. "You're not going in?"

I furrowed my brow. My feet went still, but I stared at the vardo and could not tear my gaze away to look at my friend. "Did he say anything else? Anything to indicate I would be put in harm's way?"

"No," Dora admitted. "Anna, I have communed with spirits often, as have all my sisters. I have only been frightened like this twice before, and both times, it was a trick."

I shook my head, trying to throw off the odd feeling enveloping me, and at last looked at Dora, bewildered. "You do not believe Alesky to be genuine?"

"I do not know whether the *spirit* was genuine," she said. "A spirit, yes. One which sounded like Father, yes. Nevertheless, there are malevolent spirits alongside the benevolent ones. We call them seducing spirits. They utter falsehoods as easily as you might speak your name."

"Which is why I feared playing with necromancy in the first place," I admitted.

"Let us be sensible about this," I said, my words slurred. "If the spirit was Fletcher, he has given a warning we can do little about. Death comes when it will and takes all equally."

Dora nodded. "You're right, Anna. And, if it was a spirit of falsehood, the warning is best ignored, but we should go back and tell the others. Sarah may have a different thought on the matter."

We found a carriage, though I felt sick at the thought of leaving. Perhaps a spirit was seducing me, but my head never fully cleared, and the strange pulling sensation tugged harder at my belly the further we rode toward the hotel.

Sarah was sitting in her room with Grace and Victoria when we arrived. "Where are the others?" Dora asked as soon as we stepped across the room's threshold.

"Naomi is out with her young Mr. Bailey," Grace answered. "He is quite an agreeable fellow. He spoke with us at length today and invited both Naomi and Mary for a night out. The three of them went to supper."

"And Isabella?" Dora wondered.

"Tramping around somewhere with some man or other." Victoria waved a hand in disgust. "She doesn't care a whit about her reputation. Do you know she didn't even come home last night?"

Dora ignored this and fell into a chair beside the bed. "Dora had a bit of a fright this evening," I said.

"What happened?" Victoria giggled wickedly. "Did the gypsy tell Dora that young man she's been kissing has a wife and four babes at home?"

"Tell them, Anna," Dora moaned, and I saw her hands were shaking.

"We went to Natalia, the Gypsy Queen, first," I said. "She gave Dora a reading and asked her to leave when my turn came."

Grace and Sarah exchanged a secretive look at this, but said nothing, so I went on, "Dora left to visit Alesky, a spiritualist fortune teller."

I continued the tale, speaking as quickly as I could until Sarah raised her hand in her usual impatient way. "If it was Father, we must know. I do not wish to leave the show before the season ends, but we cannot continue traveling with the circus while trying to avoid the trains. They are the only possible means of conveyance. Horses and wagons would never keep pace."

She looked around at her sisters, but stared directly into my eyes as she said, "Someone will have to go back."

Fear clawed at my chest like a dog trapped indoors. This felt like my final test. Would I stay, or would I return? Would I admit to all I had experienced and open myself to it, or would I deny it completely? Was I servant, or was I sister?

I closed my eyes, breaking Sarah's gaze, and slowly nodded my head in agreement. As Natalia had said, I made my choice before I entered her wagon. I did not believe I cared for the riches and fame that came with performing, but I desperately wanted the comfort of a permanent home—devotion and affection from the only family I would ever know the rest of my days.

"I shall return." Bile rose from my belly as I formed the words. "If one of you will come with me."

"Two are better than one," Grace agreed. "I will go with you."

"Go and be quick." Sarah's mouth went thin and her eyes grew dark. "The travelers are used to packing up and fleeing in a matter of hours. Grace, take my pocketbook with you. You may have need of it."

There were few carriages out as the stars began appearing in the sky. Standing under one of the streetlamps lining the road, we were at last spotted by a cab, which we entered hastily and made our way back to the caravan. Grace paid the cab to stay as we rushed to Alesky's wagon.

A plump woman stood in front of the door as if waiting for us. She crossed her broad arms across her ample bosom and glared. "No," she said, in an accent as thick as Natalia's had been.

"My sister—" Grace began.

"Alesky," the woman shouted, cutting her off, "that woman came back, as you say. Tell Sergie, he must go behind to bed."

"Tell them go away," a man's rough voice called from inside.

"Yes," she agreed. "You go now."

"I can give you more coins," Grace insisted.

"No coins," the woman paused. "Paper, perhaps, but much of it. You cause trouble. Frighten my boy."

"It wasn't me," Grace said. "My sister was here before."

"All the same," the woman turned.

"Twenty dollars?" Grace held out a bill.

The woman turned back. "Fifty," she said firmly. "But still, I ask my husband. He not wanting your ghosts."

"Go and ask," Grace said. "The money will pay for bread for your son for many days. Perhaps even a slice of cake or two."

The woman narrowed her eyes but said no more. I knew she would make her husband agree. These people lived hand to mouth, and the summer had been a rainy one, without much work for itinerant farmhands, let alone tourists seeking their fortune.

At last, an arm stuck out of the red and gold door, beckoning us to come in. When we ducked in to enter the small wagon, the woman held out her hand. Grace took a bill from Sarah's pocketbook and handed it to her. The woman spat on the floor to both her left and right in rapid succession. "I go back behind curtain also," she said. "Protect my Sergie."

Her husband, Alesky, sat in a chair, cradling his head in his hands. "Many spirits travel with you," he groaned, refusing to look up.

"Is my father among them?" Grace asked.

"He pushes to come," Alesky said, groaning. "I hold him back. He is too strong. Too loud." He covered his ears, and I wondered what Fletcher might be yelling at him.

Though the night was yet warm, the small, round windows lining the wagon's walls laced with frost. I closed my eyes for a moment as the scent of stale beer and cinnamon filled my nostrils. I knew it was Fletcher's spirit, for no other could conjure that peculiar combination of smells. I also recalled Naomi's warning that the cinnamon was actually incense, a portent of death.

"Please, I beg you. Allow my father to speak," Grace whispered, sitting beside Alesky. Her breath hung in the air as the room chilled.

Alesky wrapped his arms around his waist and moaned, as if in pain. Unsure how to persuade him further, Grace looked up to me, pleading for my aid. I pulled a chair over and sat between them. I held Grace's hand in my right and Alesky's hand in my left.

"All will be well," I soothed the frightened man. "Fletcher is only a spirit, and not a false one. He can bring no harm to you or your family. I promise."

Alesky squeezed my hand. "You have the gift?"

I licked my lips and replied carefully, "Perhaps. I am unsure. I can sense the ... aroma Fletcher's presence. In truth, I might attempt to call upon him myself, but I am untrained and know little of Spiritualism."

"Do not summon him then." Alesky tightened his broad, calloused hand again, a bit too forcefully this time. "He is powerful. Nearly standing here next to me. Most are wisps. Balls of light, only. Thin. This man? He thick. Much strength. Many words to say."

Alesky shook his head. The pulling sensation in my belly strained and nausea gripped me. Was it a seducing spirit, a short-lived moment of insanity, or curiosity only? I could never say, but the impulse to call Fletcher overcame me.

"Come forth," I demanded. "You have frightened this man and your daughter. Explain yourself. Tell us more clearly what your words mean."

The gypsy gave a great gasp, and a choking sound emitted from his throat as he fought to hold Fletcher back. He let go of my hand and gripped the table. His head was thrown backward, and his mouth gaped open. "Girls," he rasped. "My girls. And not my girls."

"Father?" Grace asked.

"A big death is coming. A large one. Watch the trains," Fletcher said with Alesky's lips.

"Should we leave the circus?" Grace probed. "Should we find other work?"

"No," he said. "Yes.... No... Not yet."

Grace and I gaped at one another. What did this mean?

"Mary will feel the death," he said. "The blackness will be hardest on her as always. She sees beyond the curtain. She communes with us too easily. Watch the trains. Do not stray from the circus until Mary tells you it is time. I will speak to her."

"Gently," I said, and dug my fingers into Alesky's arm, hoping Fletcher would feel it. When I drew blood with my fingernails, the man's eyes grew wide. I insisted, "You terrify her. You plague her with worry and panic."

"Gently," the voice echoed. "Gently. Yes. I will speak to Mary in whispers." Each word hissed, fading as Fletcher receded and left Alesky limp from the effort.

Grace and I moved to go, but Alesky flopped forward again. This time, speaking in a softer, more feminine tone.

"What did he tell you?" Alesky's mouth squeaked.

"Mother?" Grace gasped.

"You cannot trust all his words," this new spirit said. "He is a tricky one and will not bend to your will."

"Mother?" Grace was crying now.

"You know. You know what he was like in life. He fed on fear and anger, too. He feeds even now!" Alesky's mouth gave up a great scream, and I was reminded of the panthers.

I heard commotion in the back. Alesky slumped forward again, finished this time.

"Go," I said, pushing Grace to her feet. "Now, before another spirit comes and Alesky's wife murders us both."

The path back to the main thoroughfare was dark, and we now had only the pale light of the moon to guide our swift feet. Grace tripped over a stone, but it was a small one, and I caught her arm before she fell. Rushing back to the carriage, we were out of breath, but I was pleased to see the driver had been true to his word and had stayed until we returned.

The pulling at my navel had ceased, but my head still felt swathed in a hazy veil of silk, and the buzzing had returned to my ears.

I fought to regain my composure. "What shall I tell the others?" I asked Grace as soon as we were seated in the coach.

"Everything but the last," she said. "Mother has only spoken to me once before, and I do not know whether that was her. My father was not the best man when he walked on this earth, but it seems his message was for protection, not harm."

"I do not think we should tell Mary," I said.

She considered this. "No. She will know of the death when it comes, as shall we all, if it is so great. Telling her will only cause her to slip further from us before the designated time."

After a few moments longer, Grace held my hand in hers. "You did well, Anna. We believed you to have gifts, but we were unsure you would accept them."

"The mentalist Natalia told me the same," I replied. "I cannot say I wish to do that again..." I trailed off.

"But, you seem more alive tonight than you have been for several weeks," Grace finished my unspoken thought.

"I have felt adrift," I admitted. "It is so much."

"Your life has changed these months." She stroked my head as if I were a child. "You have grown from a child to a woman faster than you believed possible. You have become a sister to us, and nearly a mother to Mary. And the circus itself, with its endless trains and tents, can be tiring."

"And bewitching," I countered.

"Bewitching and entrancing," Grace agreed. "It has a magic all its own."

We remained silent until the carriage came to a stop in front of the hotel. Then, we slowly paced up the steps, disinclined to tell the rest of the family the events of the evening.

***

The morning after our encounters with the gypsies, who were indeed gone from the circus grounds before the sun rose, Sarah spoke to me between performances.

"I think you have chosen to join us?" her stern face stirred into a soft smile.

"I have," I said. "After seeing more of what this life would truly be like, as you suggested."

She put an arm around my shoulder, and we walked together awhile. "I would have allowed you to sing with us as a substitute," she said. "But I feared they would not let you back in the house if you did not agree to open yourself to Spiritualism as we do."

My eyes grew wide. "Your sisters would not have welcomed me in their home?"

"No," she patted my arm, assuring me. "Not my sisters. We have come to think of you as one of us. No. The spirits, you know. They are heavy in the air all around the place."

"Your father?" I asked.

"Father, Mother, our brother Charles... though he shunned home when he was alive and has rarely come back. Our family, of course, but others, too. Others who were there before the mansion, and more since. Spiritualism works on the principle of magnetism. The house draws them in... or perhaps we do it. In any case, the dead sense a gathering of souls and know their presence is not unwelcome."

"And they want to be heard," I guessed.

Sarah's mouth drew in as if I had said something sour. "Yes," she admitted at last.

"But they are not all—"

"There will be much time for questions later," Sarah stopped my words. "For now, we must begin your lessons... no, not in Spiritualism. You can read a book or two when our travels have ended, and we are back at home. No. I refer to your singing lessons. And acting, too. I cannot teach you to dance, but the younger girls dance prettily, and though they are not trained, they can teach you."

"Thank you," I said.

"I suppose you are also wondering about payment," she declared. For once, the Sutherland trick of reading minds seemed to be defective, for I had thought of nothing but my gratitude.

"I didn't—" I started.

"We have agreed that once you are ready, we will each take one day off a week," Sarah forged ahead. "That will give you plenty of practice. You can substitute for me on Sunday, Isabella on Monday, Grace on Tuesday, Naomi on Wednesday, Dora on

Thursday, and Mary on Friday. That will allow you Saturday as a day of rest."

"What about Victoria?" I asked.

Just then, Victoria walked by, giving me a sneer. "Victoria refuses to give up her place on the stage to a red-headed snippet upstart who can't sing," she said. Turning up her nose, she strode back the way she had come.

Sarah laughed. "I would pay no attention to that sentiment. Victoria doesn't like to give up her place in the lights for any of us. Sometimes, I do believe I created a monster with that one. Isabella, too. They are much prone to dramatics."

"It shows their talent," I tried.

"It shows a lack of common sense," Sarah corrected. "As to your salary, we have each agreed to give up twenty dollars apiece in payment for your services... all except for Victoria, for whom you will not substitute in any case."

I held my breath. One hundred and forty dollars a week? Could this be in jest? "No, I'm quite serious," Sarah read my thoughts correctly this time. "Each of us is paid one hundred fifty a week at the circus, and we thought it fitting we pay you the same—a bit more, when it comes to what we're giving up, but close enough nonetheless. It is only temporary until I can talk to Barnum about hiring you full-time. I think a trial period of a month should be sufficient."

"I hope I can prove myself in that time," I said, praying it was true.

Should I begin writing to Faith again? I wondered. *If Mother did not marry, Faith might still need my financial support.*

"What an odd thought," Sarah said, as if I had asked her about it. "I suppose you can send some money to your sister, or give it away to charity, if you like. I thought you would spend the first of it on more clothes. The dresses you have are wearing thin as we travel."

Or perhaps some diamonds, as Victoria is always buying, my mind leapt to the most lavish thing it could possibly think of.

Sarah looked thoroughly amused. "Why not?" she chortled. "Baubles as well as bread. Money enough for both."

I wished for a moment I could read people as easily, then hid the thought from her. It was enough to be instructed in the arts of the stage. I could not take more upon me yet.

***

As we moved into Maine, and the warmth of summer turned to the cool of autumn, Sarah instructed me in the theatrical arts. We practiced mornings and evenings until we were both exhausted from the effort. It seemed I could sing the central alto parts and even some of the mezzo soprano, but I could not stretch my range into the upper notes without some difficulty, and the lower registers gave me nearly as much trouble.

"It's of no account," she said. "Your tone is clear, as I said before. You know the words and you're beginning to emote properly so that the audience can feel your passion as you sing. You've said Natalia told you about a gift for imitation. Think of each song as if it were being sung by a character in a play. Embody each speaker in a new way. Show her thoughts on your face."

I sang through "Sailing, Sailing," and Sarah stopped me in the middle of the rousing chorus.

Try it this way, she said, "The sailor's life is bold and free, His home is on the rolling sea; And never heart more true or brave, Than his who launches on the wave!"

Sarah also sang alto, and her voice was the easiest for me to reproduce. I stressed the words "free" and "sea," just as she had, and made the same sweeping motions with my arms at the end.

It was quite a challenge, but after going through the song twice more, she at last proclaimed, "Well, Anna Louise, I don't know if you're ready, but Dora declared to me she would run away from the circus if she didn't have a day off to see her young man."

"She finally told you all about him?" I put my hands under my chin, eager to hear the rest.

"His name is Frederick, but you'll have to hear the story from her lips... or Naomi's if she isn't preoccupied with her own Harry." Sarah laughed and rolled her eyes.

When Sarah laughed her throaty chuckle, she had the same streak of fun and exuberance as I had seen in her younger siblings. I only wished she would let it out more often.

Instead, she returned to the business at hand. "Tomorrow is Thursday, and you shall substitute in for Dora. Her usual parts are much easier than some of the others. She seems more built for business than performing, but there will be time for that later. For now, use Isabella's hand mirror to practice your facial expressions, and find a costume for tomorrow."

She paused before leaving my room to add, "Something grand, I should think. Maybe even borrow jewels from Victoria, if she will allow it. I want you to feel as regal as a queen when you walk across that stage."

The next morning, I could see why Sarah wished me to be more finely arrayed. It was not for the benefit of the crowd only. It was to increase my dwindling confidence.

I looked out at the first cluster of spectators as the other acts performed. The eyes of the audience transfixed on the stage as if mesmerized. Their heads seemed to move to the left or right in one accord. Simultaneously, they lifted their hands to applaud. It was as if I was watching a conglomeration of Siamese twins with one hundred heads attached to the same body.

At last, I saw Dora enter the tent, holding the arm of a dark-haired man I supposed to be Frederick. It was a surprise to see them there, but I was more than a little pleased.

She waved at me, and I began to wave back when Isabella pulled me backstage behind the curtain. "Don't make a spectacle of yourself before we go on," she snapped. "And don't take attention away from whoever's on now."

"Isabella," I whispered. "I am more uneasy than I imagined."

"Does it feel as if there is a bird or butterfly fluttering in your stomach?" she asked, clutching me around the middle.

"Yes," I gasped.

"So, it should." She released me. "Take that nervous excitement and *use* it. Put the tension into your performance as you sing. Naomi is different and Dora, too. They feel easy and free on stage, and their freedom gives life to their comical pieces. When *you* feel easy and free, your passion fades and your work becomes lifeless. I have noticed this about you, even in practice."

"Thank you," I said. Her words soothed me for a moment, until Sarah came over.

"We're not doing the four numbers as planned," Sarah said. "Mary says Anna should sing a solo first, or she won't come onto the stage at all."

"Really?" I asked. "The first time I mentioned going on stage with you, she said I should not be 'her Anna' anymore and cried. She hasn't spoken a word to me about our rehearsals since I began studying with you. I'm surprised she approves."

Isabella spat, and I wondered why everyone thought Sarah to be the mannish one. "It's just a lot of nonsense," she said. "Mary is too old to be playing games like this. Someone ought to teach her not to interfere with our entertainments."

Isabella moved, prepared to show Mary a piece of her mind, but Sarah stopped her. "Don't," Sarah warned, holding Isabella's arm. "Wait until after Father's portend comes to pass. Then, there will be time for admonishments and arguments. For now, we acquiesce to the child's demands, much as it pains me."

"We are better when not completely rehearsed," I said. "Working on instinct and intuition rather than a schedule printed out to the letter." I looked pointedly at Isabella, "*I* have noticed this about the group, even in practice."

Sarah considered this. "You may be correct, Anna, though I should hardly go on stage without some plan. What if we begin with—"

Her words died as Professor Everett announced us. Both women smiled at me as if to say, "Well, now we can test your little theories, can we not?" and we proceeded to the front.

The applause lifted and swelled as we stepped across the stage. I first noticed the lights, which I had hardly considered as a member of the audience. They were bright and hot upon my face, making my already perspiring brow drip great beads of sweat from my forehead.

I looked out into the sea of faces, trying to find Dora again. When I could not, I decided to focus my gaze upon the pole that held up the back of the tent. My mouth went dry as the audience quieted. The feeling in my belly I had perceived in Alesky's cart returned. Suddenly, it felt as if a firm hand was pushing me forward.

My eyes shifted from the pole to the people before me. Remembering Isabella's last bit of advice, I closed my eyes, and let the passion in my belly fill my throat.

What happened next was a surprise to all of us, for from my lips came the sweet notes of the hymn my father had often sang to me before I slept. "Abide with me, fast falls the eventide. The darkness deepens, Lord with me abide. When other helpers fail, and comforts flee, Help of the helpless, O abide with me."

It was the same song the girls had dedicated to their father in a performance months before, and I knew my choice was the right one when they joined in for the second verse.

As the song came to a close, the audience was silent for a few terrible seconds before bursting into an ovation such as I had never experienced before. I fell back in line amongst the others as Sarah and Mary came forward to sing the next tune. Tears came to the corners of my eyes. My heart was warm with gratitude, and the fluttering in my belly moved to my chest, which felt as if it would continue expanding until it exploded.

The darkness deepens, a small voice inside my mind intruded upon my joy. *Other helpers fail, and comforts flee,* the next thought came. *Where will you turn when you have given up your Lord? Where can the helpless go when they have abandoned all hope?* I could not tell whether it was my own conscience, or whether some fading soul was breaking through my reverie.

It mattered little because there were practical matters to attend to and our show was far from complete. I pushed away the thoughts and whomever brought them. Sarah and Mary's song was at an end, and I knew the quartet would be next—Victoria, Isabella, Grace, and Naomi, all singing in harmony. At the closing chorus, we would all join in, and Sarah would give the signal for us to drop our tresses.

Five minutes later, the signal came.

With the other sisters, I turned, lifted my hands, and loosed my hair. It was something I had practiced before, but the feeling then of freeing my flowing tresses was exhilarating.

I could feel my auburn locks streaming down my back as everyone watched. I felt their shock and their awe, and I reveled in the display.

It felt almost as if showing our hair was something forbidden—as if we were undressing before a horde of excited men and women, who had paid for the privilege of seeing us exposed.

There were more than a hundred people under the tent, and yet, I had never before experienced anything so intimate.

The moment was brief, and we were whisked off the stage as the next act appeared. As soon as we were behind the curtain, I sunk to the ground, panting.

"I believe Anna rather enjoyed herself," Naomi grinned. "I told you she would."

"That ruby dress was the right choice of costume," Victoria admitted. "It brought out the red in your hair even more. When I glanced over at you, it was almost as if flames ran down your back."

"Yes, yes," Sarah said. "It was quite theatrical. Now, let us go to the cook tent. The flag will soon be raised, and I should like to discuss what we will do in an hour when the next show is called."

"And I should like to see Dora and her dashing young man," Naomi laughed.

"I think we should all like that," I agreed.

As we walked over to greet them, Mary took my hand and gently squeezed it. "You did well," she whispered. "But promise me you will still be my Anna when you come off the stage. You can't be Naomi or Isabella yet."

I hugged Mary to my side, puzzled at her meaning, but determined to provide comfort. "I will always be your Anna," I promised.

"Well," Sarah's voice boomed out. "I see we are finally to meet the famous Mr. Frederick Castlemaine." She stuck out a hand to the man who had his arm around Dora's waist.

He seemed a bit overwhelmed, being with all eight of us at once, but dropped his arm in order to shake hands with the family matriarch. "A pleasure to meet you Miss Sarah. I have heard much about you from your lovely sister." He smiled but cleared his throat uncomfortably.

"We should have a dinner party," Naomi broke in. I knew she was trying to make everyone feel comfortable and tried to help her.

"Yes!" I said, trying to sound enthused. "We went to a fine dinner party with Mrs. Tom Thumb a few months ago, and Naomi has wanted to hold a similar salon ever since."

Frederick seemed to brighten at this. "I am quite partial to salons, Miss Naomi," he said. "I am sure Dora has told you of my travels through Europe as of late." He paused, and we all smiled and nodded, though of course, she had told us nothing of the sort.

Until our meeting Frederick, I did not even know his last name. I thought Dora should have taken Natalia's words more seriously, but she continued to collect her secrets like a sparrow gathering grasses for his winter nest.

"Yes," Frederick continued. "I'm from Canada, you know. The French section, of course, over in Québec. But I am quite friendly with Archibald McLellan, who practically owns the railroad you fine ladies have been riding on. He has a house over in Old Orchard Beach. You are traveling there before moving on to Portland, are you not? He let me his house while he and his wife are in England. Why don't we hold your grand salon there, Miss Naomi?"

"Do you think we might?" Naomi clapped her hands. "Can you arrange everything in time?"

"There are plenty of servants. I'm sure Dora can help me arrange things. She is such a good little manager."

Dora looked delighted at this remark and hopped up to kiss him on the cheek before remembering herself and blushing, rather demurely.

"How entirely domestic of you," Isabella said coolly. "Interesting, as you don't seem the type who would take well to traditional domesticity."

Dora's lips turned down and her brow furrowed. It pained me to see Isabella jabbing at her in this way.

"All right," Sarah took charge, stemming off an argument. "Enough of this jibber-jabber. Dora, you and Frederick go enjoy your day off. Send word tomorrow, if the house is ready for a visit. The rest of you, grab your meal quickly. We should be on stage again in twenty minutes."

Sarah shook her graying head. "And Naomi, don't let these plans distract you. I know you'll be thinking of how to arrange your salon all afternoon. It will be a silly affair with only the ten of us in attendance. Do not waste your time on such trivial matters."

"Nonsense," Frederick broke in. Sarah gave him a pointed look, and I knew it was a warning to stay out of the family business. He either did not see it or ignored it and blundered on. "Miss Naomi, no salon with me in attendance is a trivial one! Archibald's home is in the Queen Anne Italianate style. Dora and I shall drum up a feast which fits the grandeur of the house, and you shall dream up a set of themes to match, I expect. Come, Dora!" Together, they swept away.

"What a bloviating dandified—" Sarah stopped herself. Instead, she turned and gave a stern look to Naomi.

"I understand," Naomi agreed, but as soon as Sarah's back was turned, she gave me a wink, and I knew she would be preoccupied all day, trying to plot out the best routes for conversation and the most fashionable topics of the moment. She cared far more about impressing the dashing Mr. Bailey than she did entertaining the crowds, who were so easily impressed by everything under our canvas roof.

***

The next day, after I had experienced the thrill of entertaining no less than five times for the wealthy patrons of Old Orchard Beach, Maine, Dora sent three carriages to collect us for the salon. Sarah, Isabella, and Victoria took the first, Mary, Grace, and I took the second, and Naomi and Harry the third. I felt a bit forlorn at Naomi's absence as we rode, and wished she was squeezed in alongside the three of us.

As I considered this, Mary put her head on my shoulder like a small child. Grace patted my hand like a mother, and I knew that things were as they should be.

The house was nearly as grand as the Sutherland mansion, though not nearly as large. I marveled at the turrets and intricate scrollwork as Dora proudly led us to the dining room, acting for all the world like the mistress of the house.

Once we were all seated around the long table, Dora stood and said, "Frederick and I have arranged for you a five-course meal. We shall begin with Vermicelli soup, followed by leg of lamb with a tart cherry sauce, a salad course of French beans, and a selection of nuts and cheeses. We shall end the evening with custard and there are cigars and cognac for the men, should they choose to retire to the study while we ladies continue our chatter."

Dora looked quite pleased with herself and stood, staring out at us as if expecting a response. I nudged Mary under the table. We began to clap politely, and the others quickly joined in. Dora smiled. I knew she had memorized her little speech and had probably practiced it a dozen times in the hour before we arrived.

"And now," she made a sweeping gesture, "Miss Naomi Sutherland shall lead us through a series of dazzling themes that will feed our minds as we feed our bodies."

We cheered again for Naomi, who cleared her throat and declared, "Our first topic of the evening shall be issues in ladies' fashion."

Victoria sat up straighter and I knew she had many thoughts on the subject, but before she could say anything, Harry broke out into laughter. "Well, Frederick," he said, "I suppose we shall remain relatively silent tonight. I fear the topics will be more pleasing to the ladies than to us lads."

"That isn't so," Naomi said, and I feared she would be hurt, but she smiled at her beau. "The aim of a salon is for men and women to share thoughts equally. Why should not you speak of fashion just as eloquently as we speak of politics?"

"I must agree with your lovely friend," Frederick said. "Par exemple, were you aware that in London, there is a new organization which protests any fashion which deforms a woman's figure or impedes her body?"

"No." Harry grinned. "You don't say. I thought all women's dresses were made to deform and impede. It seems as if they cannot go to town without tripping over layers of skirts."

"Precisely so," Frederick agreed. "But this group would change all that. I find it a shame. If they had their way, ladies would wear nothing but bloomers and britches."

"I don't find it a shame," Victoria broke in. I was surprised because, with her love of frocks and frills, I thought she would concur with the men.

"Really? Do tell us why, Miss Victoria," Frederick said. I looked at Naomi, who seemed pleased her first topic had brought such lively discussion, but I felt ill at ease that Frederick appeared to be directing the proceedings instead of my kind, jolly sister Dora.

"I have spoken with more than one woman from that organization. They call themselves the Rational Dress Society, and they believe a perfect dress is one which is not too heavy, fails to put pressure on the body, allows freedom of movement, and is both beautiful and comfortable," Victoria explained.

"I must say, I would find those guidelines quite agreeable," Isabella said. "One cannot have grace upon the stage if one is bound up with pressure against the ribcage and the lungs. And how can one walk from one side to the other in a heavy, hot gown that restricts the legs and feet?"

This comment surprised me as well, for Isabella had been sour ever since she saw Dora and Frederick that afternoon.

As the soup tureens were removed and the next course brought forth, Naomi said, "This has been stimulating! And now, let us talk of art."

"How fantastic," Frederick's voice boomed out above the rest of us. "Are any of you aware of Claude Monet?" he began.

"I believe I—" Isabella started.

"Well, he is the most progressive painter in all of France," Frederick interrupted. "Why, I was able to see some of his work first-hand, and I can tell you..."

My mind wandered as Frederick droned on and on. First about art, then music, then politics. He had a story for every subject and two opinions for every one of ours. Though there were nine of us and only one of him, he dominated conversation throughout the entire evening.

Frederick had an unusual, flamboyant way about him and I saw most of the others were entirely captivated by it. All but

Naomi and Harry, whose usual enthusiasm grew dim as the night wore on.

At last, the custards were served. I thanked the spirits the supper was finally ending. As dessert was placed before us, I spied Naomi give her gentleman a prod with her elbow. She caught me glancing at them and raised an eyebrow.

I could feel her silently ask, "Do you wish this to be over as wholly as we do?"

In response I raised my eyebrows in return and gave a slight bob of my head, as if to say, "Unquestionably."

Harry coughed. "I have an early morning tomorrow, ladies. You will excuse me if Naomi and I depart our happy family before the night is through."

She elbowed him again and tilted her chin toward me, though no one saw, they were so enraptured by the charismatic Mr. Castlemaine.

"And I am sure we should take Anna with us," he stumbled. "We need a chaperone, and it was her first day on stage today. She looks weary, despite her determination to be her usual effervescent self."

This did have heads turning, as the family examined me for signs of fatigue or distress. "It is nothing," I said, giving what I hoped was a tired looking smile. It took not much effort, for I was tired. The thrills of the day had left me much disinclined to speak further, and perhaps this was why I felt cool toward Dora's friend.

"You should go," Sarah said. "Tomorrow there will be three performances in the afternoon. You're substituting for

Mary, and I would not have you fainting of exhaustion before the week is out. Leave while there is still a bit of light in the sky."

With her permission, we stood to exit. I saw Mary furtively looking at me, and I wondered whether she was ready to make an escape as well. Most likely, the continued society was making her weary.

As we left, I heard Sarah ask Frederick, "Now, Mr. Castlemaine, you were saying something about the Canadian Prime Minister? What does Mr. Macdonald think of the suffrage movement?"

Naomi began laughing as soon as our feet hit the pavement outside. "We could walk back," she said, "unless you are truly tired. It should only take us half an hour."

"I think fresh air should do me a bit of good," I replied. The house, and those around it had large front gardens, and I inhaled a mix of calla lilies and chrysanthemums, still in bloom even as the leaves turned from green to gold.

"Particularly after that flagrant display," Harry snorted.

"Frederick is quite something, isn't he?" Naomi took his arm and I moved to her other side as we walked down the lane.

"Did you notice how much he was drinking?" I asked.

"No," Naomi admitted, precisely as Harry said, "Yes."

"I am hesitant to admit this," Harry said. "But I was aware of Mr. Castlemaine prior to our Dora's involvement with him."

"Truly?" Naomi's eyes grew wide. "What do you know of him?"

"He is the very type of man I despise," Harry said, "an idler and an opportunist. He has no occupation and little money left, I should think, after tramping around Europe with no thought in his mind but recreation and amusement."

"Though it sounds as if he stayed with friends and spent little throughout his travels," I interjected.

"Even worse, then." Naomi shook her head. "A dilettante and a dandy who sponges off the kindness of others. I worry for our poor Dora."

"And so you should," Harry said. "Castlemaine has traveled alongside our circus before. Last year, there were rumors of his involvement with a trapeze artist. The season before that, it was a Hindoo dancer, if I'm not mistaken."

"Good Lord," I breathed.

"We shall speak with her about it, Anna," Naomi insisted.

"I do not know," I hesitated. "Dora has already been warned of false men. Telling her our true feelings might only separate her from us and further propel him into Frederick's arms."

"True enough," Harry agreed. "How would you feel, Naomi, if Anna came to you and told you I was unsuitable."

Naomi considered this. "I would think she was out of her mind," she laughed. "Unless she had good reason. Then I would simply believe her mistaken. But it is different. He is not to be compared with you."

"Well, in that I am grateful," Harry said, squeezing her to him for a moment.

"I don't just flatter you because I... care for you," Naomi stammered. "Anna agrees with me. Don't you, Anna?"

"Harry is a hard worker," I said, as if he were not standing right beside us. "He never acts with impropriety and is never secretive. He is kind and jovial," I paused, "and he allows others to talk when they are in conversation."

Harry laughed. "Perhaps I am too harsh on the man. A first impression never gives the whole picture. I should judge him by his actions and not rumors alone."

"I should judge him on his lack of decorum at supper," Naomi countered. We came to our hotel in quite a better mood than when we had left the party.

Part VII
The Fate I Had Chosen

Pictured: Miss Isabella Sutherland

October, 1885

Unfortunately, my joy and merriment ended suddenly the next day as we waited to board the train.

I was idling outside the station when Isabella sidled up to me. "Watch for Dora," she whispered. "She's going around asking everyone what they think of *her Freddie*," she said this last in a mocking high-pitched squeak.

"I thought you enjoyed his company last evening," I said, concealing my own thoughts on the subject.

"Oh, I enjoy *him*. But Dora is acting absolutely ridiculous, fawning all over Frederick as if she's already planned their wedding and named their children," she scoffed.

Before I could reply, Dora came our way and Isabella hastily made her way back to the main platform. "Anna!" Dora exclaimed. "I've been looking for you. I must ask you whether you enjoyed yourself last night?"

"The food was divine," I said, avoiding her gaze.

"But what did you think of my Freddie?" she asked.

I started to answer, but she babbled on, "Isn't he simply divine? He's a flâneur, you know—a man of leisure. After attending university, he came into an inheritance and had a true, European experience. He's strolled the streets of Paris, London, and Rome!"

Dora looked at me expectantly, and I managed to say, "Frederick seems to have a great deal of knowledge when it comes to art and literature."

"Oh, he does," she enthused. "He studied painting and sculpture, and poetry, too."

"I didn't realize," I said, coolly. "I shall have to see some of his work when we next come through Maine."

Dora beamed. "Freddie has offered to travel with the circus as we go through Canada! He's written to Mr. Archibald McLellan, saying he no longer needs to stay at his friend's home."

"Really?" I asked. *No good will come of this*, a voice inside me whispered. I nearly spoke the words out loud.

"Yes, and I'm so glad," Dora smiled. "To be frank, I've been a bit jealous of Naomi. She can see her Harry every day, but I've only been with Freddie in the few cities to which he's been able to travel, and even then, we only have a few scant hours to ourselves. He's written me letters, of course, but one cannot embrace paper."

"Or kiss it either," I could not help but add.

Dora giggled and gave my arm an affectionate squeeze. "I am glad you like him," she said.

She was so bright and happy, I could not find the heart to contradict her. Instead, I said, "Let's find the others. The train will likely be late today. Perhaps we can take a short stroll down the main thoroughfare."

***

Frederick indeed joined us as we traveled from Maine through Vermont and into Montreal. I wished to take a tour of the French-Canadian city, but Grace warned me, "If we show interest in Montreal, Frederick will have to take us on the tour. If we wait until next season, he may no longer accompany our fair sister." So, I agreed to stay with the circus instead of wandering about the city.

Later, I was glad we had not gone, for we heard that a plague of smallpox had struck the city only a few months before, and several sections of Montreal were still under quarantine. It was no wonder I thought the city a quaint, quiet place. There were few people who were both unafraid of the red death and still willing to see our show.

Thankfully, none of our company took sick, and we continued our journey through Ontario.

I still felt the exhilaration of performing each time I took to the stage, but as my part grew in our show, I found that acting, singing, and dancing all day long was tiring, and I felt I could take no more excitement. I worked the first Saturday, as Mary felt unwell, though I knew it was only from again eating too much candy. The next few Saturdays, I did nothing but sleep.

At last, I found myself with a day off in Toronto, where I felt neither exhausted nor adventurous enough to tour the city on my own. I had the entire day to leisurely walk through the circus and looked forward to becoming a member of the crowd as I had at the beginning of the season.

However, I found the morning dull. I found I longed for the eyes of the crowd upon me, for the gaze of men upon my hair as I let it spill down my back.

Walking, unnoticed among the spectators, was an oddly familiar sensation, and I found I did not like it. The morning reminded me of all the days I had spent in lethargy only a few weeks before.

I sought out Georgie, though I avoided going into the menagerie tent until after I saw the panthers wheeled out for a performance under the big top. The rest of the animals seemed calmed as I slipped in. Georgie stood in the center, grinning as he handed bags of food to children clinging to the hands of their parents.

"Miss! I hardly expected you today," he said.

"I have the day off." I smiled.

"Ooh!" a woman next to us exclaimed. She held the hand of a young girl of nine or ten. Mother and daughter were dressed identically in mauve dresses, and I almost burst into a fit of giggles when I saw the little girl's bustle was just as large as her mothers.

"I recognize you from the performance the other day in the sideshow tent!" the woman grasped my arm. "You have the most wonderful, lustrous hair! Do you have a cabinet card? My daughter Genevieve and I are collecting them. We have one for nearly all the performers."

"I am afraid I do not," I admitted.

"Not yet, anyways," Georgie said. "But the young Miss here is a great actress and singer. She even rides the camels, sometimes."

"Well, that is something! Are you going to ride a camel today, Miss Sutherland?" another woman asked.

"Oh, I...I..." I stammered, unused to my new name. I had come to the tent expressly for that purpose, but did not wish to admit my vanity. I wanted the admiration of the crowd, but now their gaze was upon me, I did not quite know what to do.

"Course she is, ain't ya, Miss?" Georgie grabbed the saddle from its corner.

I hopped upon the camel with much more ease than I had the first time, and he led me out of the tent. "Take down yer hair, Miss!" Georgie called up to me.

I didn't hesitate, but swiftly pulled the pins out and deftly loosed my braid. A gentle breeze blew toward us, and I felt my hair trail out behind me. I shook my head from side to side, delighted at the sensation.

The crowd must have been delighted as well, for I heard shouts and applause as we passed. "Come to the sideshow tent!" Georgie called. "Come see seven more Lady Godivas!"

"How long are her tresses?" a man shouted from the crowd lining our path.

"The Sutherlands got seven feet of hair each," Georgie called back. "Mr. Barnum calls 'em the seven most beautiful wonders of the world!"

"I agree!" the man replied. As I smiled down and waved at him, he put his fingers to his mouth and whistled. I blushed and turned to my other side to smile at some of the younger children walking beside us.

We made our way around the yard twice before I declared to Georgie that my arm would fall off if I waved it any longer. "And I best be getting back to feed the lion," he said.

After we returned the camel and I took a few minutes to pin my tresses back into a respectable state, I wandered to find food outside the backlot tent, where I had spent nearly all my meals. Sarah had given me my first month's pay, and I now held over five hundred dollars in my purse. I did not quite know what to do with it, but I had yet to eat one piece of fudge the entire summer and was determined to do so now.

I had eaten four pieces of fudge and half a box of popcorn when Naomi found me. "We are done for the day," she said. "Lavinia has finished also, and asked that I find you for an early supper. We're to do some shopping first. Would you like to come? Dora is off with Frederick, Sarah and Mary are tired, and Isabella is obviously not invited. But Lavinia said she would not mind Victoria's company, and requested yours especially."

I agreed at once, though I did purchase a small box of taffy first.

"I am so glad you came!" Lavinia gushed when we arrived at the circus gates. "Count Primo and I are at last getting married! Of course, I cannot find a dress in my size, but the wardrobe woman promised she would make me a wedding dress within the week, if I found material to my liking."

"Victoria has the best of taste," I said.

Victoria was not typically prone to blushing, but she did so now. "I try to keep up with the latest fashions," she said. "I am glad we are going out today, for Anna is performing with us now, and I hoped to help her find at least one new dress."

"She should have a seal coat, just as we wear," Naomi said.

Victoria's mouth quirked. "Those were quite difficult to find, but we could, perhaps, find a velvet cloak or a fur-trimmed cape."

"And she must have hats and fans and jewelry," Naomi enthused.

"You will spend the poor girl's paycheck before the sun sets," Lavinia admonished with a light laugh.

"Lavinia is correct. But I do need a new dress and a pair of gloves," I admitted. I still wore the pair with the missing button I'd worn to their performance at the opera house.

"Yes, you must have proper gloves," Victoria said. "You are part of proper society now. You have to dress the part."

We walked down the street. The main thoroughfare with its rows of shops was a few blocks away, and I took the opportunity to ask Lavinia about her history. "Lavinia, you said that you agreed to join with Mr. Barnum because of Charles, but how did you and Charles happen to meet? Were you an actress before you met him?"

"Oh, I never did say!" She clapped her small hands. "But, as I mentioned before, it was really all owing Charles, along with my cousin, and my sister, that I had any career at all."

Men and women who passed us on the street, stared. "Is that a lady or a child?" I heard a little boy ask, pointing rudely as his mother bustled him away.

Lavinia ignored this rudeness, as she must have become accustomed to it. "You see, Miss Roberts, when both my sister Minnie and I failed to grow as our taller-statured siblings had, our parents declared we should not be treated any differently than our other brothers and sisters. They built us small step-stools, so we could reach the kitchen counter to help with cooking and cleaning, and we were expected to study and do chores the same as our older brothers and sisters."

"A good thing, too," Naomi added in. "All children need to do chores, I think. My Aunt Martha used to say that doing chores helps children build character."

"Yes." Lavinia nodded. "Do you know that, for several years, Count Primo's parents treated him like an infant? They

275

might have ruined him for life if a doctor had not explained to them Primo's mental capacity was fine—above average, in fact."

"Some people can be so ignorant," Victoria said. I was surprised the older girl thought the sentiment, let alone spoke it.

Lavinia smiled sweetly. "My parents were fairly well-to-do, so they encouraged Minnie and me to learn the refinements of music and art in addition to our studies. When I was sixteen, I took the exams to become a school teacher. It was a job I thoroughly enjoyed, and I found my students respected me and learned their lessons, despite my small stature."

I paused in our walk and stared at her. "I cannot believe you had so much courage," I said. "I could never teach school. The older boys always made me nervous, coming in for only a few weeks when harvest was done, and causing such commotion. My own schoolmarm had no end of trouble with them."

"I used my words instead of the strap, which I never approved of, even when the male teachers produced it." Lavinia smiled at me, fondly. "Yet, I admit that the size of our school was one reason I had few troubles. Some of these newer schools are enormous—with children divided up by age instead of ability. If I had anything larger than our tiny one-room schoolhouse, I likely would not have enjoyed myself so much."

"Why did you decide to leave teaching, Lavinia?" Naomi asked.

Lavinia explained, "My cousin purchased a showboat. He asked Minnie and me to work as miniature dancers. It was all respectable, mind you. Some of the casino riverboats were not, especially in those days. We sang, danced, and entertained the guests—both men and women. I did not want to perform at first, but entertaining was Minnie's greatest ambition, so I agreed to go in the summer and planned to return to my little school the following fall."

She turned back to me, "However, while working on the boat, I met Charles. I had been proposed to twice before, but I turned both men down. I enjoyed being a teacher and thought I would continue doing so. In my county, teachers remain unmarried. Unmarried women take care of a town's children. Married women take care only of their own. Or, so the schoolboard thinks."

"But you fell in love?" Naomi asked. I glanced to my friend and saw she was starry-eyed listening to Lavinia's tale, no doubt thinking of Harry.

"We fell in love," Lavinia smiled.

We had nearly reached the dress shop when a man ran up to our party. "Are you Miss Victoria Sutherland?" he asked.

"Yes." Victoria blushed again, and I wondered why I so often conflated Victoria with Isabella. When they were apart, they were really nothing alike. Isabella would have stuck up her nose at the rest of us if a man showed her particular attention. Victoria was acting almost demure.

"Miss Sutherland, I am honored to be in your presence," he said. "I saw you perform at Mr. Cole's circus last year and with Mr. Barnum's circus this year. You have the voice of an angel."

"Thank you," she said. "I have a few of my cabinet cards with me, if you would like one."

"Of course," the man exclaimed. "I have an autograph book with me as well, if you would agree to sign it... and the rest of you lovely ladies, of course."

He produced a pen from his pocket and handed it to Victoria first. She handed him a cabinet card in return and began to write.

As Victoria inscribed her message, a crowd began to form around us. "I heard you sing this afternoon," a woman said. "It's Miss Naomi Sutherland, correct?"

Before Naomi could reply, the woman declared, "I liked your songs, but your voice is a bit deep. Your sister Mary hits a better range."

I wanted to slap her for her impertinence, but then she turned to me. "You were there on Friday, but not today." The woman looked me up and down. "I think red hair is ugly, but my husband thought you were a fine actress, no matter what color hair you had."

Stunned, I turned away, only to see the first man, holding out the book for me to sign. *Thank you for seeing the show,* I wrote. *I hope we will enjoy your company next season and for all the seasons after.* I signed my name, being careful to write *Anna Louise Sutherland,* for Sarah wanted to keep the pretense that I was part of the family, and she told me the stage name should be the only I answered to when traveling.

I handed the book back to the man and he read my words eagerly, saying, "Oh, I will, Miss Sutherland. Indeed, I will."

I felt a hand at the back of my head and spun around to see another man pawing at my braid. "Your hair is not ugly," he leaned in to whisper in my ear.

I wanted to move, but the crowd had grown, and at least a half-dozen people pressed in, trying to speak to Naomi, who was now singing her favorite parlor song, and Lavinia, who was excitedly describing her upcoming wedding.

"Auburn hair is divine," the man breathed. I could feel his hands running up the sides of my corset. "It is a sign of a fiery spirit, a lustful nature that cannot be quenched."

"It is a sign of being Scotch-Irish," Victoria said, grasping my hand. She raised her voice, "Ladies and gentlemen, we shall be at the circus tomorrow afternoon. Please excuse our rudeness, but Miss Lavinia needs to purchase her wedding gown today, and we must visit the shops in town before the sun sets."

The crowd departed at her decisive words. "How irritating," Victoria said. "I do enjoy being celebrated, but not when the men begin pawing at you. That is one thing you must get used to, Anna."

"I do not know whether I shall ever become accustomed to such attentions," I said.

"Men don't normally bother me," Naomi said. "Except when Victoria and Isabella are with me. I swear, Victoria, you draw men to you like flies to honey."

She laughed. "The last time I drew a man as nice as your Mr. Bailey was..." she paused. "No, I cannot remember a time. The last time I drew a man I thought I might like to court, he said, 'Your coral lips were made to kiss,' and smashed his limp lips against mine before I could accept the offer."

"Some men are so impertinent," Lavinia said. "I was proposed to three times before I met Charles. And three more times by drunkards who had filled their bellies with ale while on my cousin's showboat."

We came into a store filled from top to bottom with shelves of fabric. "However will you choose the right one?" I stared at row after row of calicos, silks, satins, and velvets.

"My namesake, Queen Victoria, got married in white," Victoria said. "All the women in Europe followed her example, and it is finally becoming the fashion here in America, though we are nearly fifty years behind the times."

Lavinia touched a roll of white silk, "Did you know that I met the queen?"

"No," I said, amazed. I had never even dreamed of meeting royalty.

She nodded, moving on to another shelf, straining her neck to look at the silks above her. "I went on tour with Charles when Mr. Barnum approached us to join his circus. As you know, I refused the first time because of Joice Heth. But this time, Barnum was taking a group of performers overseas for a European tour. They were to begin the tour with a private performance for Queen Victoria!"

Victoria and Naomi went to get a shopkeeper to procure some of the silks from the higher shelves as Lavinia continued, "I asked my mother what she thought about joining the circus, since she always impressed upon me the importance of being a proper lady. She told me to go. 'The circus has reformed,' she said. 'It used to contain nothing but hoochie coochie dancers and burlesque shows, but PT Barnum has transformed the circus into a show any respectable family can enjoy.' And so, Charles and I accepted Barnum's offer."

"What was it like meeting the queen?" I wondered.

"Like a dream," Lavinia squeezed my hand, affectionately. I went from teaching arithmetic in a tiny schoolhouse where I had to pay for my own coal, to receiving Tiffany gems and a carriage from the Queen of England herself!" Lavinia giggled, "It was more than I could have ever imagined."

I gaped as she said, "Your life could be the same, you know. I told you before, you would make a fine actress. Queen Victoria is how I chose my stage name, the Lilliputian Queen. It was she who gave me the idea. After that meeting, we seemed to become famous throughout the world! We even met President Lincoln, though I did not enjoy his company so much as the queen's."

I noticed Lavinia had the same haughty look on her face as she had when speaking of Isabella's offenses and thought it best not to inquire further. Also, it was clear that Lavinia enjoyed the approval and love of her audience more than she had let on the last time we spoke. I did not blame her for changing her mind about the circus, but it was plain that she joined the troupe because she wanted to meet the queen, not because Barnum's heart had changed, as she had previously claimed.

Thankfully, unlike the Sutherlands, Lavinia could not read my thoughts, for she merely smiled at me as we continued through the shop.

"I wore white for my first wedding, Victoria," Lavinia turned to my older friend. "And I was much younger then. Do you think I should wear white again for my second?"

Victoria considered this a moment. "No, I do not. You are older, but more importantly, you are a widow. Grey would be more appropriate, but it is most unsuitable for a celebrated actress such as yourself."

"Is mauve still in style?" I asked. "I saw a woman wearing a mauve dress today. The color would look well on Lavinia."

"Mauve would be perfect," Victoria said.

"It seems Anna has been learning lessons from you as well as Sarah," Naomi beamed. "If only she would listen to me in matters of literature."

"Naomi Sutherland. You know very well I read nearly every book you give me," I slapped her playfully.

"Indeed, you do," she laughed. "We must stop at a bookshop after this. There is a new volume on Spiritism by German philosopher Eduard von Hartmann."

"The author of the famous treatise Philosophy of the Unconscious?" Lavinia asked.

"The very same," Naomi said. "I cannot wait to read the newest book."

I felt lost in the conversation, as I had heard of neither the man nor his work. Victoria must have felt the same, for she rolled her eyes and grabbed up a bolt of mauve satin. "This is just the thing," she broke into the conversation.

Lavinia cooed over the fabric. "Puffed sleeves and a frilled collar," Victoria said. "Don't show your décolletage as you did before. I saw the photographs. It looked well on you, but it is not in style anymore."

"Thank you," Lavinia said. She bought the small amount of fabric she needed, and then Victoria insisted I buy several yards for my own needs.

"It will suit you on stage," she promised.

After I made the purchase, a jolt of pleasure shot through me which felt very much like when I received applause for one of my songs or dramatic readings. I had just spent twenty dollars on fabric for a dress that was not even yet made! And I had plenty left for whatever else I might desire. Having such wealth made me feel as if a whole new world was open to me.

In the next shop, I bought both short and long gloves and a green day dress, which Naomi insisted would match my eyes exactly and make men gaze into them more intently. I did not know whether I wanted men to gaze into my eyes, but before I could protest, we were on to the milliner's, where I purchased two hats—one to go with the day dress and a tall, almost gaudy bonnet with a crushed velvet well and a flourish of feathers, which I thought looked like a man's top hat, but which Victoria insisted would, "Stand out on stage and bring drama to your performance."

As we walked to the bookstore, Lavinia told me, "You know, after Charles died, I stopped performing for several months."

"Did you go back to teaching?" I asked.

"No," she said. "I continued spending money the way I had when we were performing. But the General always took care of our finances. I had no notion of the value of a dollar back then, and I found myself nearly impoverished before the year was out."

I raised my eyebrows, confused as to why she was confessing this to me now. "You should warn your employers," Lavinia whispered. "If you can do so in a gentle, delicate way, of course. And you should be wary yourself."

"Do you believe the Sutherlands to be in trouble?" I asked. "Or myself? I have only just earned my wages for the month. I am not on the verge of poverty yet."

"Many of us in the circus come from humble means," Lavinia said, "and when we come into a large amount of money, we are not always as wise with it as we could be. As there are seven... now eight women in your group, you earn eight times more than most of the others in the show. I have seen the diamonds they wear during performances. Unless I am quite mistaken, they are not made of paste."

"That is true," I admitted. "And the mansion in Cambria is as extravagant as our costumes."

Lavinia nodded as if she knew this fact already. "The problem is that audiences are fickle," she said. "There is already talk that the Armless Wonder will not last the season. Last year, we had six Sioux Indians traveling with us, including Standing Elk and his wife. They were popular, until people tired of them. And your Sutherlands took over for Madam Milo, The Long-Haired Wonder."

"Because why have one long-haired wonder when you can have seven," I pronounced, grimly.

"Precisely," Lavinia said. "I never know now whether I will go out of fashion, or whether Count Primo will pass away like my Charles. I have taken great pains to learn from my mistakes. My lifestyle may seem lavish, but I assure you, I save much more than I spend, and you and your new family should do the same."

I nodded and promised to heed her advice. But only a few moments later, I could not help but procure the emerald pendant Victoria pointed out in the window of a jewelry store we passed. My heart beat with delight when I thought of how it would look with my new day dress.

I went in and tried it on before making the purchase. "Though the jewelry might be more suitable for evening attire, I think you should wear it with your new dress," Naomi said. "The color matches exactly, as if the two were meant to be sold together."

"Absolutely," I breathed. "And I could wear it on stage."

"Yes," Victoria agreed. "It would set nicely against Isabella's yellow dress. You can borrow it from her wardrobe on her days off."

I bought the necklace at once and could not help but get the matching earrings besides, though my ears were not yet pierced. Naomi and Victoria beamed in appreciation for my taste, but I did notice little Lavinia, scowling in the corner of the store. I made sure not to look her in the eye until we were at dinner and our purchases safely in a carriage on the way back to our hotel.

**

The next morning, we were all together in the train station, milling about, watching the canvas men, managers, and other laborers putting everything in order.

Train schedules are notoriously inaccurate. This was an aphorism I had already learned the truth of in my months touring with the circus. Unfortunately, a train came early that day as we waited to travel from Toronto to London.

The eight of us were walking outside the station looking down the track as if waiting for something to happen. Then, the scream of the train whistle cut through the air. It was not the passenger train we were expecting, but a great freight train, which would not stop at the station.

Since our train was not expected for another thirty minutes, the animal handlers were unprepared for the threat. The herd of elephants were gathered together on the track. As the whistle sounded its warning, a panic went up among the men.

The roaring locomotive made its way around the bend, rushing toward the elephants at a great speed.

Harry, who had been speaking with Naomi, tore off at a run. He ripped off his jacket and began to wave it, wildly, trying to flag down the train.

It was too late. The train could not stop in time.

Jumbo's trainer, a man by the name of Matthew Scott, hastily pushed the elephants off the track. Tom Thumb, the dwarf elephant became frightened and refused to follow.

Just as the engine was almost upon the Dwarf, Jumbo broke free from his constraints and hurled his wide body between the Dwarf and the train.

Jumbo was a magnificent creature—the tallest and strongest animal I had ever seen. But he was no match for a freight locomotive.

The train crashed into the elephant, crushing him to the ground in a matter of seconds. His sacrifice was the dwarf's salvation. The smaller elephant was hurled into the air, but was able to limp away from the blood-drenched scene.

Standing directly behind me, Mary began to wail. I may have echoed her, but I could not be certain. No one person could be heard over the chaos and the death cries of the great elephant.

The train still could not stop. It dragged Jumbo's broken body down the tracks for what seemed like miles.

Grace turned and vomited on the ground before me. I nearly did the same. As the other performers ran to see whether the great creature could be saved, we eight huddled around each other.

"A great death," Dora breathed the fortune teller's words.

"Why didn't he tell me?" Mary sank to the ground, shaking. She began rocking back and forth, and I knew we had to rescue her before she left us completely. We were in a foreign country, and I worried someone might insist Mary go to a hospital, particularly if she had a breakdown in the middle of the street.

"I saw Father's death and Topsy's. I even saw Anna coming before she came. Why did I not see this? Why did no one tell me?" she reached up to tear the hair from her head.

I bent down close to Mary's ear, so she alone could hear me. "I asked him not to," I admitted.

"What?" she blinked at me through her tears.

"I am sorry. It was weeks ago. Fletcher spoke to Dora first, then to Grace and me. He said he was going to tell you a great death was coming. I asked him not to. I asked him to be gentle."

She looked at me, and I could not detect her mood. Was she pleased or furious?

"It is well," she said. "But now, he calls to me, and there is so much pain, I can hardly stand it."

"Your father?" I felt confused.

"The elephant," she said, and I felt her slipping through the thin curtain.

I moved over as more of the girls crouched down. One by one, they placed a hand on Mary's back as if trying to give her strength.

"So tired," she whimpered, her voice taking on an odd tone. "Tired. Smoke. The little one. Small. Afraid. Whistle. Smoldering horse. Broken. Weary."

I peeked my eyes open and whispered to Naomi, "Is she truly conjuring the—"

287

"Shh," she warned, and I shut my eyes again.

"Weary!" Mary shouted, and her body writhed. "Cuts on legs. Flies living in open sores. Ivory breaking piece by piece, flaking off. Tired. Tired of gray walls. Tired of dirt roads. Tired of shouts and commands. Tired of hooks and pushing and prodding."

She clawed at her skirts, and I saw welts ripping her stockings and drawing across her calves.

"We must remove her from this place." Victoria pulled her hand away, and Mary's body jerked again.

"Hurry, while they are consumed with the accident. This is an irreparable loss. It will take them much time to..." Sarah's voice caught in her throat, but we all knew her unspoken words. "It will take them much time to clean it."

It was a horrible, logical thought in the midst of what was incomprehensible. Mary was communing with the elephant as his spirit left the world. She not only knew his thoughts; her empathy reached so far as to feel his pain. I hoped the scars would not last past the night.

Unnoticed by any in the crowd, we carried Mary from the train station back to the hotel. Sarah requested the usual eight rooms, though I presumed we would spend most of our time in one, or at least that I would. I still felt it my duty to protect and care for the child, and guilt at not warning her ate away at me.

Could I have spared her this pain? I asked silently.

"No," Mary groaned in reply. "Only prolonged my anxiety until it came. You did the correct—Oh! Oh!" Mary's words twisted into screams of agony.

"Whatever is the matter with her?" the hotel clerk pursed his lips.

"Epilepsy," Sarah and I said together.

"I see." The man relaxed. "My mum's cousin had the same affliction. Poor dear. Take her up to your room quickly then. One of our boys will fetch your things."

Once we moved Mary to the bed, her arms and legs flailed wildly. Just in time, I remembered her inclination for scratching at her own face in times like these and grasped her wrists in my hands.

We carried Mary into the room and laid her on the bed. There was a window directly across from us, and I could see our reflections, dim in the light of day. In the glass, I thought I could see some sort of halo around Mary's body. When I blinked, the halo shifted and disappeared.

Grace saw where I was looking, then looked back down at Mary's shuddering form. She placed her hands on Mary's belly and closed her eyes. "She has moved too deep," Grace said. "The elephant has passed now, but there are three... no. There are four other spirits trying to speak through her."

"What shall we do?" I looked around to each pale face.

"We shall put our hands on her again," Sarah decided. "Let the dead move and speak through you, girls, and I shall do the same. Sometimes the spirits merely want to be heard. If we allow them to have their say, they will likely leave us."

Six sets of hands were placed onto our fallen sister. I continued holding Mary's wrists while Grace stayed at her middle. Naomi grasped her shoulders and Sarah moved to place one hand gently on each side of her head. Dora and Victoria took her legs.

No sooner were we all assembled then Mary's back arched, and she shrieked again. This time, her screams sounded more angry than pained.

"Kardec says we must go into a state of waking somnambulism," Sarah explained to me, ignoring her sister's cries. "We must clear our conscious minds and practice mesmerism."

In one voice, the sisters began to chant, "We freely give up our liberty to communicate with you, great spirits. We allow you to manifest yourselves freely."

They repeated this chant over and over until I, too, was caught up in it. After a time, I felt a pleasant, almost euphoric state of peace. In my mind's eye, I saw a sun-dappled beach of white sand. Gentle waves rolled in, and a flock of four blue herons swept past, the breeze from their wings gently ruffling my loosed hair.

My lips continued moving. Though I no longer felt what I was saying, I could faintly hear the others repeating the same words in a regular, easy rhythm.

Suddenly, a coldness came over me. The vista before me went dark as clouds rolled in and a clap of thunder sounded.

The chanting stopped, and my eyes flew open. "Betrayal!" the word came from my lips, though it was not my voice which spoke it.

"Betrayal!" Victoria cried in another voice not her own.

She was followed by first Grace and then Naomi. The word became almost a second incantation. I vomited it up over and over, unable to stop myself.

"Enough," Sarah bellowed through our roaring cries. "Spirits, you have had your say. No one here wishes to speak with you any longer."

"You shall not have a voice again within these walls," Dora yelled.

My jaw snapped shut and the shouting ceased. The lamps flickered, and the stench of sulfur filled the room. After a few moments, the air cleared. Mary's body went limp and she gave one last shudder before going completely still.

In the now quiet room, we could hear her breathing as she fell into a dreamless sleep.

We looked at each other in wonder at the powerful act we had just witnessed. Then, as if disciples around the table at the Last Supper, our wonder turned to dread.

Glancing around the room, each one of us realized the same thing. First, that we had, mercifully, helped our sister. Second, that one of our other sisters was missing.

In the commotion and confusion of the afternoon, where had Isabella gone? And why wasn't she with us?

**

As far as I knew, no one said anything to Isabella once she returned later that evening, acting as if nothing were out of the ordinary.

I, too, attempted to act as if everything was the same as usual. Nevertheless, I could see plainly that the elephant's death had taken all the energy and life out of the entire circus company.

They performed admirably in front of patrons, but the backlot was calmer than in previous days, and mealtimes nearly silent.

We traveled with the circus for a week longer until we reached Buffalo, where two flags were raised at the cook tent, signaling all the performers to gather together.

The Sutherland family stood at the back of the assembly, as if we knew what was to come and did not want to hear it, though we were compelled to.

Wearing a red top hat a size too large for his head, Nicholas Foster, one of the Museum managers, stood atop the center table. "I realize we are still all in mourning," he echoed. "Jumbo's death is an irreparable loss, which affects us all. He touched our hearts just as he touched the hearts of those who paid to see him. He was the greatest, and possibly most expensive, attraction this circus will ever know."

There were murmurs of agreement, and Foster pressed forward. "I have good news, which I hope will bring you cheer! Mr. Barnum, Mr. Scott, Mr. Bailey, and I have made the decision to put Jumbo back in the show the way he would have wanted. His spirit lives on and now, so will he."

The swarm of performers buzzed with confused anticipation. "Ladies and gentlemen," Foster paused, "boys and girls. I am pleased to announce that the bones of Jumbo the elephant have been preserved and will travel with us wherever we go! He shall be found under the Museum tent, and people from miles around can see and touch him as they did before."

"What's more," he said. "Mr. Barnum has purchased Alice, Jumbo's wife, from the London Zoo! She is nearly as tall as her husband and is bound to bring in even more notice as the largest female elephant of her kind!"

The company went hog-wild. Thunderous applause shook the tent, and there were whoops of joy and stomping feet as men whistled and women danced with delight. Their glee was driven merely by money. They were glad their paychecks would not be cut from a lack attendance at the show. Now, they need no longer worry.

We eight seemed to be the only ones not rejoicing, and after a few minutes, our family left the cook tent. Mary walked a few paces ahead of the rest of our group, and I wondered whether she wanted a moment to herself, but as soon as we were within a few feet of the crowd, she turned to face us.

"Disgusting!" Mary screamed and stomped her feet.

Her body shook with fury. Only Mary truly understood what the poor animal had been through. The scars of the bullwhip still showed in thin white lines across her legs. Her teeth had become infected as Jumbo's tusks had, and we had discussed taking her to have them examined, though she assured us the symptoms would dissipate.

"It is nearly as bad as Joice Heth," I agreed.

"I would not compare a slave to an elephant," Victoria countered, "but I will say that Joice was able to find rest at the end of her days. Jumbo will not."

"No," Mary choked back tears. "He won't. He will be trapped here, living out every horrible performance until his spirit is left even more broken than his body."

"The circus continues until October," Dora began.

"And we shall not be with it," Mary said, firmly. "We are close enough to home now. We can take a packet boat and travel on the canal from Buffalo to Lockport, then take a stagecoach into Cambria."

"Or walk, for that matter," Naomi said. "We did it enough times in our youth, and I could use the time to think."

"I am too weary to walk," Sarah admitted.

"We are all weary," Grace agreed. "And tired of the train most of all. Let us go by water, as Mary suggested."

"I shall stay one more night in the city." Isabella's thin, pretty face turned away from the rest of us, and I knew she would not be dissuaded. I also knew the others were too exhausted to care. We were growing accustomed to her disappearances.

"Do what you will." Sarah waved in her usual, dismissive way.

I thought Victoria might stay with her, as they often did things in pairs, but she seemed not to care for whatever dalliances Isabella had planned. Instead, she turned to Naomi. "What will you tell Harry?" she asked.

"The truth." Naomi shrugged. "As much as he is able to hear. I've seen him little since the accident. He may stay with the circus, but I think..." Naomi's cheeks grew red. She did not want to say what had plainly been on her mind for several weeks.

"I think you are right," Victoria said. "I have had enough proposals of my own to know when one is coming. Just be sure you have an answer ready for him when it comes. And be sure it is the right answer."

Naomi left to find Harry, and I turned to Dora, "What will you tell Frederick?"

"I know he has traveled far to watch our shows." Dora bit her lip. "He may be displeased at our absence."

"If he cares for you, I think he will not mind," I said, hoping this might test the man's mettle.

"True enough," said Sarah. "Invite him to the house. He can stay in one of the guest rooms a few weeks before deciding what to do with himself."

Dora glanced around. "Freddie was going to arrive later this afternoon, but there is a telephone at his hotel."

"And one in the rail station," Victoria said. "I saw it earlier. It's not too far from here, Dora. Go, call him, and see if he will join us in Cambria tomorrow."

As soon as Dora left, Sarah moved back to the task at hand. "Barnum has been away, but I will tell Mr. James Bailey we are leaving. People move in and out so easily. They will accept our early departure. Buffalo is indeed the Queen City, a bustling place, filled with entertainments. They are sure to replace us within the week."

"Sarah, if you go to find Mr. Bailey, and the others go to collect our things from the hotel, I will go ahead of you all and book us passage on the short voyage," Grace offered.

Victoria and I agreed while Isabella slipped away as the final arrangements were made. I saw the train of Isabella's yellow dress as she disappeared through the crowd, and a voice whispered to me that she would not return to us soon.

***

We embarked upon a canal boat first. I had never sailed on the canal before, and I was calmed both by the floating houses we passed and by the locks, which filled slowly and patiently before allowing us through to the next section of wide, tranquil water.

After arriving in Lockport, we boarded a horse-drawn tram, which had become all the rage over the past months. We also found that, in our absence, the town had seen its first electric lights installed in both Chester's Mill and Weaver's Drug Store. This was followed by nearly all the other shops in town, whose proprietors hoped to keep up with the latest fashions.

"I would have those lights in the house," Dora told me. She bit her lip, and I knew she was thinking of the money lost by leaving the circus so precipitously.

Harry came with us on the journey, refusing to leave Naomi's side. He was a bit seasick on the little packet boat, though the canal was calmer than a river.

Ever ready to stir up trouble, Victoria sidled up to Harry and asked, "Are you going to become a man about town while our sweet Naomi loses her voice singing for her supper?"

I thought Harry might take offense. Instead, he wiped his brow with a handkerchief and stood taller. "I have enough saved up for three years, if I live modestly. But of course, I should find a job before then. Tomorrow, if I'm able."

He chuckled in his usual way, but there seemed to be some concern in his eyes, and I wondered how much of our Spiritualist activities Naomi had described to him. I needn't have worried, for later, as I sat on the deck, watching the small towns pass by, Harry sat next to me and took a little box from his pocket.

"Already?" I whispered.

He opened the box halfway, and I peeked inside. There in the center was a delicate gold ring with a small topaz in the center. "Do you think she will like it?" Harry's eyes were wide with hope, and he again took out a handkerchief to wipe away the beads of sweat from his brow.

I closed my hand over his. "She will love it," I promised. "Just as she loves you."

He flushed and thanked me. "I planned to take her to Niagara Falls tonight," he whispered. "In July, they finished the state park. I thought perhaps we could ride there before I... before I ask for her hand."

"The scenery could not be lovelier," I said.

"And we could get a house in Cambria nearby the rest of you," Harry continued.

I nearly cried at this. I wanted to be happy for my friend, but her joy would be my misery. I could not bear the idea of Naomi being gone from us—even a few miles away. I realized it was a silly thought, as I had six others as companions, but I could not keep it from my mind.

I closed my eyes for a moment and breathed in the autumn air. "Let her go. All is well," a small voice seemed to murmur in my ear.

As before, I could not discern whether the words came from my conscience or a departed soul. Either way, I felt comforted. I opened my eyes and smiled up at Harry. "I think you will have a very happy life," I said.

"I hope so, Anna Louise. I certainly hope so." He ran back to his intended, and I sat, lost in reverie.

Harry forgot his grand schemes of visiting Niagara and proposed before we stepped off the boat, though the ride lasted only a few hours. As it happened, he had shown the ring to everyone. Once we all approved, he simply could not contain his nervous excitement.

Naomi departed the vessel, beaming like a child at Christmas. The topaz ring glinted prettily on her finger. It showed how well Harry knew his betrothed. Victoria would have wanted diamonds. Sarah a simple gold band. Naomi was neither flashy nor plain.

Later, Victoria told me, "I thought at first Naomi's ring was chintzy, but in the language of gems, topaz is a symbol of love and affection. It is said to aid one's sweetness of disposition."

I did not know whether stones could aid anything, but if the stone symbolized affection, it was exactly the right choice for Naomi.

In contrast, Frederick Castlemaine did not travel with us. Dora said he had business in Buffalo, which would keep him all afternoon. I could not think of what business this was, since the man had no clear occupation, unless we had been mistaken about him and he had investments or private business of which we were unaware.

"He will meet with us late in the evening or sometime tomorrow." Dora's shoulders slumped.

Difficult as it was for me to watch Harry and Naomi, it was doubly so for Dora. Their relationship was happy and easy. Harry's constant, loving attentions must have been a sharp contrast to Frederick and Dora's courtship, where her Freddie seemed to care only for his own needs and comforts. The difference was that Naomi would always be first in Harry's heart, whereas in Freddie's heart, no one would come before himself.

Proof of this came the next evening. Harry and Naomi had taken one of the carriages for a ride—unchaperoned this time, as they were engaged.

The rest of us went into the parlor to practice our songs, though we hardly knew where we would be singing, now the circus was behind us.

Dora stared out the parlor window, waiting for her beloved to arrive, just as she had stared and waited all day and the night before. At last, the trotting of a horse could be heard outside.

"He's come!" Dora bounced in her seat.

"Don't jump to greet him," Victoria called to her. "He made you wait long enough. You should do the same to him."

"She is correct," Grace said. "I think your Freddie is charming, but I do not care for the way he has tarried in coming this evening."

"Don't be over-eager," Sarah threw her oar in the mix.

"Don't answer the door," Mary whispered. She looked afraid, and I opened my mouth to inquire further, but she shook her head, refusing to elaborate.

Before a decision could be made, Mrs. Poole entered the parlor. We expected her to cheerfully announce Mr. Frederick Castlemaine. Instead, her lips went thin and her brow furrowed. Silently, she walked over to Dora and handed her a letter. "For you, Miss," she said.

As the housekeeper bustled away, she did not leave before giving me a scrutinizing look. Since we had come back, Mrs. Poole refused to speak to me, but gave me only glares and exacting glances. I could not understand her newly adopted attitude toward me and wanted to follow her out to confront her on the issue.

As it was, I could not, for Dora stood, shaking, as she read the letter. And I needed to care for my sister instead of worrying over the shifting moods of our staff.

"What is it?" I asked. "What's wrong?"

"Frederick has eloped." Dora's face went gray.

"Kitty, no!" Mary exclaimed.

The rest of us stared, unable to comprehend this startling turn of events. Frederick was clearly not the best match for our pretty sister, but we had not expected such a....

"Betrayal," Victoria, Grace, and I said at once.

"I am sorry," Dora whimpered through her tears. "There is more. I should explain. He... he..."

Dora crumpled back into her chair and dropped the letter, unable to go on. I picked it up as she threw an arm over her face, sobbing.

"My God," I said.

"What is it?" Sarah demanded.

"He has eloped... with Isabella."

"No!" the other girls protested.

"He admits to seeing me on Thursdays and Saturdays and Isabella on Mondays and Fridays," Dora cried.

"And a host of others in between, no doubt," Victoria interjected.

"He says he loves us both, dearly, but..." Dora's words became unintelligible through her tears.

"Oh, my poor little Kitty," Mary sunk beside her sister and began stroking her hair. Grace moved to her other side.

Victoria and Sarah looked at me, eyebrows raised. "He says he loves them both, dearly," I continued, reading the missive, "but Isabella is with child, and he feels he must marry her, though his heart is with Dora also."

We all sat around the great room. After an hour of stunned weeping, Dora's tears dried. She rose like a specter and seemed to float out of the room toward the staircase.

"Will she attempt to take her own life?" I felt compelled to ask.

"She is going to the attic, I think," Sarah said. "If I am not much mistaken, she wishes to commune with the spirits and determine the next steps on her path."

"I shall go with her," I offered.

"I think not," Grace stood. "You have a gift, Anna, but you are unpracticed and untrained as yet. I do not want you deceived by anyone who might come to you."

"And I do not want you crossing too far, as I often cannot help but do," Mary added.

"I will do it," Victoria offered. I was surprised, for I often assumed Victoria was nothing but the spoiled, moody girl who had thrown dishes in a tantrum only a few months before. *I have grown up*, I thought. *Why shouldn't she?*

I acquiesced to the requests to stay behind, but as Victoria followed Dora up the stairs, I vowed to read every book on Spiritualism I could find. I resolved never to be left behind again.

***

It was another letter which brought joy back into the household a few months later. Since the news of Isabella's betrayal with Dora's beau, no one in the house seemed to have any shred of happiness, save Naomi, who tried to hold back her delight as she planned out the details of her extravagant wedding. The rest of us were listless and uninterested in singing or performing, though Sarah roused herself enough to rouse us for a half hour of practice each afternoon.

To combat her own melancholy, Mary had begun purchasing cats. She had eighteen of them before the first flakes of snow appeared in the sky. Though she said she would train the kittens as part of a circus act, I more than once spied her underneath a pile of the soft, furry creatures, and guessed they were comforting her more often than she was training them.

Victoria was often gone in the mornings. She returned with more and more packages until I thought her room must be bursting at the seams with hats and dresses.

For her part, Grace had taken to volunteering at the local hospital. She said, "Now we have wealth and leisure, we may as well put our time to good use. I cannot bear to sit around the house moping all day when there are others whose needs are so much greater than my own."

So, I was often left with Sarah who, when she was not directing our already-capable housekeeper in the ways of properly keeping a house, was consumed with teaching me as much about Spiritualism as I was willing to learn.

I sat and read for hours, attuning my own spirit to those around me. My dreams became ever more bright and vivid, and I sought out visions in my daily meditations. Soon, I became adept at sensing the energies of the dead, both those bright orbs who would help, and those dark forces who might harm. I found the more I practiced, the more I could control the voices that fluttered throughout the upper rooms of the house.

My intuition grew greater and, not only did the ghosts speak to me, I was sometimes able to have them do my bidding as well. A message to Mary about what she should name her newest mewling kitten. A whisper to Dora, trying to bring her cheer. A note on a song to Sarah from someone who wished to hear it.

Small things at first. But I could feel my talents growing and became eager for the power they might bring me.

Dora had taken to her rooms, allowing no one but Mrs. Poole in, and only then to bring her meals, which she ate little of. When she at last emerged, it was several weeks after Isabella's departure and the first dusting of snow covered the ground.

Harry had left for the week to visit family and make arrangements for permanent residence in Lockport, so there were only the five of us sisters sitting around the long walnut table, and I feared another somber meal was upon us.

I nearly clapped my hands in joy and relief when I saw Dora coming into the dining room for supper. She stood statelier than before. The baby fat had gone from her cheeks, making her look much older and wiser than her years, and her previous elfish temperament had gone, replaced with a more serious demeanor.

Dora sat at the head of the long, walnut table, a seat which Sarah acquiesced without protest, though I knew she would be too proud and stubborn to do it a second time.

"I have spoken to Mother," Dora declared. "She says it will be alright."

"Thank goodness for that," Mary breathed.

"Mother says that Frederick has not stopped loving me, and as soon as he and Isabella have returned from their honeymoon, he will begin writing to me again."

Grace opened her mouth to protest, but Dora continued, "There will be no child. Neither for me, nor for Isabella."

She paused, smiling at each one of us in turn. "Do not fret, sisters. She cannot lose what was never there to begin with."

I let out a breath I did not realize I had been holding. "Then, he will leave her, and you will take him back?" I asked.

"No." She shook her head. "As I have said in the past, I have no need for motherhood, and I do not wish to be shackled to a husband. I care more for business than men, and I should not want anyone to interfere with that. Not even Freddie."

"Especially not Freddie," Victoria quipped.

"I still love him, and he loves me, and I have decided to take Aunt Martha's part in this."

"Dora!" Grace exclaimed. "Surely, you cannot mean it?"

"I do mean it," Dora insisted. "We shall share him. Isabella will have the status she desires as the wife of a wealthy man. And I shall have all the love and affection I desire whenever I want it. There is no reason I should shun Frederick simply because he loves my sister as much as myself. As there will be no children involved to take the shaming chatter of villagers as we did, I see no harm in such an arrangement."

"Mother and Martha were perfectly happy," I was surprised to hear Sarah agree. "But if I were you, I would write to Martha about it before making any rash decisions. Her last two letters inquired as to your health. Write back to her and ask what path you should take."

"That is wise counsel, Sarah, thank you," Dora said. "I shall write to her in the morning."

When Dora agreed, our group lapsed into an easy silence, feeling more comfortable than we had since before Naomi's engagement.

After a few calm moments, I felt it time to make my announcement. "Another message is imminent," I said. "A letter of some sort. One which will change our lives... but for the better, this time. I was told of its import yesterday, and I can feel it now. I believe it will soon arrive—"

My words were stopped by the rapping of the door knocker. We fell silent as Mrs. Poole moved to greet the stranger outside.

Within seconds, she ran into the dining room, face shining. "Misses! You will not guess! I am sorry, but I could not help to read it when I saw the words."

"What is it, Shannon?" Sarah said, using the woman's Christian name in her irritation."

"It's a telegram, Miss. And I should say, it's the most wonderful telegram there ever was!"

Victoria hopped up and grabbed it from the woman's shaking hands. "You must come back to the circus next season," she began to read. "We are taking the big top to London. Your presence has been requested for a special performance before Her Royal Majesty, Queen Victoria, and His Royal Highness, the Prince of Wales!"

We broke out into screams of delight! Then, all of us fell to laughing, for we seemed to transform from somber adults to joyous children in a matter of seconds.

"The Queen of England," Sarah crowed. "We shall have something to say to the people in town now, shan't we, girls?"

"No one will look down on us any longer," Mary agreed.

"We must make sure to practice," I said, worrying about my still-thin voice and unsure steps on stage.

As soon as I said it, I wondered whether I would be performing before the queen. I was not truly one of the Seven Sutherland Sisters, except in the hearts of my adopted family.

I did not need to worry long as Sarah comforted me in her usual, gentlemanly way. She slapped me on the back and said, "Don't fear, Anna. We'll soon get you ready."

Dinner was forgotten as the party began chattering and making plans. First, there was the question of whether only the eight of us would travel—the seven of us sisters plus Henry—or whether we should invite Isabella and Frederick. A telegram could be sent, or perhaps a telephone call might be made, now there was one in the house. Surely, the pair would be at a hotel. Surely, Isabella would want to come along.

Then, the conversation turned to other, practical matters, and I decided to leave the girls in the parlor, discussing whether we should take the RMS Britannic, which was fast, but was used mainly for carrying immigrants, or the RMS Majestic, which was slower, but far more elegant.

My mind felt cluttered with all the talk. I wanted to consult the spirits on the matter.

I went to the upper attic. As soon as I stepped across the threshold, the air grew thick with a warm, humid air, though outside the winter air was sharp and thin, and snow covered the ground like a bitter mother, pulling a white sheet over unwanted children as she tucked them into bed.

Even without the change in temperature, I could sense an apparition hovering just above me. It did not feel like Fletcher, whose presence still came violently, despite my insistence he be gentle. This felt more pleasant. A feminine spirit, I thought. As if to confirm my suspicions, a perfume of strawberries and honeysuckle wafted by.

I went to the rocking chair, which sat in the corner, and rested for a moment, closing my eyes. She, whomever she was, seemed to put a comforting hand on my shoulder. An image of summer came to my mind, soft rays of sunshine glinting over my hair.

The eight of us were bathing at a beach. Though it was not one we had been to before, I recognized the landscape from my first trance, the night Jumbo died.

I seemed to be standing on a rock or small crest of a hill just above the sands. As the flock of herons flew by, I looked down to watch my family. Isabella was there bathing and Frederick as well. He appeared content to talk to his wife and Dora equally. As Dora had said, neither seemed to mind, so I decided not to take offense to the matter either.

"Good," the spirit spoke in soft tones. "You shall all go. The other one is in New Jersey, but she senses when she is needed and will call soon."

"Will either boat bring us to harm?" I whispered.

"No," she breathed, and I felt her essence shift from kindness to amusement.

"But we should enjoy the luxury liner more?" I felt the corners of my lips turn up. "I understand."

I rose and moved to leave, hoping to share my insights with my sisters. And yet, I felt as if there were another presence calling me back into the room, refusing to let me go.

Suddenly, there was a stabbing at my neck. I tried to turn, but fell down in pain. Closing my eyes, I could perceive the shade of a young man in a blue coat with gold buttons down the front.

I gave another cry of pain, feeling this time as if my legs were stabbed. *I will not be like Mary,* I said to myself as my mind fought off the spirit. *I will keep my rational mind.*

"Be gone," I whispered. Pushing myself up at my elbows, I said it louder. "Be gone! You are able to hurt me no longer."

The stabbing ceased, but the crow seated outside the window gave a great, boisterous, "Caw!" and I sensed the murderous spirit had traveled into the bird, who had chosen to stay in the cold, rather than chasing the sun as his brothers did.

I walked over to examine the bird more closely, for it seemed familiar to me somehow. As I approached the window, I noticed someone on the sidewalk below. A young girl in a cream wool coat rushed toward the house, her blonde braids trailing out behind her.

I recognized her as a girl from town—Amelia Dove, if I was not mistaken. She was a sweet pixie-like child, who sang in the church choir. I realized I should not have thought of her as a child any longer, for she was at least fourteen, though still small for her age.

A chill came over me. I turned to where the kindly female spirit had been. "Is she in trouble?"

"No," the inaudible answer sounded in my mind. "Only wanting a few extra coins before Christmas."

I made a note to send a turkey to her family, and perhaps some bread, along with a few small gifts. Considering what to do next, I fingered the emerald necklace, which lay at my throat.

I had fame, riches and power now, yes, and family, too. I had chosen my life as a Sutherland sister, and I found comfort in my new home.

But my future had been sealed for me the day my father died. Now, I led a charmed existence, but not it was the one I would have chosen had he lived. For all its glitter, my life also held a darkness I could never fully escape.

Yet, I could protect this innocent girl from the same fate. I opened the window and turned my face to the crow.

He gave a second loud "Caw!"

I answered back in two sharp whistles and jerked my head toward Amelia, who was searching through the snow to see the source of the noise.

Before the young girl realized what was happening, the crow was upon her, stabbing his beak into the soft flesh of her hands as she tried to beat him off. I could not help but give a sad smile as Amelia screamed.

When Amelia at last escaped and ran back toward home, I shut the window, knowing the creature gave the girl enough of a fright, she would never walk our way again.

Coming Soon:

Sutherland Book Two:

The Eighth Sister

Pictured: An Advertisement Announcing the Sutherland Sisters Before Her Majesty, Queen Victoria and His Royal Highness, the Prince of Wales

May, 1886

When I began communing with the spirits, I believed myself to be under a particular protection, provided to me by the women I had come to know as sisters.

But real ghosts don't always whisper simple, soft replies like gentle lullabies. And they grow discontented haunting the shadowy corners of dusty rooms. Real ghosts envelop you in a blanket of pretty promises, giving warmth until your brow sweats with fever, providing comfort until your smothered lungs scream for air.

There may be answers among the dead, but spirits mislead and deceive as often as they guide, and who can discern when dreams turn to nightmares? It is like slowly drinking a tall glass of cool, fresh milk and lamenting when it curdles in your mouth.

The sound of gunfire in the night awoke me from such a dream the first night Frederick Castlemaine returned to the Sutherland Mansion with his bride.

I sat up in bed, shaking in fright. My first thought was that someone in the house had taken their own life, or perhaps the life of another. We were not to meet with the circus for a few more weeks, and everyone seemed to itch with anticipation.

At Christmastime, Naomi and Harry had married in spectacular fashion and had moved into a small, modest house in Lockport. With Naomi's jovial spirit gone from the Sutherland mansion, and Isabella still away with her new husband, the rest of us grew irritable easily.

Victoria had stormed her way through a set of dishes in one tantrum and had burned no less than three of Grace's dresses the week before, shouting, "These are out of fashion, Grace, and you have no need of such dreadful looking sacks!"

Grace, who was usually gentle and motherly, declared Victoria a "wicked woman," and responded to her sister's outrageous actions with one of her own.

She told the moony-faced Orren Longmate, "Isabella has married, but Victoria is secretly pleased because she always fancied you."

And so, Orren had begun calling for Victoria and following her around town until Victoria declared, "Orren, I will burn your house right down to the ground if you so much look in my direction again!"

While Sarah prepared for the July performance before Queen Victoria and her son, Dora consumed her spare time writing to the now-married Frederick.

The days were bleak and cold, so Mary and I spent much of our days at leisure. We trained her cats, read books, sang songs, played games, and even ventured into town once when the snow thawed. But it soon returned, and after many months, we wearied of each other's company and began sniping at one another.

Considering this, I would not have been surprised if the house's impatience and irritation turned to violence. In one form or another, it seemed violence always haunted the mansion's halls.

Heart beating in my chest, I leapt from my bed to grab a lantern, only to remember I was no longer in my father's tiny parsonage with Faith sleeping in the trundle bed beside me.

Lamps flickered in the hallway, and there was no need of another light.

"Should I be careful?" I asked the air, though I sensed no spirits beside me.

As I expected, no answer came, and I creeped to the staircase. Looking down to the front door, I could see figures milling about the porch. I was unsure what to make of this until one of the figures bent over, howling in laughter.

Recognizing the voice, I returned to my room and threw a dressing robe over the top of my nightgown, not wanting to appear indecent.

I rushed down the stairs and stumbled as I opened the door. "There you are, Anna," Frederick's deep voice bellowed. "We wondered how many shots it would take to wake you. I guessed three." He winked. "But Dora knew just the one would do. And here you are!"

He hugged me with his thick arms in a most coarse, familiar manner, slurring his words.

Isabella took no notice of her husband's over-familiarity with another woman. "Freddie and I stopped at Naomi and Harry's first. We thought we'd pick them up in our carriage, so we could all be together to celebrate!"

"Celebrate your return?" I asked.

"Of course!" Frederick picked me up this time and spun me around twice before setting my feet back on firm ground.

"Now," he said, "I saw a wagon come this way, and damned if I'm not going to shoot the spokes right out of it!"

The others laughed and began talking of travel plans. All but Harry and Naomi, who stood on either side of me. "Is he drunk?" I whispered.

"No. Much worse," Harry confided. "Naomi and I believe it is morphine. We saw him use a syringe in the carriage on the way here."

"Isabella said nothing about it," Naomi sighed. "And I do not think Dora knows. "Nor do I have any wish to tell her."

"No," I agreed. "Though the last time we failed to warn Dora about her beloved Mr. Castlemaine, she nearly starved herself to death."

"True enough," Naomi conceded.

I wished to talk more, but the party demanded our attention as a wagon did indeed roll by. Frederick fired two loud shots, and the crack of the gun was followed by the cracking of the wagon—first the back wheel and then the axel.

The horses pulling the wagon were spooked, but could not run, as the wagon in their charge was now firmly planted in the ground. This frightened them even more, and they neighed and whinnied, rearing up and kicking their front legs in the air.

"What in the name of Heavenly Glory?" a man's voice sounded. He jumped from the front of the wagon, screaming and cursing all of us.

"Oh, dear," said Grace. "It's Doctor Hubbard. I do hope he is on his way home only, and not going to any emergency."

"I hope he was," Isabella snipped. "Remember when Mother grew ill, and he refused to treat her because she hadn't enough coins in her pocket? As far as I'm concerned, that man and his patients can rot.

The doctor shouted, "How dare you, sir? Do I look like a thief, come in the night to cause you injury?"

"I don't know what you look like," Frederick called back. "But I can guess by your bowlegs and thick neck that I could thrash you before you could say 'Jack Robinson.'"

The man spluttered until Grace broke in, trying to play peacemaker as always. "Doctor, I promise Frederick meant no harm."

"Meant no harm?" the man spluttered. "Meant no harm? I've been sitting with the Widow Murphy these last hours as she left this world. Now, as I make my way home, I must be degraded? My wagon destroyed?"

"If you'll only—" Grace tried again.

"And what if someone else should call?" Hubbard yelled.

"Come inside," Sarah said. "You can stay here tonight, and we shall have Mr. Longmate and Mr. Gorman repair your cart in the morning."

The man stopped in his approach and began backing away. "No," he said, voice shaking, "I'll not stay in that house with its ghosts and ghouls. You are unnatural. All of you!" He turned and ran back the way he had come.

At his final words, a rich, alto voice sounded in my mind. "Let him walk back to town," it sighed. "He is of no consequence. Go inside and rest. You have much to say and more to do, but it can all wait until morning."

In one accord, the eight of us whispered, "Yes," and silently filed inside, the men trailing behind us.

Author's Note: On Fact & Fiction

Unlike my other novels, this book has been the result of many years of obsession and study. I have been unsuccessfully trying to get the Seven Sutherland Sisters out of my mind since I was eight-years-old, so I sincerely hope that readers enjoy the story as much as I enjoyed telling it. Ultimately, I felt their story deserving of the "long treatment," and rather than leaving out any vital details, I decided to share the rest of their haunting tale in *Sutherland Book II: The Eighth Sister*, which will be published next year.

In my mind, the true story of the Sutherlands has always been a tragic twist on a Cinderella tale. The Sutherland Sisters' impoverished beginnings, sudden fame, and ultimate decline demonstrate the American propensity to consume celebrity.

We idolize the famous. Then, when they crumble under the pressure of living up to our expectations, we devastate and dispose of them... only to replace our fallen idols with new faces who serve to repeat the cycle.

It is an intriguing and dangerous pattern we find ourselves caught up in. Actors, politicians, athletes, and musicians rise and fall at the whim of the public. Women, in particular, are consumed in a distinctly different fashion than men and find their bodies displayed and devoured with a regularity much more savage than their male counterparts.

Considering this, I wanted to tell the story of this family of women who both reveled in and struggled with new-found celebrity.

The real Sutherlands were interested in Spiritualism, and tales of their meetings with mediums, their staunch refusals to bury bodies of their dead loved ones, and their extravagant funerals have circulated in my hometown of Lockport, New York for over a hundred years.

While the ghosts of the women's past literally haunt them in this novel, I think a comparison can be made to celebrities today. They often try to escape their pasts by answering the call to fame. Consider, for example, how many change their names, take on alter egos, hide the darker parts of their past, or sell pieces of themselves for the right role. Tales of the casting couch and the more recent "Me Too" movement testify to these occurrences.

Similarly, the circus of performers and sideshow freaks, of which the Sutherlands were a part, accentuates and exaggerates the gaze of the public in a way that society was unable to replicate until the dawn of reality television and online commentary. Therefore, though the Sutherland sisters were born before the Civil War, I believe they have much to teach us today.

Some of the seemingly outlandish details of this novel are indeed true. The sisters refused to bury their father until city officials were forced to intervene. While he was buried in a humble grave with little ceremony, Topsy the dog had a funeral procession led by horses wearing gold-plated horseshoes (at least one of which was stolen by a local boy, who wanted a souvenir).

They did build a mansion beyond compare for anything in that part of New York at the time, and they had seven maids to attend them during the circus. Their excess included purchasing seal coats in summer, buying steaks for their animals, and breaking and replacing multiple sets of fine china.

It is also true that Mary did have a history of ferocious fits and was plagued by a serious mental illness, which prevented her from performing. Because of this and an increasingly demanding schedule, the women employed several substitutes who pretended to be part of the family. Anna Louise Roberts was one of the first hired for this position.

However, this book is primarily a work of fiction, and I have not endeavored to tell a mere history of the Seven Sutherland Sisters. As a result, although their pictures appear among these pages, many details of their lives have been left out or rearranged to fit the narrative.

In particular, I altered some of Anna Louise Roberts' history. In real life, Anna Louise was a stand-in performer who often traveled with the sisters, but they found her while holding auditions to replace Naomi when she became pregnant with her first child. In a similar manner, they found another woman, Hannah Corwin, while auditioning to replace Victoria, who ran off with a nineteen-year-old boy when she herself was over fifty.

While Anna did perform with the Sutherlands, I could find little about her history. Thus, I created Anna's backstory as an impoverished minister's daughter and told the Sutherland tale through her eyes because I did not feel that any of the Sutherland women could give a trustworthy, unbiased account of their lives.

I attempted to write this book three times before, taking one of the sisters as a narrator in two versions and a multiple first-person perspective in the third. All of these attempts failed, for I found the Sutherlands could not clearly see the problems and disfunctions in their own family, particularly since many of them were touched by mental illness. Since I wanted a more reliable narrator who was close to the family, I chose Anna to tell the tale.

I also altered the dates of the girls' births because much happened in their lives over a longer period of time. For narrative purposes, I wanted some of the girls a bit younger than they were in real life. Though records in those days were not kept as clearly as they are now, in 1885, Mary would have been approximately 23 instead of 13. Naomi and Dora, 27; Grace, 31; Isabella, 33; Victoria, 36; and Sarah, 40, as she is in the book.

I also changed the date of Fletcher Sutherland's demise. Fletcher did not die until 1888 and was integral in developing the brand of hair care products that added to the family's growing fortunes, which will be explored further in the second book in this two-book series.

Sarah was the driving force behind the ladies' initial success as a singing group. Meanwhile, with the help of Henry Bailey, Dora Sutherland managed much of the family's wealth, and not only ran several stores selling their products, but expanded the product lines beyond the original hair grower formula to eventually include shampoo, dandruff cure, hair color, scalp cleaner, and more.

In real life, Fletcher often tried to take center stage. In the novel, I wanted to showcase the women's accomplishments rather than their father's.

However, other details of Fletcher's life are accurate. He married Mary Brink in 1844, but then lived with both Mary and her sister Martha. Children were born to both women. In particular, many believed that Isabella and the single brother of the Sutherland family, Charles, were both the children of Martha.

Fletcher was a minister and politician, but his affairs were notorious, and a combination of his philandering and his support of the South in the Civil War led the family to a life of poverty.

Surprisingly, much like their mother, Dora and Isabella seemed to have a similar relationship with Frederick Castlemaine. As is shown in my novel, Castlemaine courted one sister and married the other, but appeared to be romantically attached to both in an odd arrangement that may have seemed normal to the sisters. These details were unchanged.

For a more pure, historical account of the women, I direct readers to *The Seven Sutherland Sisters* by Clarence O. Lewis and *The Amazing Seven Sutherland Sisters: A Biography of America's First Celebrity Models* by Brandon M. Stickney, two thoroughly-researched works well worth reading.

I am also grateful to the Niagara Historical Society and the Lockport Public Library and the teams of amazing staff and volunteers in both locations, who allowed me into their archives during the research phase of this book and gave me much-needed advice and information about the Sutherland family.

I am also grateful to the Ringling Circus Museum in Sarasota, Florida. I visited the museum twice during my research, and I believe much of the rich, period detail captured in the book is a result of those visits. The descriptions of the unloading of the trains, the costumes, and the performances as they would have been in 1885 could not have been written had it not been for the museum's wonderful displays and amazing archives of posters and other materials. In particular, the poster of the photographs of Jumbo's demise and the poster portraying the exhibition of his bones helped me to fully convey how wonderful and terrible the circus was at the time.

In the book, the route taken by the circus was precise only due to Sideshow World and the Circus Historical Society, both of which have a wealth of resources online. If you love the circus and can't make it to Florida, their records are well worth the read.

I also must extend thanks to my teachers in the Lockport CLASS (Creative Learning Applied to Special Strengths) program. In fourth grade, we studied the Seven Sutherland Sisters in CLASS and completed a research project about the family which included a book and a theatrical, full-cast audio radio program. The Sutherlands piqued my interest even back then, and I always hoped to write a novel that would illustrate their story with the rich detail it deserved...

However, I must admit, as I quoted my grandmother in the first page of this book, "I wasn't told the rest of it until much later." So, while I was aware of the dog's funeral, the propensity to throw dishes during fights, and the hair that made the women famous, please do not think my fourth-grade teachers ever touched upon spiritualism or polygamy in our classroom!

Finally, I must also thank my husband Stephen, my parents Karen and Dennis, my brother Tim, and my grandmother Lois. During my writing process, I often found the Sutherland history to be overwhelming. I can honestly say that without my family's continued encouragement, this book would never have been finished. Thank you all for your love and support.

Made in the USA
Columbia, SC
26 September 2018